PENGUIN BOOKS

Deception

Roald Dahl is best known for his mischievous, wildly inventive stories for children. But throughout his life he was also a prolific and acclaimed writer of stories for adults. These sinister, surprising tales continue to entertain, amuse and shock generations of readers even today.

Deception

ROALD DAHL

PENGUIN BOOKS

PENGUIN BOOKS

UK | USA | Canada | Ireland | Australia
India | New Zealand | South Africa

Penguin Books is part of the Penguin Random House group of companies
whose addresses can be found at global.penguinrandomhouse.com.

These stories have been previously published in a variety of publications.
Details of each story's original publication are provided at the start of each
chapter and constitute an extension of this copyright page.
This collection first published in Penguin Books 2016

002

Set in 12.5/14.75 pt Garamond MT Std
Typeset by Jouve (UK), Milton Keynes
Printed in Great Britain by Clays Ltd, St Ives plc

A CIP catalogue record for this book is available from the British Library

ISBN: 978-1-405-93300-1

www.greenpenguin.co.uk

Contents

My Lady Love, My Dove

First published in *The New Yorker* (21 June 1952)

It has been my habit for many years to take a nap after lunch. I settle myself in a chair in the living-room with a cushion behind my head and my feet up on a small square leather stool, and I read until I drop off.

On this Friday afternoon, I was in my chair and feeling as comfortable as ever with a book in my hands – an old favourite, Doubleday and Westwood's *The Genera of Diurnal Lepidoptera* – when my wife, who has never been a silent lady, began to talk to me from the sofa opposite. 'These two people,' she said, 'what time are they coming?'

I made no answer, so she repeated the question, louder this time.

I told her politely that I didn't know.

'I don't think I like them very much,' she said. 'Especially him.'

'No, dear, all right.'

'Arthur. I said I don't think I like them very much.'

I lowered my book and looked across at her lying with her feet up on the sofa, flipping over the pages of some fashion magazine. 'We've only met them once,' I said.

'A dreadful man, really. Never stopped telling jokes, or stories, or something.'

'I'm sure you'll manage them very well, dear.'

I

'And she's pretty frightful, too. When do you think they'll arrive?'

Somewhere around six o'clock, I guessed.

'But don't *you* think they're awful?' she asked, pointing at me with her finger.

'Well . . .'

'They're *too* awful, they really are.'

'We can hardly put them off now, Pamela.'

'They're absolutely the end,' she said.

'Then why did you ask them?' The question slipped out before I could stop myself and I regretted it at once, for it is a rule with me never to provoke my wife if I can help it. There was a pause, and I watched her face, waiting for the answer – the big white face that to me was something so strange and fascinating there were occasions when I could hardly bring myself to look away from it. In the evenings sometimes – working on her embroidery, or painting those small intricate flower pictures – the face would tighten and glimmer with a subtle inward strength that was beautiful beyond words, and I would sit and stare at it minute after minute while pretending to read. Even now, at this moment, with that compressed acid look, the frowning forehead, the petulant curl of the nose, I had to admit that there was a majestic quality about this woman, something splendid, almost stately; and so tall she was, far taller than I – although today, in her fifty-first year, I think one would have to call her big rather than tall.

'You know very well why I asked them,' she answered sharply. 'For bridge, that's all. They play an absolutely first-class game, and for a decent stake.' She glanced up and saw me watching her. 'Well,' she said, 'that's about the way you feel too, isn't it?'

'Well, of course, I . . .'

'Don't be a fool, Arthur.'

'The only time I met them I must say they did seem quite nice.'

'So is the butcher.'

'Now Pamela, dear – please. We don't want any of that.'

'Listen,' she said, slapping down the magazine on her lap, 'you saw the sort of people they were as well as I did. A pair of stupid climbers who think they can go anywhere just because they play good bridge.'

'I'm sure you're right, dear, but what I don't honestly understand is why –'

'I keep telling you – so that for once we can get a decent game. I'm sick and tired of playing with rabbits. But I really can't see why I should have these awful people in the house.'

'Of course not, my dear, but isn't it a little late now –'

'Arthur?'

'Yes?'

'Why for God's sake do you always argue with me? You *know* you disliked them as much as I did.'

'I really don't think you need worry, Pamela. After all, they seemed quite a nice well-mannered young couple.'

'Arthur, don't be pompous.' She was looking at me hard with those wide grey eyes of hers, and to avoid them – they sometimes made me quite uncomfortable – I got up and walked over to the French windows that led into the garden.

The big sloping lawn out in front of the house was newly mown, striped with pale and dark ribbons of green. On the far side, the two laburnums were in full flower at last, the long golden chains making a blaze of colour against the darker trees beyond. The roses were out too, and the scarlet begonias, and in the long herbaceous border all my lovely hybrid lupins, columbine, delphinium, sweet-william, and the huge, pale, scented iris. One of the gardeners was coming up the drive from his lunch. I could see the roof of his cottage through the trees and beyond it to one side, the place where the drive went out through the iron gates on the Canterbury road.

My wife's house. Her garden. How beautiful it all was! How peaceful! Now, if only Pamela would try to be a little less solicitous of my welfare, less prone to coax me into doing things for my own good rather than for my own pleasure, then everything would be heaven. Mind you, I don't want to give the impression that I do not love her – I worship the very air she breathes – or that I can't manage her, or that I am not the captain of my ship. All I am trying to say is that she can be a trifle irritating at times, the way she carries on. For example, those little mannerisms of hers – I do wish she would drop them all, especially the way she has of pointing a finger at me to emphasize a phrase. You must remember that I am a man who is built rather small, and a gesture like this, when used to excess by a person like my wife, is apt to intimidate. I sometimes find it difficult to convince myself that she is not an overbearing woman.

'Arthur!' she called. 'Come here.'

'What?'

'I've just had a most marvellous idea. Come here.'

I turned and went over to where she was lying on the sofa.

'Look,' she said, 'do you want to have some fun?'

'What sort of fun?'

'With the Snapes.'

'Who are the Snapes?'

'Come on,' she said. 'Wake up. Henry and Sally Snape. Our week-end guests.'

'Well?'

'Now listen. I was lying here thinking how awful they really are . . . the way they behave . . . him with his jokes and her like a sort of love-crazed sparrow . . .' She hesitated, smiling slyly, and for some reason, I got the impression she was about to say a shocking thing. 'Well – if that's the way they behave when they're in front of us, then what on earth must they be like when they're alone together?'

'Now wait a minute, Pamela –'

'Don't be an ass, Arthur. Let's have some fun – some real fun for once – tonight.' She had half raised herself up off the sofa, her face bright with a kind of sudden recklessness, the mouth slightly open, and she was looking at me with two round grey eyes, a spark dancing slowly in each.

'Why shouldn't we?'

'What do you want to do?'

'Why, it's obvious. Can't you see?'

'No, I can't.'

'All we've got to do is put a microphone in their room.'

I admit I was expecting something pretty bad, but when

she said this I was so shocked I didn't know what to answer.

'That's exactly what we'll do,' she said.

'Here!' I cried. 'No. Wait a minute. You can't do that.'

'Why not?'

'That's about the nastiest trick I ever heard of. It's like – why, it's like listening at keyholes, or reading letters, only far far worse. You don't mean this seriously, do you?'

'Of course I do.'

I knew how much she disliked being contradicted but there were times when I felt it necessary to assert myself, even at considerable risk. 'Pamela,' I said, snapping the words out sharply, 'I forbid you to do it!'

She took her feet down from the sofa and sat up straight. 'What in God's name are you trying to pretend to be, Arthur? I simply don't understand you.'

'That shouldn't be too difficult.'

'Tommyrot! I've known you do lots of worse things than this before now.'

'Never!'

'Oh yes I have. What makes you suddenly think you're a so much nicer person than I am?'

'I've never done things like that.'

'All right, my boy,' she said, pointing her finger at me like a pistol. 'What about the time at the Milfords' last Christmas? Remember? You nearly laughed your head off and I had to put my hand over your mouth to stop them hearing us. What about that for one?'

'That was different,' I said. 'It wasn't our house. And they weren't our guests.'

'It doesn't make any difference at all.' She was sitting very upright, staring at me with those round grey eyes, and the chin was beginning to come up high in a peculiarly contemptuous manner. 'Don't be such a pompous hypocrite,' she said. 'What on earth's come over you?'

'I really think it's a pretty nasty thing, you know, Pamela. I honestly do.'

'But listen, Arthur. I'm a *nasty* person. And so are you – in a secret sort of way. That's why we get along together.'

'I never heard such nonsense.'

'Mind you, if you've suddenly decided to change your character completely, that's another story.'

'You've got to stop talking this way, Pamela.'

'You see,' she said, 'if you really *have* decided to reform, then what on earth am I going to do?'

'You don't know what you're saying.'

'Arthur, how could a nice person like you want to associate with a stinker?'

I sat myself down slowly in the chair opposite her, and she was watching me all the time. You understand, she was a big woman, with a big white face, and when she looked at me hard, as she was doing now, I became – how shall I say it – surrounded, almost enveloped by her, as though she were a great tub of cream and I had fallen in.

'You don't honestly want to do this microphone thing, do you?'

'But of course I do. It's time we had a bit of fun around here. Come on, Arthur. Don't be so stuffy.'

'It's not right, Pamela.'

'It's just as right' – up came the finger again – 'just as

right as when you found those letters of Mary Probert's in her purse and you read them through from beginning to end.'

'We should never have done that.'

'*We!*'

'You read them afterwards, Pamela.'

'It didn't harm anyone at all. You said so yourself at the time. And this one's no worse.'

'How would *you* like it if someone did it to *you*?'

'How could I *mind* if I didn't know it was being done? Come on, Arthur. Don't be so flabby.'

'I'll have to think about it.'

'Maybe the great radio engineer doesn't know how to connect the mike to the speaker?'

'That's the easiest part.'

'Well, go on then. Go on and do it.'

'I'll think about it and let you know later.'

'There's no time for that. They might arrive any moment.'

'Then I won't do it. I'm not going to be caught red-handed.'

'If they come before you're through, I'll simply keep them down here. No danger. What's the time, anyway?'

It was nearly three o'clock.

'They're driving down from London,' she said, 'and they certainly won't leave till after lunch. That gives you plenty of time.'

'Which room are you putting them in?'

'The big yellow room at the end of the corridor. That's not too far away, is it?'

'I suppose it could be done.'

'And by the by,' she said, 'where are you going to have the speaker?'

'I haven't said I'm going to do it yet.'

'My God!' she cried, 'I'd like to see someone try and stop you now. You ought to see your face. It's all pink and excited at the very prospect. Put the speaker in our bedroom, why not? But go on – and hurry.'

I hesitated. It was something I made a point of doing whenever she tried to order me about, instead of asking nicely. 'I don't like it, Pamela.'

She didn't say any more after that; she just sat there, absolutely still, watching me, a resigned, waiting expression on her face, as though she were in a long queue. This, I knew from experience, was a danger signal. She was like one of those bomb things with the pin pulled out, and it was only a matter of time before – bang! and she would explode. In the silence that followed, I could almost hear her ticking.

So I got up quietly and went out to the workshop and collected a mike and a hundred and fifty feet of wire. Now that I was away from her, I am ashamed to admit that I began to feel a bit of excitement myself, a tiny warm prickling sensation under the skin, near the tips of my fingers. It was nothing much, mind you – really nothing at all. Good heavens, I experience the same thing every morning of my life when I open the paper to check the closing prices on two or three of my wife's larger stockholdings. So I wasn't going to get carried away by a silly joke like this. At the same time, I couldn't help being amused.

I took the stairs two at a time and entered the yellow

room at the end of the passage. It had the clean, unlived-in appearance of all guest rooms, with its twin beds, yellow satin bedspreads, pale-yellow walls and golden-coloured curtains. I began to look around for a good place to hide the mike. This was the most important part of all, for whatever happened, it must not be discovered. I thought first of the basket of logs by the fireplace. Put it under the logs. No – not safe enough. Behind the radiator? Or on top of the wardrobe? Under the desk? None of these seemed very professional to me. All might be subject to chance inspection because of a dropped collar stud or something like that. Finally, with considerable cunning, I decided to put it inside the springing of the sofa. The sofa was against the wall, near the edge of the carpet, and my lead wire could go straight under the carpet over to the door.

I tipped up the sofa and slit the material underneath. Then I tied the microphone securely up among the springs, making sure that it faced the room. After that, I led the wire under the carpet to the door. I was calm and cautious in everything I did. Where the wire had to emerge from under the carpet and pass out of the door, I made a little groove in the wood so that it was almost invisible.

All this, of course, took time, and when I suddenly heard the crunch of wheels on the gravel of the drive outside, and then the slamming of car doors and the voices of our guests, I was still only halfway down the corridor, tacking the wire along the skirting. I stopped and straightened up, hammer in hand, and I must confess that I felt afraid. You have no idea how unnerving that noise was to me. I experienced the same sudden stomachy feeling of fright as when a bomb once dropped the other side of the village during the war, one afternoon, while I was working quietly in the library with my butterflies.

Don't worry, I told myself. Pamela will take care of these people. She won't let them come up here.

Rather frantically, I set about finishing the job, and soon I had the wire tacked all along the corridor and through into our bedroom. Here, concealment was not so important, although I still did not permit myself to get careless, because of the servants. So I laid the wire under the carpet and brought it up unobtrusively into the back of the radio. Making the final connections was an elementary technical matter and took me no time at all.

Well – I had done it. I stepped back and glanced at the little radio. Somehow, now, it looked different – no longer a silly box for making noises but an evil little creature that crouched on the table top with a part of its own body reaching out secretly into a forbidden place far away. I switched it on. It hummed faintly but made no other sound. I took my bedside clock, which had a loud tick, and carried it along to the yellow room and placed it on the floor by the sofa. When I returned, sure enough the radio creature was ticking away as loudly as if the clock were in the room – even louder.

I fetched back the clock. Then I tidied myself up in the bathroom, returned my tools to the workshop and prepared to meet the guests. But first, to compose myself, and so that I would not have to appear in front of them with the blood, as it were, still wet on my hands, I spent five minutes in the library with my collection. I concentrated on a tray of the lovely *Vanessa cardui* – the 'painted lady' – and made a few notes for a paper I was preparing entitled 'The Relation between Colour Pattern and Framework of Wings', which I intended to read at the next meeting of our society in Canterbury. In this way I soon regained my normal grave, attentive manner.

When I entered the living-room, our two guests, whose names I could never remember, were seated on the sofa. My wife was mixing drinks.

'Oh, *there* you are, Arthur,' she said. 'Where *have* you been?'

I thought this was an unnecessary remark. 'I'm so sorry,' I said to the guests as we shook hands. 'I was busy and forgot the time.'

'We all know what *you've* been doing,' the girl said, smiling wisely. 'But we'll forgive him, won't we, dearest?'

'I think we should,' the husband answered.

I had a frightful, fantastic vision of my wife telling them, amidst roars of laughter, precisely what I had been doing upstairs. She *couldn't* – she *couldn't* have done that! I looked round at her and she too was smiling as she measured out the gin.

'I'm sorry we disturbed you,' the girl said.

I decided that if this was going to be a joke then I'd better join in quickly, so I forced myself to smile with her.

'You must let us see it,' the girl continued.

'See what?'

'Your collection. Your wife says that they are absolutely beautiful.'

I lowered myself slowly into a chair and relaxed. It was

ridiculous to be so nervous and jumpy. 'Are you interested in butterflies?' I asked her.

'I'd love to see yours, Mr Beauchamp.'

The Martinis were distributed and we settled down to a couple of hours of talk and drink before dinner. It was from then on that I began to form the impression that our guests were a charming couple. My wife, coming from a titled family, is apt to be conscious of her class and breeding, and is often hasty in her judgement of strangers who are friendly towards her – particularly tall men. She is frequently right, but in this case I felt that she might be making a mistake. As a rule, I myself do not like tall men either; they are apt to be supercilious and omniscient. But Henry Snape – my wife had whispered his name – struck me as being an amiable simple young man with good manners whose main preoccupation, very properly, was Mrs Snape. He was handsome in a long-faced, horsy sort of way, with dark-brown eyes that seemed to be gentle and sympathetic. I envied him his fine mop of black hair, and caught myself wondering what lotion he used to keep it looking so healthy. He did tell us one or two jokes, but they were on a high level and no one could have objected.

'At school,' he said, 'they used to call me Scervix. Do you know why?'

'I haven't the least idea,' my wife answered.

'Because cervix is Latin for nape.'

This was rather deep and it took me a while to work out.

'What school was that, Mr Snape?' my wife asked.

'Eton,' he said, and my wife gave a quick little nod of

approval. Now she will talk to him, I thought, so I turned my attention to the other one, Sally Snape. She was an attractive girl with a bosom. Had I met her fifteen years earlier I might well have got myself into some sort of trouble. As it was, I had a pleasant enough time telling her all about my beautiful butterflies. I was observing her closely as I talked, and after a while I began to get the impression that she was not, in fact, quite so merry and smiling a girl as I had been led to believe at first. She seemed to be coiled in herself, as though with a secret she was jealously guarding. The deep-blue eyes moved too quickly about the room, never settling or resting on one thing for more than a moment; and over all her face, though so faint that they might not even have been there, those small downward lines of sorrow.

'I'm so looking forward to our game of bridge,' I said, finally changing the subject.

'Us too,' she answered. 'You know, we play almost every night, we love it so.'

'You are extremely expert, both of you. How did you get to be so good?'

'It's practice,' she said. 'That's all. Practice, practice, practice.'

'Have you played in any championships?'

'Not yet, but Henry wants very much for us to do that. It's hard work, you know, to reach that standard. Terribly hard work.' Was there not here, I wondered, a hint of resignation in her voice? Yes, that was probably it; he was pushing her too hard, making her take it too seriously, and the poor girl was tired of it all.

At eight o'clock, without changing, we moved in to dinner. The meal went well, with Henry Snape telling us some very droll stories. He also praised my Richebourg '34 in a most knowledgeable fashion, which pleased me greatly. By the time coffee came, I realized that I had grown to like these two youngsters immensely, and as a result I began to feel uncomfortable about this microphone business. It would have been all right if they had been horrid people, but to play this trick on two such charming young persons as these filled me with a strong sense of guilt. Don't misunderstand me. I was not getting cold feet. It didn't seem necessary to stop the operation. But I refused to relish the prospect openly as my wife seemed now to be doing, with covert smiles and winks and secret little noddings of the head.

Around nine thirty, feeling comfortable and well fed, we returned to the large living-room to start our bridge. We were playing for a fair stake – ten shillings a hundred – so we decided not to split families, and I partnered my wife the whole time. We all four of us took the game seriously, which is the only way to take it, and we played silently, intently, hardly speaking at all except to bid. It was not the money we played for. Heaven knows, my wife had enough of that, and so apparently did the Snapes. But among experts it is almost traditional that they play for a reasonable stake.

That night the cards were evenly divided, but for once my wife played badly, so we got the worst of it. I could see that she wasn't concentrating fully, and as we came along towards midnight she began not even to care. She kept glancing up at me with those large grey eyes of hers, the eyebrows raised, the nostrils curiously open, a little gloating smile around the corner of her mouth.

Our opponents played a fine game. Their bidding was masterly, and all through the evening they made only one mistake. That was when the girl badly overestimated her partner's hand and bid six spades. I doubled and they went three down, vulnerable, which cost them eight hundred points. It was just a momentary lapse, but I remember that Sally Snape was very put out by it, even though her husband forgave her at once, kissing her hand across the table and telling her not to worry.

Around twelve thirty my wife announced that she wanted to go to bed.

'Just one more rubber?' Henry Snape said.

'No, Mr Snape. I'm tired tonight. Arthur's tired, too. I can see it. Let's all go to bed.'

She herded us out of the room and we went upstairs, the four of us together. On the way up, there was the usual talk about breakfast and what they wanted and how they were to call the maid. 'I think you'll like your room,' my wife said. 'It has a view right across the valley, and the sun comes to you in the morning around ten o'clock.'

We were in the passage now, standing outside our own bedroom door, and I could see the wire I had put down that afternoon and how it ran along the top of the skirting down to their room. Although it was nearly the same colour as the paint, it looked very conspicuous to me. 'Sleep well,' my wife said. 'Sleep well, Mrs Snape. Good night, Mr Snape.' I followed her into our room and shut the door.

'Quick!' she cried. 'Turn it on!' My wife was always like that, frightened that she was going to miss something. She had a reputation, when she went hunting – I never go myself – of always being right up with the hounds whatever the cost to herself or her horse for fear that she might miss a kill. I could see she had no intention of missing this one.

The little radio warmed up just in time to catch the noise of their door opening and closing again.

'There!' my wife said. 'They've gone in.' She was standing in the centre of the room in her blue dress, her hands clasped before her, her head craned forward, intently listening, and the whole of the big white face seemed somehow to have gathered itself together, tight like a wineskin.

Almost at once the voice of Henry Snape came out of the radio, strong and clear. 'You're just a goddam little fool,' he was saying, and this voice was so different from the one I remembered, so harsh and unpleasant, it made me jump. 'The whole bloody evening wasted! Eight hundred points – that's eight pounds between us!'

'I got mixed up,' the girl answered. 'I won't do it again, I promise.'

'What's *this*!' my wife said. 'What's going on?' Her mouth was wide open now, the eyebrows stretched up high, and she came quickly over to the radio and leaned forward, ear to the speaker. I must say I felt rather excited myself.

'I promise, I promise I won't do it again,' the girl was saying.

'We're not taking any chances,' the man answered grimly. 'We're going to have another practice right now.'

'Oh no, please! I couldn't stand it!'

'Look,' the man said, 'all the way out here to take money off this rich bitch and you have to go and mess it up.'

My wife's turn to jump.

'The second time this week,' he went on.

'I promise I won't do it again.'

'Sit down. I'll sing them out and you answer.'

'No, Henry, *please*! Not all five hundred of them. It'll take three hours.'

'All right, then. We'll leave out the finger positions. I think you're sure of those. We'll just do the basic bids showing honour tricks.'

'Oh Henry, must we? I'm so tired.'

'It's absolutely essential you get them perfect,' he said. 'We have a game every day next week, you know that. And we've got to eat.'

'What is this?' my wife whispered. 'What on earth is it?'

'Shhh!' I said. 'Listen!'

'All right,' the man's voice was saying. 'Now we'll start from the beginning. Ready?'

'Oh Henry, *please*!' She sounded very near to tears.

'Come on, Sally. Pull yourself together.'

Then, in a quite different voice, the one we had been used to hearing in the living-room, Henry Snape said, '*One* club.' I noticed that there was a curious lilting emphasis on the word 'one', the first part of the word drawn out long.

'Ace queen of clubs,' the girl replied wearily. 'King jack of spades. No hearts, and ace jack of diamonds.'

'And how many cards to each suit? Watch my finger positions carefully.'

'You said we could miss those.'

'Well – if you're quite sure you know them?'

'Yes, I know them.'

A pause, then 'A *club*.'

'King jack of clubs,' the girl recited. 'Ace of spades. Queen jack of hearts, and ace queen of diamonds.'

Another pause, then 'I'll say *one* club.'

'Ace king of clubs . . .'

'My heavens alive!' I cried. 'It's a bidding code! They show every card in the hand!'

'Arthur, it couldn't be!'

'It's like those men who go into the audience and borrow something from you and there's a girl blindfolded on the stage and from the way he phrases the question she can tell him exactly what it is – even a railway ticket, and what station it's from.'

'It's impossible!'

'Not at all. But it's tremendous hard work to learn. Listen to them.'

'I'll go *one heart*,' the man's voice was saying.

'King queen ten of hearts. Ace jack of spades. No diamonds. Queen jack of clubs . . .'

'And you see,' I said, 'he tells her the *number* of cards he has in each suit by the position of his fingers.'

'How?'

'I don't know. You heard him saying about it.'

'My *God*, Arthur! Are you sure that's what they're doing?'

'I'm afraid so.' I watched her as she walked quickly over to the side of the bed to fetch a cigarette. She lit it with her back to me and then swung round, blowing the smoke up at the ceiling in a thin stream. I knew we were going to have to do something about this, but I wasn't quite sure what because we couldn't possibly accuse them without revealing the source of our information. I waited for my wife's decision.

'Why, Arthur,' she said slowly, blowing out clouds of smoke. 'Why, this is a *mar-vellous* idea. D'you think *we* could learn to do it?'

'What!'

'Of course. Why not?'

'Here! No! Wait a minute, Pamela . . .' but she came swiftly across the room, right up close to me where I was standing, and she dropped her head and looked down at me – the old look of a smile that wasn't a smile, at the corners of the mouth, and the curl of the nose, and the big full grey eyes staring at me with their bright black centres, and then they were grey, and all the rest was white-flecked, with hundreds of tiny red veins – and when she looked at me like this, hard and close, I swear to you it made me feel as though I were drowning.

'Yes,' she said. 'Why not?'

'But Pamela . . . Good heavens . . . No . . . After all . . .'

'Arthur, I do wish you wouldn't *argue* with me all the time. That's exactly what we'll do. Now, go fetch a deck of cards; we'll start right away.'

The Mildenhall Treasure

First published in *Saturday Evening Post* (September 1947)

Around seven o'clock in the morning, Gordon Butcher got out of bed and switched on the light. He walked barefoot to the window and drew back the curtains and looked out.

This was January and it was still dark, but he could tell there hadn't been any snow in the night.

'That wind,' he said aloud to his wife. 'Just listen to that wind.'

His wife was out of bed now, standing beside him near the window, and the two of them were silent, listening to the swish of the icy wind as it came sweeping in over the fens.

'It's a nor'easter,' he said.

'There'll be snow for certain before nightfall,' she told him. 'And plenty of it.'

She was dressed before him, and she went into the next room and leaned over the cot of her six-year-old daughter and gave her a kiss. She called out a good morning to the two other older children in the third room, then she went downstairs to make breakfast.

At a quarter to eight, Gordon Butcher put on his coat, his cap and his leather gloves, and walked out of the back door into the bitter early-morning winter weather. As he moved through the half-daylight over the yard to the shed where his bicycle stood, the wind was like a knife on his cheek. He wheeled out the bike and mounted and began to ride down the middle of the narrow road, right into the face of the gale.

Gordon Butcher was thirty-eight. He was not an ordinary farm labourer. He took orders from no man unless he wished. He owned his own tractor, and with this he ploughed other men's fields and gathered other men's harvests under contract. His thoughts were only for his wife, his son, his two daughters. His wealth was in his small brick house, his two cows, his tractor, his skill as a ploughman.

Gordon Butcher's head was very curiously shaped, the back of it protruding like the sharp end of an enormous egg, and his ears stuck out, and a front tooth was missing on the left side. But none of this seemed to matter very much when you met him face to face in the open air. He looked at you with steady blue eyes that were without any malice or cunning or greed. And the mouth didn't have those thin lines of bitterness around the edges which one so often sees on men who work the land and spend their days fighting the weather.

His only eccentricity, to which he would cheerfully admit if you asked him, was in talking aloud to himself when he was alone. This habit, he said, grew from the fact that the kind of work he did left him entirely by himself for ten hours a day, six days a week. 'It keeps me company,' he said, 'hearing me own voice now and again.'

He biked on down the road, pedalling hard against the brutal wind.

'All right,' he said, 'all right, why don't you blow a bit? Is that the best you can do? My goodness me, I hardly know you're there this morning!' The wind howled around him and snapped at his coat and squeezed its way through the pores of the heavy wool, through his jacket underneath, through his shirt and vest, and it touched his bare skin with an icy fingertip.

'Why,' he said, 'it's lukewarm you are today. You'll have to do a sight better than that if you're going to make *me* shiver.'

And now the darkness was diluting into a pale-grey morning light, and Gordon Butcher could see the cloudy roof of the sky very low above his head and flying with the wind. Grey-blue the clouds were, flecked here and there with black, a solid mass from horizon to horizon, the whole thing moving with the wind, sliding past above his head like a great grey sheet of metal unrolling. All around him lay the bleak and lonely fen-country of Suffolk, mile upon mile of it that went on for ever.

He pedalled on. He rode through the outskirts of the little town of Mildenhall and headed for the village of West Row where the man called Ford had his place.

He had left his tractor at Ford's the day before because his next job was to plough up four and a half acres on Thistley Green for Ford. It was not Ford's land. It is important to remember this, but Ford was the one who had asked him to do the work.

Actually, a farmer called Rolfe owned the four and a half acres.

Rolfe had asked Ford to get it ploughed because Ford, like Gordon Butcher, did ploughing jobs for other men.

The difference between Ford and Gordon Butcher was that Ford was somewhat grander. He was a fairly prosperous small-time agricultural engineer who had a nice house and a large yard full of sheds filled with farm implements and machinery. Gordon Butcher had only his one tractor.

On this occasion, however, when Rolfe had asked Ford to plough up his four and a half acres on Thistley Green, Ford was too busy to do the work so he hired Gordon Butcher to do it for him.

There was no one about in Ford's yard when Butcher rode in. He parked his bike, filled up his tractor with paraffin and petrol, warmed the engine, hitched the plough behind, mounted the high seat and drove out to Thistley Green.

The field was not half a mile away, and around eight thirty Butcher drove the tractor in through the gate on to the field itself. Thistley Green was maybe a hundred acres all told, with a low hedge running round it. And although it was actually one large field, different parts of it were owned by different men. These separate parts were easy to define because each was cultivated in its own way. Rolfe's plot of four and a half acres was over to one side near the southern boundary fence. Butcher knew where it was and he drove his tractor round the edge of the field, then inward until he was on the plot.

The plot was barley stubble now, covered with the short and rotting yellow stalks of barley harvested last autumn, and only recently had it been broad-sheared so that now it was ready for the plough.

'Deep-plough it,' Ford had said to Butcher the day

before. 'It's for sugar-beet. Rolfe's putting sugar-beet in there.'

They only plough about four inches down for barley, but for sugar-beet they plough deep, to ten or twelve inches. A horse-drawn plough can't plough as deep as that. It was only since motor-tractors came along that the farmers had been able to deep-plough properly. Rolfe's land had been deep-ploughed for sugar-beet some years before this, but it wasn't Butcher who had done the ploughing and no doubt the job had been skimped a bit and the ploughman had not gone quite as deep as he should. Had he done so, what was about to happen today would have happened then, and that would have been a different story.

Gordon Butcher began to plough. Up and down the field he went, lowering the plough deeper and deeper each trip until at last it was cutting twelve inches into the ground and turning up a smooth even wave of black earth as it went.

The wind was coming faster now, rushing in from the killer sea, sweeping over the flat Norfolk fields, past Saxthorpe and Reepham and Honingham and Swaffham and Larling and over the border to Suffolk, to Mildenhall and to Thistley Green where Gordon Butcher sat upright high on the seat of his tractor, driving back and forth over the plot of yellow barley stubble that belonged to Rolfe. Gordon Butcher could smell the sharp crisp smell of snow not far away, he could see the low roof of the sky – no longer flecked with black, but pale and whitish grey – sliding by overhead like a solid sheet of metal unrolling.

'Well,' he said, raising his voice above the clatter of the tractor, 'you are surely fashed at somebody today. What an almighty fuss it is now of blowin' and whistlin' and freezin'. Like a woman,' he added. 'Just like a woman does sometimes in the evening,' and he kept his eye upon the line of the furrow, and he smiled.

At noon he stopped the tractor, dismounted and fished in his pocket for his lunch. He found it and sat on the ground in the lee of one of the huge tractor-wheels. He ate large pieces of bread and very small pieces of cheese. He had nothing to drink, for his only Thermos had got smashed by the jolting of the tractor two weeks before, and in wartime, for this was in January 1942, you could not buy another anywhere. For about fifteen minutes he sat on the ground in the shelter of the wheel and ate his lunch. Then he got up and examined his peg.

Unlike many ploughmen, Butcher always hitched his plough to the tractor with a wooden peg so that if the plough fouled a root or a large stone, the peg would simply break at once, leaving the plough behind and saving the shares from serious damage. All over the black fen country, just below the surface, lie enormous trunks of ancient oak trees, and a wooden peg will save a ploughshare many times a week out there. Although Thistley Green was well-cultivated land, field-land, not fen-land, Butcher was taking no chances with his plough.

He examined the wooden peg, found it sound, mounted the tractor again, and went on with his ploughing.

The tractor nosed back and forth over the ground, leaving a smooth black wave of soil behind it. And still the wind blew colder but it did not snow.

Around three o'clock the thing happened.

There was a slight jolt, the wooden peg broke, and the tractor left the plough behind. Butcher stopped, dismounted and walked back to the plough to see what it had struck. It was surprising for this to have happened here, on field-land. There should be no oak trees underneath the soil in this place.

He knelt down beside the plough and began to scoop the soil away around the point of the ploughshare. The lower tip of the share was twelve inches down. There was a lot of soil to be scooped up. He dug his gloved fingers into the earth and scooped it out with both hands. Six inches down . . . eight inches . . . ten inches . . . twelve. He slid his fingers along the blade of the ploughshare until they reached the forward point of it. The soil was loose and crumbly, and it kept falling back into the hole he was digging. He could not therefore see the twelve-inch-deep point of the share. He could only feel it. And now he could feel that the point was indeed lodged against something solid. He scooped away more earth. He enlarged the hole. It was necessary to see clearly what sort of an obstacle he had struck. If it was fairly small, then perhaps he could dig it out with his hands and get on with the job. If it was a tree-trunk he would have to go back to Ford's and fetch a spade.

'Come on,' he said aloud. 'I'll have you out of there, you hidden demon, you rotten old thing.' And suddenly, as the gloved fingers scraped away a final handful of black earth, he caught sight of the curved rim of something flat, like the rim of a huge thick plate sticking up out of the soil. He rubbed the rim with his fingers and he rubbed again. Then all at once, the rim gave off a greenish glint, and Gordon Butcher bent his head closer and closer still, peering down into the little hole he had dug with his hands. For one last time, he rubbed the rim clean with his fingers, and in a flash of light, he saw clearly the unmistakable blue-green crust of ancient buried metal, and his heart stood still.

It should be explained here that farmers in this part of Suffolk, and particularly in the Mildenhall area, have for years been turning up ancient objects from the soil. Flint arrowheads from very long ago have been found in considerable numbers, but more interesting than that, Roman pottery and Roman implements have also been found. It is known that the Romans favoured this part of the country during their occupation of Britain, and all local farmers are therefore well aware of the possibility of finding something interesting during a day's work. And so there was a kind of permanent awareness among Mildenhall people of the presence of treasure underneath the earth of their land.

Gordon Butcher's reaction, as soon as he saw the rim of that enormous plate, was a curious one. He immediately drew away. Then he got to his feet and turned his back on what he had just seen. He paused only long enough to switch off the engine of his tractor before he walked off fast in the direction of the road.

He did not know precisely what impulse caused him to stop digging and walk away. He will tell you that the only thing he can remember about those first few seconds was the whiff of danger that came to him from that little patch of greenish blue. The moment he touched it with his fingers, something electric went through his body, and there came to him a powerful premonition that this was a thing that could destroy the peace and happiness of many people.

In the beginning, all he had wished was to be away from it, and to leave it behind him and be done with it for ever. But after he had gone a few hundred yards or so, he began to slow his pace. At the gate leading out from Thistley Green, he stopped.

'What in the world is the matter with you, Mr Gordon Butcher?' he said aloud to the howling wind. 'Are you frightened or something? No, I'm not frightened. But I'll tell you straight, I'm not keen to handle this alone.'

That was when he thought of Ford.

He thought of Ford at first because it was for him that he was working. He thought of him second because he knew that Ford was a kind of collector of old stuff, of all the old stones and arrowheads which people kept digging up from time to time in the district, which they brought to Ford and which Ford placed upon the mantel in his parlour. It was believed that Ford sold these things, but no one knew or cared how he did it.

Gordon Butcher turned towards Ford's place and walked fast out of the gate on to the narrow road, down the road around the sharp left-hand corner and so to the house. He found Ford in his large shed, bending over a damaged harrow, mending it. Butcher stood by the door and said, 'Mr Ford!'

Ford looked around without straightening his body.

'Well, Gordon,' he said, 'what is it?'

Ford was middle-aged or a little older, bald-headed,

long-nosed, with a clever foxy look about his face. His mouth was thin and sour, and when he looked at you, and when you saw the tightness of his mouth and the thin, sour line of his lips, you knew that this was a mouth that never smiled. His chin receded, his nose was long and sharp and he had the air about him of a sour old crafty fox from the woods.

'What is it?' he said, looking up from the harrow.

Gordon Butcher stood by the door, blue-cheeked with cold, a little out of breath, rubbing his hands slowly one against the other.

'The tractor left the plough behind,' he said quietly. 'There's metal down there. I saw it.'

Ford's head gave a jerk. 'What kind of metal?' he said sharply.

'Flat. Quite flat like a sort of huge plate.'

'You didn't dig it out?' Ford had straightened up now and there was a glint of eagles in his eyes.

Butcher said, 'No, I left it alone and came straight on here.'

Ford walked quickly over to the corner and took his coat off the nail. He found a cap and gloves, then he found a spade and went towards the door. There was something odd, he noticed, in Butcher's manner.

'You're sure it was metal?'

'Crusted up,' Butcher said. 'But it was metal all right.'

'How deep?'

'Twelve inches down. At least the top of it was twelve inches down. The rest is deeper.'

'How d'you know it was a plate?'

'I don't,' Butcher said. 'I only saw a little bit of the rim. But it looked like a plate to me. An enormous plate.'

Ford's foxy face went quite white with excitement. 'Come on,' he said. 'We'll go back and see.'

The two men walked out of the shed into the fierce, ever-mounting fury of the wind. Ford shivered.

'Curse this filthy weather,' he said. 'Curse and blast this filthy freezing weather,' and he sank his pointed foxy face deep into the collar of his coat and began to ponder upon the possibilities of Butcher's find.

One thing Ford knew which Butcher did not know. He knew that back in 1932 a man called Lethbridge, a lecturer in Anglo-Saxon Antiquities at Cambridge University, had been excavating in the district and that he had actually unearthed the foundations of a Roman villa on Thistley Green itself. Ford was not forgetting that, and he quickened his pace. Butcher walked beside him without speaking and soon they were there. They went through the gate and over the field to the plough, which lay about ten yards behind the tractor.

Ford knelt down beside the front of the plough and peered into the small hole Gordon Butcher had dug with his hands. He touched the rim of green-blue metal with a gloved finger. He scraped away a bit more earth. He leaned farther forward so that his pointed nose was right down the hole. He ran fingers over the rough green surface. Then he stood up and said, 'Let's get the plough out of the way and do some digging.' Although there were fireworks exploding in his head and shivers running all over his body, Ford kept his voice very soft and casual.

Between them they pulled the plough back a couple of yards.

'Give me the spade,' Ford said, and he began cautiously to dig the soil away in a circle about three feet in diameter around the exposed patch of metal. When the hole was two feet deep, he threw away the spade and used his hands. He knelt down and scraped the soil away, and gradually the little patch of metal grew and grew until at last there lay exposed before them the great round disc of an enormous plate. It was fully twenty-four inches in diameter. The lower point of the plough had just caught the raised centre rim of the plate, for one could see the dent.

Carefully Ford lifted it out of the hole. He got to his feet, and stood wiping the soil away from it, turning it over and over in his hands. There was nothing much to see, for the whole surface was crusted over with a thick layer of a hard greenish-blue substance. But he knew that it was an enormous plate or dish of great weight and thickness. It weighed about eighteen pounds!

Ford stood in the field of yellow barley stubble and gazed at the huge plate. His hands began to shake. A tremendous and almost unbearable excitement started boiling up inside him and it was not easy for him to hide it. But he did his best.

'Some sort of a dish,' he said.

Butcher was kneeling on the ground beside the hole. 'Must be pretty old,' he said.

'Could be old,' Ford said. 'But it's all rusted up and eaten away.'

'That don't look like rust to me,' Butcher said. 'That greenish stuff isn't rust. It's something else . . .'

'It's green rust,' Ford said rather superbly, and that ended the discussion.

Butcher, still on his knees, was poking about casually in the now three-feet-wide hole with his gloved hands. 'There's another one down here,' he said.

Instantly, Ford laid the great dish on the ground. He knelt beside Butcher, and within minutes they had unearthed a second large green-encrusted plate. This one was a shade smaller than the first, and deeper. More of a bowl than a dish.

Ford stood up and held the new find in his hands. Another heavy one. And now he knew for certain they were on to something absolutely tremendous. They were on to Roman Treasure, and almost without question it was pure silver. Two things pointed to its being pure silver. First the weight, and second, the particular type of green crust caused by oxidation.

How often is a piece of Roman silver discovered in the world?

Almost never any more. And had pieces as large as this *ever* been unearthed before?

Ford wasn't sure, but he very much doubted it.

Worth millions it must be.

Worth literally millions of pounds.

His breath, coming fast, was making little white clouds in the freezing atmosphere.

'There's still more down here, Mr Ford,' Butcher was

saying. 'I can feel bits of it all over the place. You'll need the spade again.'

The third piece they got out was another large plate, somewhat similar to the first. Ford placed it in the barley stubble with the other two.

When Butcher felt the first flake of snow upon his cheek he looked up and saw over to the northeast a great white curtain drawn across the sky, a solid wall of snow flying forward on the wings of the wind.

'Here she comes!' he said, and Ford looked round and saw the snow moving upon them and he said, 'It's a blizzard. It's a filthy stinking blizzard!'

The two men stared at the blizzard as it raced across the fens towards them. Then it was on them, and all around was snow and snowflakes in the eyes and ears and mouth and down the neck and all around. And when Butcher glanced down at the ground a few seconds later it was already white.

'That's all we want,' Ford said. 'A filthy rotten stinking blizzard,' and he shivered and sank his sharp and foxy face deeper into the collar of his coat. 'Come on,' he said. 'See if there's any more.'

Butcher knelt down again and poked around in the soil, then in the slow and casual manner of a man having a lucky dip in a barrel of sawdust, he pulled out another plate and held it out to Ford. Ford took it and placed it with the other three. Now Ford knelt down beside Butcher and began to dip into the soil with him.

For a whole hour the two men stayed out there digging and scratching in that little three-foot patch of soil. And during that hour they found and laid upon the ground beside them *no less than thirty-four separate pieces*! There were dishes, bowls, goblets, spoons, ladles and several other things, all of them crusted over but each one recognizable for what it was. And all the while the blizzard swirled around them and the snow gathered in little mounds upon their caps and on their shoulders and the flakes melted on their faces so that rivers of icy water trickled down their necks. A large globule of half-frozen liquid dangled continuously, like a snow drop, from the end of Ford's pointed nose.

They worked in silence. It was too cold to speak. And as one precious article after the other was unearthed, Ford laid them carefully on the ground in rows, pausing every now and then to wipe the snow away from a dish or a spoon which was in danger of being completely covered.

At last Ford said, 'That's the lot, I think.'

'Yes.'

Ford stood up and stamped his feet on the ground. 'Got a sack in the tractor?' he said, and while Butcher walked over to fetch the sack, he turned and gazed upon the four-and-thirty pieces lying in the snow at his feet. He counted them again. If they were silver, which they surely must be, and if they were Roman, which they undoubtedly were, then this was a discovery that would rock the world.

Butcher called to him from the tractor, 'It's only a dirty old sack.'

'It'll do.'

Butcher brought the sack over and held it open while Ford carefully put the articles into it. They all went in except one. The massive two-foot plate was too large for the neck of the sack.

The two men were really cold now. For over an hour they had knelt and scratched about out there in the open field with the blizzard swirling around them. Already, nearly six inches of snow had fallen. Butcher was half frozen. His cheeks were dead-white, blotched with blue, his feet were numb like wood, and when he moved his legs he could not feel the ground beneath his feet. He was much colder than Ford. His coat and clothes were not so thick, and ever since early morning he had been sitting high up on the seat of the tractor, exposed to the bitter wind. His blue-white face was tight and unmoving. All he wanted was to get home to his family and to the fire that he knew would be burning in the grate.

Ford, on the other hand, was not thinking about the cold. His mind was concentrated solely upon one thing – how to get possession for himself of this fabulous treasure. His position, as he knew very well, was not a strong one.

In England there is a very curious law about finding any kind of gold or silver treasure. This law goes back hundreds of years, and is still strictly enforced today. The law states that if a person digs up out of the ground, even out of his own garden, a piece of metal that is either *gold* or *silver*, it automatically becomes what is known as Treasure Trove and is the property of the Crown. The Crown doesn't in these days mean the actual King or Queen. It means the country or the government. The law also states that it is a criminal offence to conceal such a find. You are simply not allowed to hide the stuff and keep it for yourself. You must report it at once, preferably to the police. And if you do report it at once, you as the finder will be entitled to receive from the government in money the full amount of the market value of the article. You are not required to report the digging up of other metals. You are allowed to find as much valuable pewter, bronze, copper or even platinum as you wish, and you can keep it all, but not gold or silver.

The other curious part of this curious law is this: it is the person who *discovers* the treasure in the first place who gets the reward from the government. The owner of the land gets nothing – unless of course the finder is trespassing on the land when he makes the discovery. But if the finder of the treasure has been hired by the owner to do a job on his land, then he, the finder, gets all the reward.

In this case, the finder was Gordon Butcher. Farthermore, he was not trespassing. He was performing a job which he had been hired to do. This treasure therefore belonged to Butcher and to no one else. All he had to do was to take it and show it to an expert, who would immediately identify it as silver, then turn it in to the police. In time, he would receive from the government one hundred per cent of its value – perhaps a million pounds.

All this left Ford out in the cold and Ford knew it. He had no rights whatsoever to the treasure by law. Thus, as he must have told himself at the time, his only chance of getting hold of the stuff for himself lay in the fact that Butcher was an ignorant man who didn't know the law and who did not anyway have the faintest idea of the value of the find. The probability was that in a few days Butcher would forget all about it. He was too simple-minded a fellow, too artless, too trusting, too unselfish to give the matter much thought.

Now, out there in the desolate snow-swept field, Ford bent down and took hold of the huge dish with one hand. He raised it but he did not lift it. The lower rim remained resting on the snow. With his other hand, he grasped the top of the sack. He didn't lift that either. He just held it. And there he stooped amid the swirling snowflakes, both hands embracing, as it were, the treasure, but not actually taking it. It was a subtle and canny gesture. It managed somehow to signify ownership before ownership had been discussed. A child plays the same game when he reaches out and closes his fingers over the biggest chocolate éclair on the plate and then says, 'Can I have this one, Mummy?' He's already got it.

'Well, Gordon,' Ford said, stooping over, holding the sack and the great dish in his gloved fingers. 'I don't suppose you want any of this old stuff.'

It was not a question. It was a statement of fact framed as a question.

The blizzard was still raging. The snow was falling so densely the two men could hardly see one another.

'You ought to get along home and warm yourself up,' Ford went on. 'You look frozen to death.'

'I *feel* frozen to death,' Butcher said.

'Then you get on that tractor quick and hurry home,' said the thoughtful, kind-hearted Ford. 'Leave the plough here and leave your bike at my place. The important thing is to get back and warm yourself up before you catch pneumonia.'

'I think that's just what I will do, Mr Ford,' Butcher said. 'Can you manage all right with that sack? It's mighty heavy.'

'I might not even bother about it today,' Ford said casually. 'I just might leave it here and come back for it another time. Rusty old stuff.'

'So long then, Mr Ford.'

''Bye, Gordon.'

Gordon Butcher mounted the tractor and drove away into the blizzard.

Ford hoisted the sack on to his shoulder, and then, not without difficulty, he lifted the massive dish with his other hand and tucked it under his arm.

'I am carrying,' he told himself, as he trudged through the snow, 'I am now carrying what is probably the biggest treasure ever dug up in the whole history of England.'

When Gordon Butcher came stamping and blowing through the back door of his small brick house late that afternoon, his wife was ironing by the fire. She looked up and saw his blue-white face and snow-encrusted clothes.

'My goodness, Gordon, you look froze to death!' she cried.

'I am,' he said. 'Help me off with these clothes, love. My fingers aren't hardly working at all.'

She took off his gloves, his coat, his jacket, his wet shirt. She pulled off his boots and socks. She fetched a towel and rubbed his chest and shoulders vigorously all over to restore the circulation. She rubbed his feet.

'Sit down there by the fire,' she said, 'and I'll get you a hot cup of tea.'

Later, when he was settled comfortably in the warmth with dry clothes on his back and the mug of tea in his hand, he told her what had happened that afternoon.

'He's a foxy one, that Mr Ford,' she said, not looking up from her ironing. 'I never did like him.'

'He got pretty excited about it all, I can tell you that,' Gordon Butcher said. 'Jumpy as a jack-rabbit he was.'

'That may be,' she said. 'But you ought to have had more sense than to go crawling about on your hands and knees in a freezing blizzard just because Mr Ford said to do it.'

'I'm all right,' Gordon Butcher said, 'I'm warming up nicely now.'

And that, believe it or not, was about the last time the subject of the treasure was discussed in the Butcher household for some years.

The reader should be reminded that this was wartime, 1942. Britain was totally absorbed in the desperate war against Hitler and Mussolini. Germany was bombing England, and England was bombing Germany, and nearly every night Gordon Butcher heard the roar of motors from the big aerodrome at nearby Mildenhall as the bombers took off for Hamburg, Berlin, Kiel, Wilhelmshaven or Frankfurt. Sometimes he would wake in the early hours and hear them coming home, and sometimes the Germans flew over to bomb the aerodrome, and the Butcher house would shake with the *crumph* and crash of bombs not far away.

Butcher himself was exempt from military service. He was a farmer, a skilled ploughman, and they had told him when he volunteered for the Army in 1939 that he was not wanted. The island's food supplies must be kept going, they told him, and it was vital that men like him stay on their jobs and cultivate the land.

Ford, being in the same business, was also exempt. He was a bachelor, living alone, and he was thus able to live a secret life and to do secret things within the walls of his home.

And so, on that terrible snowy afternoon when they dug up the treasure, Ford carried it home and laid everything out on a table in the back room.

Thirty-four separate pieces! They covered the entire table. And by the look of it, they were in marvellous condition. Silver does not rust. The green crust of oxidation can even be protection for the surface of the metal underneath. And with care, it could all be removed.

Ford decided to use an ordinary domestic silver polish known as Silvo, and he bought a large stock of it from the ironmonger's shop in Mildenhall. Then he took first the great two-foot plate which weighed more than eighteen pounds. He worked on it in the evenings. He soaked it all over with Silvo. He rubbed and rubbed. He worked patiently on this single dish every night for more than sixteen weeks.

At last, one memorable evening, there showed beneath his rubbing a small area of shining silver, and on the silver, raised up and beautifully worked, there was a part of a man's head.

He kept at it, and gradually the little patch of shining metal spread and spread, the blue-green crust crept outwards to the edges of the plate, until finally the top surface of the great dish lay before him in its full glory, covered all over with a wondrous pattern of animals and men and many odd legendary things.

Ford was astounded by the beauty of the great plate. It was filled with life and movement. There was a fierce face with tangled hair, a dancing goat with a human head, there were men and women and animals of many kinds cavorting around the rim, and no doubt all of them told a story.

Next, he set about cleaning the reverse side of the plate. Weeks and weeks it took. And when the work was completed and the whole plate on both sides was shining like a star, he placed it safely in the lower cupboard of his big oak sideboard and locked the cupboard door.

One by one, he tackled the remaining thirty-three pieces. A mania had taken hold of him now, a fierce compulsion to make every item shine in all its silver brilliance. He wanted to see all thirty-four pieces laid out on the big table in a dazzling array of silver. He wanted that more than anything else, and he worked desperately hard to achieve his wish.

He cleaned the two smaller dishes next, then the large fluted bowl, then the five long-handled ladles, the goblets, the wine-cups, the spoons. Every single piece was cleaned with equal care and made to shine with equal brilliance, and when they were all done, two years had passed and it was 1944.

But no strangers were allowed to look. Ford discussed the matter with no man or woman, and Rolfe, the owner of the plot on Thistley Green where the treasure had been found, knew nothing except that Ford, or someone Ford had hired, had ploughed his land extremely well and very deep.

One can guess why Ford hid the treasure instead of reporting it to the police as Treasure Trove. Had he reported it, it would have been taken away and Gordon Butcher would have been rewarded as the finder. Rewarded with a fortune. So the only thing Ford could do was to hang on to it and hide it in the hope, presumably, of selling it quietly to some dealer or collector at a later date.

It is possible, of course, to take a more charitable view and assume that Ford kept the treasure solely because he loved beautiful things and wanted to have them around him. No one will ever know the true answer.

Another year went by.

The war against Hitler was won.

And then, in 1946, just after Easter, there was a knock on the door of Ford's house. Ford opened it.

'Why hello, Mr Ford. How are you after all these years?'

'Hello, Dr Fawcett,' Ford said. 'You been keeping all right?'

'I'm fine, thank you,' Dr Fawcett said. 'It's been a long time, hasn't it?'

'Yes,' Ford said. 'That old war kept us all pretty busy.'

'May I come in?' Dr Fawcett asked.

'Of course,' Ford said. 'Come on in.'

Dr Hugh Alderson Fawcett was a keen and learned

archaeologist who before the war had made a point of visiting Ford once a year in search of old stones or arrowheads. Ford had usually collected a batch of such items during the twelve months and he was always willing to sell them to Fawcett. They were seldom of great value, but now and again something quite good had turned up.

'Well,' said Fawcett, taking off his coat in the little hall. 'Well, well, well. It's been nearly seven years since I was here last.'

'Yes, it's been a long time,' Ford said.

Ford led him into the front room and showed him a box of flint arrowheads which had been picked up in the district. Some were good, others not so good. Fawcett picked through them, sorted them, and a deal was done.

'Nothing else?'

'No, I don't think so.'

Ford wished fervently that Dr Fawcett had never come. He wished even more fervently that he would go away.

It was at this point that Ford noticed something that made him sweat. He saw suddenly that he had left lying on the mantel over the fireplace the two most beautiful of the Roman spoons from the treasure hoard. These spoons had fascinated him because each was inscribed with the name of a Roman girl child to whom it had been given, presumably as a christening present, by Roman parents who had been converted to Christianity. One name was Pascentia, the other was Papittedo. Rather lovely names.

Ford, sweating with fear, tried to place himself between Dr Fawcett and the mantelpiece. He might even, he thought, be able to slip the spoons into his pocket if he got the chance.

He didn't get the chance.

Perhaps Ford had polished them so well that a little flash of reflected light from the silver caught the doctor's eye. Who knows? The fact remains that Fawcett saw them. The moment he saw them, he pounced like a tiger.

'Great heavens alive!' he cried. 'What are these?'

'Pewter,' Ford said, sweating more than ever. 'Just a couple of old pewter spoons.'

'Pewter?' cried Fawcett, turning one of the spoons over in his fingers. 'Pewter! You call this *pewter*?'

'That's right,' Ford said. 'It's pewter.'

'You know what this is?' Fawcett said, his voice going high with excitement. 'Shall I tell you what this *really* is?'

'You don't have to tell me,' Ford said, truculent. 'I know what it is. It's old pewter. And quite nice, too.'

Fawcett was reading the inscription in Roman letters on the scoop of the spoon. 'Papittedo!' he cried.

'What's that mean?' Ford asked him.

Fawcett picked up the other spoon. 'Pascentia,' he said. 'Beautiful! These are the names of Roman children! And these spoons, my friend, are made of solid silver! Solid Roman silver!'

'Not possible,' Ford said.

'They're magnificent!' Fawcett cried out, going into raptures. 'They're perfect! They're unbelievable! Where on earth did you find them? It's most important to know where you found them! Was there anything else?' Fawcett was hopping about all over the room.

'Well . . .' Ford said, licking dry lips.

'You must report them at once!' Fawcett cried. 'They're

Treasure Trove! The British Museum is going to want these and that's for certain! How long have you had them?'

'Just a little while,' Ford told him.

'And *who* found them?' Fawcett asked, looking straight at him. 'Did you find them yourself or did you get them from somebody else? This is vital! The finder will be able to tell us all about it!'

Ford felt the walls of the room closing in on him and he didn't quite know what to do.

'Come on, man! Surely you know where you got them! Every detail will have to come out when you hand them in. Promise me you'll go to the police with them at once?'

'Well . . .' Ford said.

'If you don't, then I'm afraid I shall be forced to report it myself,' Fawcett told him. 'It's my duty.'

The game was up now and Ford knew it. A thousand questions would be asked. How did you find it? When did you find it? What were you doing? Where was the exact spot? Whose land were you ploughing? And sooner or later, inevitably, the name of Gordon Butcher would have to come into it. It was unavoidable. And then, when Butcher was questioned, he would remember the size of the hoard and tell them all about it.

So the game was up. And the only thing to do at this point was to unlock the doors of the big sideboard and show the entire hoard to Dr Fawcett.

Ford's excuse for keeping it all and not turning it in would have to be that he thought it was pewter. So long as he stuck to that, he told himself, they couldn't do anything to him.

Dr Fawcett would probably have a heart attack when he saw what there was in that cupboard.

'There is actually quite a bit more of it,' Ford said.

'Where?' cried Fawcett, spinning round. 'Where, man, where? Lead me to it!'

'I really thought it was pewter,' Ford said, moving slowly and very reluctantly forward to the oak sideboard. 'Otherwise I would naturally have reported it at once.'

He bent down and unlocked the lower doors of the sideboard. He opened the doors.

And then Dr Hugh Alderson Fawcett very nearly did have a heart attack. He flung himself on his knees. He gasped. He choked. He began spluttering like an old kettle. He reached out for the great silver dish. He took it. He held it in shaking hands and his face went as white as snow. He didn't speak. He couldn't. He was literally and physically and mentally struck absolutely dumb by the sight of the treasure.

The interesting part of the story ends here. The rest is routine. Ford went to Mildenhall police station and made a report. The police came at once and collected all thirty-four pieces, and they were sent under guard to the British Museum for examination.

Then an urgent message from the Museum to the Mildenhall police. It was far and away the finest Roman silver ever found in the British Isles. It was of enormous value. The Museum (which is really a public governmental institution) wished to acquire it. In fact, they insisted upon acquiring it.

The wheels of the law began to turn. An official inquest and hearing was arranged at the nearest large town, Bury St Edmunds. The silver was moved there under special police guard. Ford was summoned to appear before the coroner and a jury of fourteen, while Gordon Butcher, that good and quiet man, was ordered also to present himself to give evidence.

On Monday, July the first, 1946, the hearing took place, and the coroner cross-questioned Ford closely.

'You thought it was pewter?'

'Yes.'

'Even after you had cleaned it?'

'Yes.'

'You took no steps to inform any experts of the find?'

'No.'

'What did you intend to do with the articles?'

'Nothing. Just keep them.'

And when he had concluded his evidence, Ford asked permission to go outside into the fresh air because he said he felt faint. Nobody was surprised.

Then Butcher was called, and in a few simple words he told of his part in the affair.

Dr Fawcett gave his evidence, so did several other learned archaeologists, all of whom testified to the extreme rarity of the treasure. They said that it was of the fourth century after Christ; that it was the table silver of a wealthy Roman family; that it had probably been buried by the owner's bailiff to save it from the Picts and Scots who swept down from the north in about AD 365–7 and laid waste many Roman settlements. The man who buried it had probably been liquidated either by a Pict or a Scot, and the treasure had remained concealed a foot below the soil ever since. The workmanship, said the experts, was magnificent. Some of it may have been executed in England, but more probably the articles were made in Italy or in Egypt. The great plate was of course the finest piece. The head in the centre was that of Neptune, the sea-god, with dolphins in his hair and seaweed in his beard. All around him, sea-nymphs and sea-monsters gambolled. On the broad rim of the plate stood Bacchus and his attendants. There was wine and revelry. Hercules was there, quite drunk, supported by two satyrs, his lion's skin fallen from his shoulders. Pan was there, too, dancing upon his goat-legs with his pipes in his hand. And everywhere there were maenads, female devotees of Bacchus, rather tipsy women.

The court was told also that several of the spoons bore the monogram of Christ (Chi-Rho), and that the two which were inscribed with the names Pascentia and Papittedo were undoubtedly christening presents.

The experts concluded their evidence and the court adjourned. Soon the jury returned, and their verdict was astonishing. No blame was attached to anyone for anything, although the finder of the treasure was no longer entitled to receive full compensation from the Crown because the find had not been declared at once.

Nevertheless, there would probably be a measure of compensation paid, and with this in view, the finders were declared to be jointly Ford and Butcher.

Not Butcher. Ford and Butcher.

There is no more to tell other than that the treasure was acquired by the British Museum, where it now stands proudly displayed in a large glass case for all to see. And already people have travelled great distances to go and look upon those lovely things which Gordon Butcher found beneath his plough on that cold and windy winter afternoon. One day, a book or two will be compiled about them, full of suppositions and abstruse conclusions, and men who move in archaeological circles will talk for ever about the Treasure of Mildenhall.

As a gesture, the Museum rewarded the co-finders with one thousand pounds each. Butcher, the true finder, was happy and surprised to receive so much money. He did not realize that had he been allowed to take the treasure home originally, he would almost certainly have revealed its existence and would thus have become eligible to receive one hundred per cent of its value, which could have been anything between half a million and a million pounds.

Nobody knows what Ford thought about it all. He must have been relieved and perhaps somewhat surprised when he heard that the court had believed his story about pewter. But above all he must have been shattered by the loss of his great treasure. For the rest of his life he would be kicking himself for leaving those two spoons on the mantel above the fireplace for Dr Fawcett to see.

Parson's Pleasure

First published in *Esquire* (April 1958)

Mr Boggis was driving the car slowly, leaning back comfortably in the seat with one elbow resting on the sill of the open window. How beautiful the countryside, he thought; how pleasant to see a sign or two of summer once again. The primroses especially. And the hawthorn. The hawthorn was exploding white and pink and red along the hedges and the primroses were growing underneath in little clumps, and it was beautiful.

He took one hand off the wheel and lit himself a cigarette. The best thing now, he told himself, would be to make for the top of Brill Hill. He could see it about half a mile ahead. And that must be the village of Brill, that cluster of cottages among the trees right on the very summit. Excellent. Not many of his Sunday sections had a nice elevation like that to work from.

He drove up the hill and stopped the car just short of the summit on the outskirts of the village. Then he got out and looked around. Down below, the countryside was spread out before him like a huge green carpet. He could see for miles. It was perfect. He took a pad and pencil from his pocket, leaned against the back of the car, and allowed his practised eye to travel slowly over the landscape.

He could see one medium farmhouse over on the right,

back in the fields, with a track leading to it from the road. There was another larger one beyond it. There was a house surrounded by tall elms that looked as though it might be a Queen Anne, and there were two likely farms away over on the left. Five places in all. That was about the lot in this direction.

Mr Boggis drew a rough sketch on his pad showing the position of each so that he'd be able to find them easily when he was down below, then he got back into the car and drove up through the village to the other side of the hill. From there he spotted six more possibles – five farms and one big white Georgian house. He studied the Georgian house through his binoculars. It had a clean prosperous look, and the garden was well ordered. That was a pity. He ruled it out immediately. There was no point in calling on the prosperous.

In this square then, in this section, there were ten possibles in all. Ten was a nice number, Mr Boggis told himself. Just the right amount for a leisurely afternoon's work. What time was it now? Twelve o'clock. He would have liked a pint of beer in the pub before he started, but on Sundays they didn't open until one. Very well, he would have it later. He glanced at the notes on his pad. He decided to take the Queen Anne first, the house with the elms. It had looked nicely dilapidated through the binoculars. The people there could probably do with some money. He was always lucky with Queen Annes, anyway. Mr Boggis climbed back into the car, released the handbrake, and began cruising slowly down the hill without the engine.

Apart from the fact that he was at this moment disguised in the uniform of a clergyman, there was nothing very sinister about Mr Cyril Boggis. By trade he was a dealer in antique furniture, with his own shop and showroom in the King's Road, Chelsea. His premises were not large, and generally he didn't do a great deal of business, but because he always bought cheap, very very cheap, and sold very very dear, he managed to make quite a tidy little income every year. He was a talented salesman, and when buying or selling a piece he could slide smoothly into whichever mood suited the client best. He could become grave and charming for the aged, obsequious for the rich, sober for the godly, masterful for the weak, mischievous for the widow, arch and saucy for the spinster. He was well aware of his gift, using it shamelessly on every possible occasion; and often, at the end of an unusually good performance, it was as much as he could do to prevent himself from turning aside and taking a bow or two as the thundering applause of the audience went rolling through the theatre.

In spite of this rather clownish quality of his, Mr Boggis was not a fool. In fact, it was said of him by some that he probably knew as much about French, English and Italian furniture as anyone else in London. He also had surprisingly good taste, and he was quick to recognize and reject an ungraceful design, however genuine the article might be. His real love, naturally, was for the work of the great eighteenth-century English designers, Ince, Mayhew, Chippendale, Robert Adam, Manwaring, Inigo Jones, Hepplewhite, Kent, Johnson, George Smith, Lock, Sheraton and the rest of them, but even with these he occasionally drew the line. He refused, for example, to allow a single piece from Chippendale's Chinese or Gothic period to come into his showroom, and the same was true of some of the heavier Italian designs of Robert Adam.

During the past few years, Mr Boggis had achieved considerable fame among his friends in the trade by his ability to produce unusual and often quite rare items with astonishing regularity. Apparently the man had a source of supply that was almost inexhaustible, a sort of private warehouse, and it seemed that all he had to do was to drive out to it once a week and help himself. Whenever they asked him where he got the stuff, he would smile knowingly and wink and murmur something about a little secret.

The idea behind Mr Boggis's little secret was a simple one, and it had come to him as a result of something that had happened on a certain Sunday afternoon nearly nine years before, while he was driving in the country.

He had gone out in the morning to visit his old mother, who lived in Sevenoaks, and on the way back the fan-belt on his car had broken, causing the engine to overheat and the water to boil away. He had got out of the car and walked to the nearest house, a smallish farm building about fifty yards off the road, and had asked the woman who answered the door if he could please have a jug of water.

While he was waiting for her to fetch it, he happened to glance in through the door to the living-room, and there, not five yards from where he was standing, he spotted something that made him so excited the sweat began to come out all over the top of his head. It was a large oak armchair of a type that he had only seen once before in his life. Each arm, as well as the panel at the back, was supported by a row of eight beautifully turned spindles. The back panel itself was decorated by an inlay of the most delicate floral design, and the head of a duck was carved to lie along half the length of either arm. Good God, he thought. This thing is late fifteenth century!

He poked his head in further through the door, and there, by heavens, was another of them on the other side of the fireplace!

He couldn't be sure, but two chairs like that must be worth at least a thousand pounds up in London. And oh, what beauties they were!

When the woman returned, Mr Boggis introduced himself and straight away asked if she would like to sell her chairs.

Dear me, she said. But why on earth should she want to sell her chairs?

No reason at all, except that he might be willing to give her a pretty nice price.

And how much would he give? They were definitely not for sale, but just out of curiosity, just for fun, you know, how much would he give?

Thirty-five pounds.

How much?

Thirty-five pounds.

Dear me, thirty-five pounds. Well, well, that was very interesting. She'd always thought they were valuable. They were very old. They were very comfortable too. She couldn't possibly do without them, not possibly. No, they were not for sale but thank you very much all the same.

They weren't really so very old, Mr Boggis told her, and they wouldn't be at all easy to sell, but it just happened that he had a client who rather liked that sort of thing. Maybe he could go up another two pounds – call it thirty-seven. How about that?

They bargained for half an hour, and of course in the end Mr Boggis got the chairs and agreed to pay her something less than a twentieth of their value.

That evening, driving back to London in his old station-wagon with the two fabulous chairs tucked away snugly in the back, Mr Boggis had suddenly been struck by what seemed to him to be a most remarkable idea.

Look here, he said. If there is good stuff in one farmhouse, then why not in others? Why shouldn't he search for it? Why shouldn't he comb the countryside? He could do it on Sundays. In that way, it wouldn't interfere with his work at all. He never knew what to do with his Sundays.

So Mr Boggis bought maps, large-scale maps of all the counties around London, and with a fine pen he divided each of them up into a series of squares. Each of these squares covered an actual area of five miles by five, which was about as much territory, he estimated, as he could cope with on a single Sunday, were he to comb it thoroughly. He didn't want the towns and the villages. It was the comparatively isolated places, the large farmhouses and the rather dilapidated country mansions, that he was looking for; and in this way, if he did one square each Sunday, fifty-two squares a year, he would gradually cover every farm and every country house in the home counties.

But obviously there was a bit more to it than that. Country folk are a suspicious lot. So are the impoverished rich. You can't go about ringing their bells and expecting them to show you around their houses just for the asking, because they won't do it. That way you would never get beyond the front door. How then was he to gain admittance? Perhaps it would be best if he didn't let them know he was a dealer at all. He could be the telephone man, the plumber, the gas inspector. He could even be a clergyman . . .

From this point on, the whole scheme began to take on a more practical aspect. Mr Boggis ordered a large quantity of superior cards on which the following legend was engraved:

THE REVEREND

CYRIL WINNINGTON BOGGIS

President of the Society	*In association with*
for the Preservation of	*The Victoria and*
Rare Furniture	*Albert Museum*

From now on, every Sunday, he was going to be a nice old parson spending his holiday travelling around on a labour of love for the 'Society', compiling an inventory of the treasures that lay hidden in the country homes of England. And who in the world was going to kick him out when they heard that one?

Nobody.

And then, once he was inside, if he happened to spot something he really wanted, well – he knew a hundred different ways of dealing with that.

Rather to Mr Boggis's surprise, the scheme worked. In fact, the friendliness with which he was received in one house after another through the countryside was, in the beginning, quite embarrassing, even to him. A slice of cold pie, a glass of port, a cup of tea, a basket of plums, even a full sit-down Sunday dinner with the family, such things were constantly being pressed upon him. Sooner or later, of course, there had been some bad moments and a number of unpleasant incidents, but then nine years is more than four hundred Sundays, and that adds up to a great quantity of houses visited. All in all, it had been an interesting, exciting and lucrative business.

And now it was another Sunday and Mr Boggis was operating in the county of Buckinghamshire, in one of the most northerly squares on his map, about ten miles from Oxford, and as he drove down the hill and headed for his first house, the dilapidated Queen Anne, he began to get the feeling that this was going to be one of his lucky days.

He parked the car about a hundred yards from the gates and got out to walk the rest of the way. He never liked people to see his car until after a deal was completed. A dear old clergyman and a large station-wagon somehow never seemed quite right together. Also the short walk gave him time to examine the property closely from the outside and to assume the mood most likely to be suitable for the occasion.

Mr Boggis strode briskly up the drive. He was a small

fat-legged man with a belly. The face was round and rosy, quite perfect for the part, and the two large brown eyes that bulged out at you from this rosy face gave an impression of gentle imbecility. He was dressed in a black suit with the usual parson's dog-collar round his neck, and on his head a soft black hat. He carried an old oak walking-stick which lent him, in his opinion, a rather rustic easy-going air.

He approached the front door and rang the bell. He heard the sound of footsteps in the hall and the door opened and suddenly there stood before him, or rather above him, a gigantic woman dressed in riding-breeches. Even through the smoke of her cigarette he could smell the powerful odour of stables and horse manure that clung about her.

'Yes?' she asked, looking at him suspiciously. 'What is it you want?'

Mr Boggis, who half expected her to whinny any moment, raised his hat, made a little bow, and handed her his card. 'I do apologize for bothering you,' he said, and then he waited, watching her face as she read the message.

'I don't understand,' she said, handing back the card. 'What is it you want?'

Mr Boggis explained about the Society for the Preservation of Rare Furniture.

'This wouldn't by any chance be something to do with the Socialist Party?' she asked, staring at him fiercely from under a pair of pale bushy brows.

From then on, it was easy. A Tory in riding-breeches,

male or female, was always a sitting duck for Mr Boggis. He spent two minutes delivering an impassioned eulogy on the extreme Right Wing Conservative Party, then two more denouncing the Socialists. As a clincher, he made particular reference to the Bill that the Socialists had once introduced for the abolition of bloodsports in the country, and went on to inform his listener that his idea of heaven – 'though you better not tell the bishop, my dear' – was a place where one could hunt the fox, the stag and the hare with large packs of tireless hounds from morn till night every day of the week, including Sundays.

Watching her as he spoke, he could see the magic beginning to do its work. The woman was grinning now, showing Mr Boggis a set of enormous, slightly yellow teeth. 'Madam,' he cried, 'I beg of you, *please* don't get me started on Socialism.' At that point, she let out a great guffaw of laughter, raised an enormous red hand, and slapped him so hard on the shoulder that he nearly went over.

'Come in!' she shouted. 'I don't know what the hell you want, but come on in!'

Unfortunately, and rather surprisingly, there was nothing of any value in the whole house, and Mr Boggis, who never wasted time on barren territory, soon made his excuses and took his leave. The whole visit had taken less than fifteen minutes, and that, he told himself as he climbed back into his car and started off for the next place, was exactly as it should be.

From now on, it was all farmhouses, and the nearest was about half a mile up the road. It was a large half-timbered brick building of considerable age, and there was a magnificent pear tree still in blossom covering almost the whole of the south wall.

Mr Boggis knocked on the door. He waited, but no one came. He knocked again, but still there was no answer, so he wandered round the back to look for the farmer among the cowsheds. There was no one there either. He guessed that they must all still be in church, so he began peering in the windows to see if he could spot anything interesting. There was nothing in the dining-room. Nothing in the library either. He tried the next window, the living-room, and there, right under his nose, in the little alcove that the window made, he saw a beautiful thing, a semicircular card-table in mahogany, richly veneered and in the style of Hepplewhite, built around 1780.

'Ah-ha,' he said aloud, pressing his face hard against the glass. 'Well done, Boggis.'

But that was not all. There was a chair there as well, a single chair, and if he were not mistaken it was of an even finer quality than the table. Another Hepplewhite, wasn't it? And oh, what a beauty! The lattices on the back were finely carved with the honeysuckle, the husk and the paterae, the caning on the seat was original, the legs were very gracefully turned and the two back ones had that peculiar outward splay that meant so much. It was an exquisite chair. 'Before this day is done,' Mr Boggis said softly, 'I shall have the pleasure of sitting down upon that lovely seat.' He never bought a chair without doing this. It was a favourite test of his, and it was always an intriguing sight to see him lowering himself delicately into the seat, waiting for the 'give', expertly gauging the precise but infinitesimal degree of shrinkage that the years had caused in the mortise and dovetail joints.

But there was no hurry, he told himself. He would return here later. He had the whole afternoon before him.

The next farm was situated some way back in the fields, and in order to keep his car out of sight, Mr Boggis had to leave it on the road and walk about six hundred yards along a straight track that led directly into the back yard of the farmhouse. This place, he noticed as he approached, was a good deal smaller than the last, and he didn't hold out much hope for it. It looked rambling and dirty, and some of the sheds were clearly in bad repair.

There were three men standing in a close group in a corner of the yard, and one of them had two large black greyhounds with him, on leashes. When the men caught sight of Mr Boggis walking forward in his black suit and parson's collar, they stopped talking and seemed suddenly to stiffen and freeze, becoming absolutely still, motionless, three faces turned towards him, watching him suspiciously as he approached.

The oldest of the three was a stumpy man with a wide frog-mouth and small shifty eyes, and although Mr Boggis didn't know it, his name was Rummins and he was the owner of the farm.

The tall youth beside him, who appeared to have something wrong with one eye, was Bert, the son of Rummins.

The shortish flat-faced man with a narrow corrugated brow and immensely broad shoulders was Claud. Claud had dropped in on Rummins in the hope of getting a piece of pork or ham out of him from the pig that had been killed the day before. Claud knew about the killing – the noise of it had carried far across the fields – and he also knew that a man should have a government permit to do that sort of thing, and that Rummins didn't have one.

'Good afternoon,' Mr Boggis said. 'Isn't it a lovely day.'

None of the three men moved. At that moment they were all thinking precisely the same thing – that somehow or other this clergyman, who was certainly not the local fellow, had been sent to poke his nose into their business and to report what he found to the government.

'What beautiful dogs,' Mr Boggis said. 'I must say I've never been greyhound-racing myself, but they tell me it's a fascinating sport.'

Again the silence, and Mr Boggis glanced quickly from Rummins to Bert, then to Claud, then back again to Rummins, and he noticed that each of them had the same peculiar expression on his face, something between a jeer and a challenge, with a contemptuous curl to the mouth, and a sneer around the nose.

'Might I inquire if you are the owner?' Mr Boggis asked, undaunted, addressing himself to Rummins.

'What is it you want?'

'I do apologize for troubling you, especially on a Sunday.'

Mr Boggis offered his card and Rummins took it and held it up close to his face. The other two didn't move, but their eyes swivelled over to one side, trying to see.

'And what exactly might you be wanting?' Rummins asked.

For the second time that morning, Mr Boggis explained at some length the aims and ideals of the Society for the Preservation of Rare Furniture.

'We don't have any,' Rummins told him when it was over. 'You're wasting your time.'

'Now, just a minute, sir,' Mr Boggis said, raising a finger. 'The last man who said that to me was an old farmer down in Sussex, and when he finally let me into his house, d'you know what I found? A dirty-looking old chair in the corner of the kitchen, and it turned out to be worth *four hundred pounds*! I showed him how to sell it, and he bought himself a new tractor with the money.'

'What on earth are you talking about?' Claud said. 'There ain't no chair in the world worth four hundred pound.'

'Excuse me,' Mr Boggis answered primly, 'but there are plenty of chairs in England worth more than twice that figure. And you know where they are? They're tucked away in the farms and cottages all over the country, with the owners using them as steps and ladders and standing on them with hobnailed boots to reach a pot of jam out of the top cupboard or to hang a picture. This is the truth I'm telling you, my friend.'

Rummins shifted uneasily on his feet. 'You mean to say all you want to do is go inside and stand there in the middle of the room and look around?'

'Exactly,' Mr Boggis said. He was at last beginning to sense what the trouble might be. 'I don't want to pry into your cupboards or into your larder. I just want to look at the furniture to see if you happen to have any treasures here, and then I can write about them in our Society magazine.'

'You know what I think?' Rummins said, fixing him with his small wicked eyes. 'I think you're after buying the stuff yourself. Why else would you be going to all this trouble?'

'Oh, dear me. I only wish I had the money. Of course, if I saw something that I took a great fancy to, and it wasn't beyond my means, I might be tempted to make an offer. But alas, that rarely happens.'

'Well,' Rummins said, 'I don't suppose there's any harm in your taking a look around if that's all you want.' He led the way across the yard to the back door of the farm-house, and Mr Boggis followed him; so did the son, Bert, and Claud with his two dogs. They went through the kitchen, where the only furniture was a cheap deal table with a dead chicken lying on it, and they emerged into a fairly large, exceedingly filthy living-room.

And there it was! Mr Boggis saw it at once, and he stopped dead in his tracks and gave a little shrill gasp of shock. Then he stood there for five, ten, fifteen seconds at least, staring like an idiot, unable to believe, not daring to believe what he saw before him. It *couldn't* be true, not possibly! But the longer he stared, the more true it began to seem. After all, there it was standing against the wall right in front of him, as real and as solid as the house itself. And who in the world could possibly make a mistake about a thing like that? Admittedly it was painted white, but that made not the slightest difference. Some idiot had done that. The paint could easily be stripped off. But good God! Just look at it! And in a place like this!

At that point, Mr Boggis became aware of the three men, Rummins, Bert and Claud, standing together in a group over by the fireplace, watching him intently. They had seen him stop and gasp and stare, and they must have seen his face turning red, or maybe it was white, but in any event they had seen enough to spoil the whole goddam business if he didn't do something about it quick. In a flash, Mr Boggis clapped one hand over his heart, staggered to the nearest chair, and collapsed into it, breathing heavily.

'What's the matter with you?' Claud asked.

'It's nothing,' he gasped. 'I'll be all right in a minute. Please – a glass of water. It's my heart.'

Bert fetched him the water, handed it to him, and stayed close beside him, staring down at him with a fatuous leer on his face.

'I thought maybe you were looking at something,' Rummins said. The wide frog-mouth widened a fraction farther into a crafty grin, showing the stubs of several broken teeth.

'No, no,' Mr Boggis said. 'Oh dear me, no. It's just my heart. I'm so sorry. It happens every now and then. But it goes away quite quickly. I'll be all right in a couple of minutes.'

He *must* have time to think, he told himself. More important still, he must have time to compose himself thoroughly before he said another word. Take it gently, Boggis. And whatever you do, keep calm. These people may be ignorant, but they are not stupid. They are suspicious and wary and sly. And if it is really true – no it *can't* be, it *can't* be true . . .

He was holding one hand up over his eyes in a gesture of pain, and now, very carefully, secretly, he made a little crack between two of the fingers and peeked through.

Sure enough, the thing was still there, and on this occasion he took a good long look at it. Yes – he had been right the first time! There wasn't the slightest doubt about it! It was really unbelievable!

What he saw was a piece of furniture that any expert would have given almost anything to acquire. To a layman, it might not have appeared particularly impressive, especially when covered over as it was with dirty white paint, but to Mr Boggis it was a dealer's dream. He knew, as does every other dealer in Europe and America, that among the most celebrated and coveted examples of eighteenth-century English furniture in existence are the three famous pieces known as 'The Chippendale Commodes'. He knew their history backwards – that the first was 'discovered' in 1920, in a house at Moreton-on-the-Marsh, and was sold at Sotheby's the same year; that the other two turned up in the same auction rooms a year later, both coming out of Rainham Hall, Norfolk. They all fetched enormous prices. He couldn't quite remember the exact figure for the first one, or even the second, but he knew for certain that the last one to be sold had fetched thirty-nine hundred guineas. And that was in 1921! Today the same piece would surely be worth ten thousand pounds. Some man, Mr Boggis couldn't remember his name, had made a study of these commodes fairly recently and had proved that all three must have come from the same workshop, for the veneers were all from the same log, and the same set of templates had been used in the construction of each. No invoices had been found for any of them, but all the experts were agreed that these three commodes could have been executed only by Thomas Chippendale himself, with his own hands, at the most exalted period in his career.

And here, Mr Boggis kept telling himself as he peered cautiously through the crack in his fingers, here was the fourth Chippendale Commode! And *he* had found it! He would be rich! He would also be famous! Each of the other three was known throughout the furniture world by a special name – the Chastleton Commode, the First Rainham Commode, the Second Rainham Commode. This one would go down in history as the Boggis Commode! Just imagine the faces of the boys up there in London when they got a look at it tomorrow morning! And the luscious offers coming in from the big fellows over in the West End – Frank Partridge, Mallett, Jetley and the rest of them! There would be a picture of it in *The Times*, and it would say, 'The very fine Chippendale Commode which was recently discovered by Mr Cyril Boggis, a London dealer . . .' Dear God, what a stir he was going to make!

This one here, Mr Boggis thought, was almost exactly similar to the Second Rainham Commode. (All three, the Chastleton and the two Rainhams, differed from one another in a number of small ways.) It was a most impressive handsome affair built in the French Rococo style of Chippendale's Director period, a kind of large fat chest-of-drawers set upon four carved and fluted legs that raised it about a foot from the ground. There were six drawers in all, two long ones in the middle and two shorter ones on either side. The serpentine front was magnificently ornamented along the top and sides and bottom, and also vertically between each set of drawers, with intricate carvings of festoons and scrolls and clusters. The brass handles, although partly obscured by white paint, appeared to be superb. It was, of course, a rather 'heavy' piece, but the design had been executed with such elegance and grace that the heaviness was in no way offensive.

'How're you feeling now?' Mr Boggis heard someone saying.

'Thank you, thank you, I'm much better already. It passes quickly. My doctor says it's nothing to worry about really so long as I rest for a few minutes whenever it happens. Ah yes,' he said, raising himself slowly to his feet. 'That's better. I'm all right now.'

A trifle unsteadily, he began to move around the room examining the furniture, one piece at a time, commenting upon it briefly. He could see at once that apart from the commode it was a very poor lot.

'Nice oak table,' he said. 'But I'm afraid it's not old enough to be of any interest. Good comfortable chairs, but quite modern, yes, quite modern. Now this cupboard, well, it's rather attractive, but again, not valuable. This chest-of-drawers' – he walked casually past the Chippendale Commode and gave it a little contemptuous flip with his fingers – 'worth a few pounds, I dare say, but no more. A rather crude reproduction, I'm afraid. Probably made in Victorian times. Did you paint it white?'

'Yes,' Rummins said. 'Bert did it.'

'A very wise move. It's considerably less offensive in white.'

'That's a strong piece of furniture,' Rummins said. 'Some nice carving on it too.'

'Machine-carved,' Mr Boggis answered superbly, bending down to examine the exquisite craftsmanship. 'You can tell it a mile off. But still, I suppose it's quite pretty in its way. It has its points.'

He began to saunter off, then he checked himself and turned slowly back again. He placed the tip of one finger against the point of his chin, laid his head over to one side, and frowned as though deep in thought.

'You know what?' he said, looking at the commode, speaking so casually that his voice kept trailing off. 'I've just remembered . . . I've been wanting a set of legs something like that for a long time. I've got a rather curious table in my own little home, one of those low things that people put in front of the sofa, sort of a coffee-table, and last Michaelmas, when I moved house, the foolish movers damaged the legs in the most shocking way. I'm very fond of that table. I always keep my big Bible on it, and all my sermon notes.'

He paused, stroking his chin with the finger. 'Now I was just thinking. These legs on your chest-of-drawers might be very suitable. Yes, they might indeed. They could easily be cut off and fixed on to my table.'

He looked around and saw the three men standing absolutely still, watching him suspiciously, three pairs of eyes, all different but equally mistrusting, small pig-eyes for Rummins, large slow eyes for Claud, and two odd eyes for Bert, one of them very queer and boiled and misty pale, with a little black dot in the centre, like a fish-eye on a plate.

Mr Boggis smiled and shook his head. 'Come, come, what on earth am I saying? I'm talking as though I owned the piece myself. I do apologize.'

'What you mean to say is you'd like to buy it,' Rummins said.

'Well . . .' Mr Boggis glanced back at the commode, frowning. 'I'm not sure. I might . . . and then again . . . on second thoughts . . . no . . . I think it might be a bit too much trouble. It's not worth it. I'd better leave it.'

'How much were you thinking of offering?' Rummins asked.

'Not much, I'm afraid. You see, this is not a genuine antique. It's merely a reproduction.'

'I'm not so sure about that,' Rummins told him. 'It's been in *here* over twenty years, and before that it was up at the Manor House. I bought it there myself at auction when the old Squire died. You can't tell me that thing's new.'

'It's not exactly new, but it's certainly not more than about sixty years old.'

'It's more than that,' Rummins said. 'Bert, where's that bit of paper you once found at the back of one of them drawers? That old bill.'

The boy looked vacantly at his father.

Mr Boggis opened his mouth, then quickly shut it again without uttering a sound. He was beginning literally to shake with excitement, and to calm himself he walked over to the window and stared out at a plump brown hen pecking around for stray grains of corn in the yard.

'It was in the back of that drawer underneath all them rabbit-snares,' Rummins was saying. 'Go on and fetch it out and show it to the parson.'

When Bert went forward to the commode, Mr Boggis turned round again. He couldn't stand not watching him. He saw him pull out one of the big middle drawers, and he noticed the beautiful smooth way in which the drawer slid open. He saw Bert's hand dipping inside and rummaging around among a lot of wires and strings.

'You mean this?' Bert lifted out a piece of folded yellowing paper and carried it over to the father, who unfolded it and held it up close to his face.

'You can't tell me this writing ain't bloody old,' Rummins said, and he held the paper out to Mr Boggis, whose whole arm was shaking as he took it. It was brittle and it crackled slightly between his fingers. The writing was in a long sloping copperplate hand:

Edward Montagu, Esq.   *Dr*
                                           To Thos. Chippendale
A large mahogany Commode Table of exceeding fine wood, very rich carvd, set upon fluted legs, two very neat shapd long drawers in the middle part and two ditto on each side, with rich chasd Brass Handles and Ornaments, the whole compleatly finished in the most exquisite taste . . . £87

Mr Boggis was holding on to himself tight and fighting to

suppress the excitement that was spinning round inside him and making him dizzy. Oh God, it was wonderful! With the invoice, the value had climbed even higher. What in heaven's name would it fetch now? Twelve thousand pounds? Fourteen? Maybe fifteen or even twenty? Who knows?

Oh, boy!

He tossed the paper contemptuously on to the table and said quietly, 'It's exactly what I told you, a Victorian reproduction. This is simply the invoice that the seller – the man who made it and passed it off as an antique – gave to his client. I've seen lots of them. You'll notice that he doesn't say he made it himself. That would give the game away.'

'Say what you like,' Rummins announced, 'but that's an old piece of paper.'

'Of course it is, my dear friend. It's Victorian, late Victorian. About eighteen ninety. Sixty or seventy years old. I've seen hundreds of them. That was a time when masses of cabinet-makers did nothing else but apply themselves to faking the fine furniture of the century before.'

'Listen, Parson,' Rummins said, pointing at him with a thick dirty finger, 'I'm not saying as how you may not know a fair bit about this furniture business, but what I *am* saying is this: How on earth can you be so mighty sure it's a fake when you haven't even seen what it looks like underneath all that paint?'

'Come here,' Mr Boggis said. 'Come over here and I'll show you.' He stood beside the commode and waited for them to gather round. 'Now, anyone got a knife?'

Claud produced a horn-handled pocket knife, and Mr Boggis took it and opened the smallest blade. Then, working with apparent casualness but actually with extreme care, he began chipping off the white paint from a small area on the top of the commode. The paint flaked away cleanly from the old hard varnish underneath, and when he had cleared away about three square inches, he stepped back and said, 'Now, take a look at that!'

It was beautiful – a warm little patch of mahogany, glowing like a topaz, rich and dark with the true colour of its two hundred years.

'What's wrong with it?' Rummins asked.

'It's processed! Anyone can see that!'

'How can you see it, Mister? You tell us.'

'Well, I must say that's a trifle difficult to explain. It's chiefly a matter of experience. My experience tells me that without the slightest doubt this wood has been processed with lime. That's what they use for mahogany, to give it that dark aged colour. For oak, they use potash salts, and for walnut it's nitric acid, but for mahogany it's always lime.'

The three men moved a little closer to peer at the wood. There was a slight stirring of interest among them now. It was always intriguing to hear about some new form of crookery or deception.

'Look closely at the grain. You see that touch of orange in among the dark red-brown. That's the sign of lime.'

They leaned forward, their noses close to the wood, first Rummins, then Claud, then Bert.

'And then there's the patina,' Mr Boggis continued.

'The what?'

He explained to them the meaning of this word as applied to furniture.

'My dear friends, you've no idea the trouble these rascals will go to to imitate the hard beautiful bronze-like appearance of genuine patina. It's terrible, really terrible, and it makes me quite sick to speak of it!' He was spitting each word sharply off the tip of the tongue and making a sour mouth to show his extreme distaste. The men waited, hoping for more secrets.

'The time and trouble that some mortals will go to in order to deceive the innocent!' Mr Boggis cried. 'It's perfectly disgusting! D'you know what they did here, my friends? I can recognize it clearly. I can almost *see* them doing it, the long, complicated ritual of rubbing the wood with linseed oil, coating it over with French polish that has been cunningly coloured, brushing it down with pumice-stone and oil, beeswaxing it with a wax that contains dirt and dust, and finally giving it the heat treatment to crack the polish so that it looks like two-hundred-year-old varnish! It really upsets me to contemplate such knavery!'

The three men continued to gaze at the little patch of dark wood.

'Feel it!' Mr Boggis ordered. 'Put your fingers on it! There, how does it feel, warm or cold?'

'Feels cold,' Rummins said.

'Exactly, my friend! It happens to be a fact that faked patina is always cold to the touch. Real patina has a curiously warm feel to it.'

'This feels normal,' Rummins said, ready to argue.

'No, sir, it's cold. But of course it takes an experienced and sensitive fingertip to pass a positive judgement. You couldn't really be expected to judge this any more than I could be expected to judge the quality of your barley. Everything in life, my dear sir, is experience.'

The men were staring at this queer moon-faced clergyman with the bulging eyes, not quite so suspiciously now because he did seem to know a bit about his subject. But they were still a long way from trusting him.

Mr Boggis bent down and pointed to one of the metal drawer-handles on the commode. 'This is another place where the fakers go to work,' he said. 'Old brass normally has a colour and character all of its own. Did you know that?'

They stared at him, hoping for still more secrets.

'But the trouble is that they've become exceedingly skilled at matching it. In fact it's almost impossible to tell the difference between "genuine old" and "faked old". I don't mind admitting that it has me guessing. So there's not really any point in our scraping the paint off these handles. We wouldn't be any the wiser.'

'How can you possibly make new brass look like old?' Claud said. 'Brass doesn't rust, you know.'

'You are quite right, my friend. But these scoundrels have their own secret methods.'

'Such as what?' Claud asked. Any information of this nature was valuable, in his opinion. One never knew when it might come in handy.

'All they have to do,' Mr Boggis said, 'is to place these

handles overnight in a box of mahogany shavings satur-
ated in sal ammoniac. The sal ammoniac turns the metal
green, but if you rub off the green, you will find underneath it a fine soft silvery-warm lustre, a lustre identical to
that which comes with very old brass. Oh, it is so bestial,
the things they do! With iron they have another trick.'

'What do they do with iron?' Claud asked, fascinated.

'Iron's easy,' Mr Boggis said. 'Iron locks and plates and
hinges are simply buried in common salt and they come
out all rusted and pitted in no time.'

'All right,' Rummins said. 'So you admit you can't tell
about the handles. For all you know, they may be hundreds and hundreds of years old. Correct?'

'Ah,' Mr Boggis whispered, fixing Rummins with two
big bulging brown eyes. 'That's where you're wrong. Watch
this.'

From his jacket pocket, he took out a small screwdriver.
At the same time, although none of them saw him do it,
he also took out a little brass screw which he kept well
hidden in the palm of his hand. Then he selected one
of the screws in the commode – there were four to each
handle – and began carefully scraping all traces of white
paint from its head. When he had done this, he started
slowly to unscrew it.

'If this is a genuine old brass screw from the eighteenth
century,' he was saying, 'the spiral will be slightly uneven
and you'll be able to see quite easily that it has been hand-
cut with a file. But if this brasswork is faked from more
recent times, Victorian or later, then obviously the screw
will be of the same period. It will be a mass-produced,

machine-made article. Anyone can recognize a machine-made screw. Well, we shall see.'

It was not difficult, as he put his hands over the old screw and drew it out, for Mr Boggis to substitute the new one hidden in his palm. This was another little trick of his, and through the years it had proved a most rewarding one. The pockets of his clergyman's jacket were always stocked with a quantity of cheap brass screws of various sizes.

'There you are,' he said, handing the modern screw to Rummins. 'Take a look at that. Notice the exact evenness of the spiral? See it? Of course you do. It's just a cheap common little screw that you yourself could buy today in any ironmonger's in the country.'

The screw was handed round from the one to the other, each examining it carefully. Even Rummins was impressed now.

Mr Boggis put the screwdriver back in his pocket together with the fine hand-cut screw that he'd taken from the commode, and then he turned and walked slowly past the three men towards the door.

'My dear friends,' he said, pausing at the entrance to the kitchen, 'it was so good of you to let me peep inside your little home – so kind. I do hope I haven't been a terrible old bore.'

Rummins glanced up from examining the screw. 'You didn't tell us what you were going to offer,' he said.

'Ah,' Mr Boggis said. 'That's quite right. I didn't, did I? Well, to tell you the honest truth, it's all a bit too much trouble. I think I'll leave it.'

'How much would you give?'

'You mean that you really wish to part with it?'

'I didn't say I wished to part with it. I asked you how much.'

Mr Boggis looked across at the commode, and he laid his head first to one side, then to the other, and he frowned, and pushed out his lips, and shrugged his shoulders, and gave a little scornful wave of the hand as though to say the thing was hardly worth thinking about really, was it?

'Shall we say . . . ten pounds. I think that would be fair.'

'Ten pounds!' Rummins cried. 'Don't be so ridiculous, Parson, *please*!'

'It's worth more'n that for firewood!' Claud said, disgusted.

'Look here at the bill!' Rummins went on, stabbing that precious document so fiercely with his dirty forefinger that Mr Boggis became alarmed. 'It tells you exactly what it cost! Eighty-seven pounds! And that's when it was new. Now it's antique it's worth double!'

'If you'll pardon me, no, sir, it's not. It's a second-hand reproduction. But I'll tell you what, my friend – I'm being rather reckless, I can't help it – I'll go up as high as fifteen pounds. How's that?'

'Make it fifty,' Rummins said.

A delicious little quiver like needles ran all the way down the back of Mr Boggis's legs and then under the soles of his feet. He had it now. It was his. No question about that. But the habit of buying cheap, as cheap as it was humanly possible to buy, acquired by years of necessity and practice, was too strong in him now to permit him to give in so easily.

'My dear man,' he whispered softly, 'I only *want* the legs. Possibly I could find some use for the drawers later on, but the rest of it, the carcass itself, as your friend so rightly said, it's firewood, that's all.'

'Make it thirty-five,' Rummins said.

'I *couldn't*, sir, I *couldn't*! It's not worth it. And I simply mustn't allow myself to haggle like this about a price. It's all wrong. I'll make you one final offer, and then I must go. Twenty pounds.'

'I'll take it,' Rummins snapped. 'It's yours.'

'Oh dear,' Mr Boggis said, clasping his hands. 'There I go again. I should never have started this in the first place.'

'You can't back out now, Parson. A deal's a deal.'

'Yes, yes, I know.'

'How're you going to take it?'

'Well, let me see. Perhaps if I were to drive my car up into the yard, you gentlemen would be kind enough to help me load it?'

'In a car? This thing'll never go in a car! You'll need a truck for this!'

'I don't think so. Anyway, we'll see. My car's on the road. I'll be back in a jiffy. We'll manage it somehow, I'm sure.'

Mr Boggis walked out into the yard and through the gate and then down the long track that led across the field towards the road. He found himself giggling quite uncontrollably, and there was a feeling inside him as though hundreds and hundreds of tiny bubbles were rising up from his stomach and bursting merrily in the top of his head, like sparkling-water. All the buttercups in the field were suddenly turning into golden sovereigns, glistening in the sunlight. The ground was littered with them, and he swung off the track on to the grass so that he could walk among them and tread on them and hear the little metallic tinkle they made as he kicked them around with his toes. He was finding it difficult to stop himself from breaking into a run. But clergymen never run; they walk slowly. Walk slowly, Boggis. Keep calm, Boggis. There's no hurry now. The commode is yours! Yours for twenty pounds, and it's worth fifteen or twenty thousand! The Boggis Commode! In ten minutes it'll be loaded into your car – it'll go in easily – and you'll be driving back to London and singing all the way! Mr Boggis driving the Boggis Commode home in the Boggis car. Historic occasion. What *wouldn't* a newspaperman give to get a picture of that! Should he arrange it? Perhaps he should. Wait and see. Oh, glorious day! Oh, lovely sunny summer day! Oh, glory be!

Back in the farmhouse, Rummins was saying, 'Fancy that old bastard giving twenty pound for a load of junk like this.'

'You did very nicely, Mr Rummins,' Claud told him. 'You think he'll pay you?'

'We don't put it in the car till he do.'

'And what if it won't go in the car?' Claud asked. 'You know what I think, Mr Rummins? You want my honest opinion? I think the bloody thing's too big to go in the car. And then what happens? Then he's going to say to hell with it and just drive off without it and you'll never see him again. Nor the money either. He didn't seem all that keen on having it, you know.'

Rummins paused to consider this new and rather alarming prospect.

'How can a thing like that possibly go in a car?' Claud went on relentlessly. 'A parson never has a big car anyway. You ever seen a parson with a big car, Mr Rummins?'

'Can't say I have.'

'Exactly! And now listen to me. I've got an idea. He told us, didn't he, that it was only the legs he was wanting. Right? So all we've got to do is to cut 'em off quick right here on the spot before he comes back, then it'll be sure to go in the car. All we're doing is saving him the trouble of cutting them off himself when he gets home. How about it, Mr Rummins?' Claud's flat bovine face glimmered with a mawkish pride.

'It's not such a bad idea at that,' Rummins said, looking at the commode. 'In fact it's a bloody good idea. Come on then, we'll have to hurry. You and Bert carry it out into the yard. I'll get the saw. Take the drawers out first.'

Within a couple of minutes, Claud and Bert had carried the commode outside and had laid it upside down in the yard amidst the chicken droppings and cow dung and mud. In the distance, halfway across the field, they could see a small black figure striding along the path towards the road. They paused to watch. There was something rather comical about the way in which this figure was conducting itself. Every now and again it would break into a trot, then it did a kind of hop, skip and jump, and once it seemed as though the sound of a cheerful song came rippling faintly to them from across the meadow.

'I reckon he's balmy,' Claud said, and Bert grinned darkly, rolling his misty eye slowly round in its socket.

Rummins came waddling over from the shed, squat and frog-like, carrying a long saw. Claud took the saw away from him and went to work.

'Cut 'em close,' Rummins said. 'Don't forget he's going to use 'em on another table.'

The mahogany was hard and very dry, and as Claud worked, a fine red dust sprayed out from the edge of the saw and fell softly to the ground. One by one, the legs came off, and when they were all severed, Bert stooped down and arranged them carefully in a row.

Claud stepped back to survey the results of his labour. There was a longish pause.

'Just let me ask you one question, Mr Rummins,' he said slowly. 'Even now, could *you* put that enormous thing into the back of a car?'

'Not unless it was a van.'

'Correct!' Claud cried. 'And parsons don't have vans, you know. All they've got usually is piddling little Morris Eights or Austin Sevens.'

'The legs is all he wants,' Rummins said. 'If the rest of it won't go in, then he can leave it. He can't complain. He's got the legs.'

'Now you know better'n that, Mr Rummins,' Claud said patiently. 'You know damn well he's going to start knocking the price if he don't get every single bit of this into the car. A parson's just as cunning as the rest of 'em when it comes to money, don't you make any mistake about that. Especially this old boy. So why don't we give him his firewood now and be done with it. Where d'you keep the axe?'

'I reckon that's fair enough,' Rummins said. 'Bert, go fetch the axe.'

Bert went into the shed and fetched a tall woodcutter's axe and gave it to Claud. Claud spat on the palms of his hands and rubbed them together. Then, with a long-armed high-swinging action, he began fiercely attacking the legless carcass of the commode.

It was hard work, and it took several minutes before he had the whole thing more or less smashed to pieces.

'I'll tell you one thing,' he said, straightening up, wiping his brow. 'That was a bloody good carpenter put this job together and I don't care what the parson says.'

'We're just in time!' Rummins called out. 'Here he comes!'

The Wonderful Story of Henry Sugar

First published in *The Wonderful
Story of Henry Sugar* (1977)

Henry Sugar was forty-one years old and unmarried. He was also wealthy. He was wealthy because he had had a rich father who was now dead. He was unmarried because he was too selfish to share any of his money with a wife.

He was six feet two inches tall, but he wasn't really as good-looking as he thought he was.

He paid a great deal of attention to his clothes. He went to an expensive tailor for his suits, to a shirtmaker for his shirts, and to a bootmaker for his shoes.

He used a costly aftershave lotion on his face, and he kept his hands soft with a cream that contained turtle oil.

His hairdresser trimmed his hair once every ten days, and he always took a manicure at the same time.

His upper front teeth had been capped at incredible expense because the originals had had a rather nasty yellowish tinge. A small mole had been removed from his left cheek by a plastic surgeon.

He drove a Ferrari car which must have cost him about the same as a country cottage.

He lived in London in the summer, but as soon as the first frosts appeared in October, he was off to the

West Indies or the South of France, where he stayed with friends. All his friends were wealthy from inherited money.

Henry had never done a day's work in his life, and his personal motto, which he had invented himself, was this: *It is better to incur a mild rebuke than to perform an onerous task.* His friends thought this was hilarious.

Men like Henry Sugar are to be found drifting like seaweed all over the world. They can be seen especially in London, New York, Paris, Nassau, Montego Bay, Cannes and St Tropez. They are not particularly bad men. But they are not good men either. They are of no real importance. They are simply a part of the decoration.

All of them, all wealthy people of this type, have one peculiarity in common: they have a terrific urge to make themselves still wealthier than they already are. The million is never enough. Nor is the two million. Always, they have this insatiable longing to get more money. And that is because they live in constant terror of waking up one morning and finding there's nothing in the bank.

These people all employ the same methods for trying to increase their fortunes. They buy stocks and shares, and watch them going up and down. They play roulette and blackjack for high stakes in casinos. They bet on horses. They bet on just about everything. Henry Sugar had once staked a thousand pounds on the result of a tortoise race on Lord Liverpool's tennis lawn. And he had wagered double that sum with a man called Esmond Hanbury on an even sillier bet, which was as follows: they let Henry's dog out into the garden and they watched it through the window. But before the dog was let out, each man had to guess beforehand what would be the first object the dog would lift its leg against. Would it be a wall, a post, a bush, or a tree? Esmond chose a wall. Henry, who had been studying his dog's habits for days with a view to making this particular bet, chose a tree, and he won the money.

With ridiculous games such as these did Henry and his friends try to conquer the deadly boredom of being both idle and wealthy.

Henry himself, as you may have noticed, was not above cheating a little on these friends of his if he saw the chance. The bet with the dog was definitely not honest. Nor, if you want to know, was the bet on the tortoise race. Henry cheated on that one by secretly forcing a little sleeping-pill powder into the mouth of his opponent's tortoise an hour before the race.

And now that you've got a rough idea of the sort of person Henry Sugar was, I can begin my story.

One summer week-end, Henry drove down from London to Guildford to stay with Sir William Wyndham. The house was magnificent, and so were the grounds, but when Henry arrived on that Saturday afternoon, it was already pelting with rain. Tennis was out, croquet was out. So was swimming in Sir William's outdoor pool. The host and his guests sat glumly in the drawing-room, staring at the rain splashing against the windows. The very rich are enormously resentful of bad weather. It is the one discomfort that their money cannot do anything about.

Somebody in the room said, 'Let's have a game of canasta for lovely high stakes.'

The others thought that a splendid idea, but as there were five people in all, one would have to sit out. They cut the cards. Henry drew the lowest, the unlucky card.

The other four sat down and began to play. Henry was annoyed at being out of the game. He wandered out of the drawing-room into the great hall. He stared at the pictures for a few moments, then he walked on through the house, bored to death at having nothing to do. Finally, he mooched into the library.

Sir William's father had been a famous book collector, and all the four walls to this huge room were lined with books from floor to ceiling. Henry Sugar was not impressed. He wasn't even interested. The only books he read were detective novels and thrillers. He ambled aimlessly round the room, looking to see if he could find any of the sort of books he liked. But the ones in Sir William's library were all leather-bound volumes with names on them like Balzac, Ibsen, Voltaire, Johnson and Pepys. Boring rubbish, the whole lot of it, Henry told himself. And he was just about to leave when his eye was caught and held by a book that was quite different from all the others. It was so slim he would never have noticed it if it hadn't been sticking out a little from the ones on either side. And when he pulled it from the shelf, he saw that it was actually nothing more than a cardboard-covered exercise-book of the kind children use at school. The cover was dark blue, but there was nothing written on it. Henry opened the exercise-book. On the first page, hand-printed in ink, it said:

A REPORT ON AN INTERVIEW
WITH IMHRAT KHAN, THE MAN WHO
COULD SEE WITHOUT HIS EYES
by
Dr John F. Cartwright
BOMBAY, INDIA
DECEMBER, 1934

That sounds mildly interesting, Henry told himself. He turned over a page. What followed was all handwritten in black ink. The writing was clear and neat. Henry read the first two pages standing up. Suddenly, he found himself wanting to read on. This was good stuff. It was fascinating. He carried the little book over to a leather armchair by the window and settled himself comfortably. Then he started reading again from the beginning.

This is what Henry read in the little blue exercise-book:

I, John Cartwright, am a surgeon at Bombay General Hospital. On the morning of the second of December, 1934, I was in the Doctors' Rest Room having a cup of tea. There were three other doctors there with me, all having a well-earned tea-break. They were Dr Marshall, Dr Phillips and Dr Macfarlane. There was a knock on the door. 'Come in,' I said.

The door opened and an Indian came in who smiled at us and said, 'Excuse me, please. Could I ask you gentlemen a favour?'

The Doctors' Rest Room was a most private place.

Nobody other than a doctor was allowed to enter it except in an emergency.

'This is a private room,' Dr Macfarlane said sharply.

'Yes, yes,' the Indian answered. 'I know that and I am very sorry to be bursting in like this, sirs, but I have a most interesting thing to show you.'

All four of us were pretty annoyed and we didn't say anything.

'Gentlemen,' he said. 'I am a man who can see without using his eyes.'

We still didn't invite him to go on. But we didn't kick him out either.

'You can cover my eyes in any way you wish,' he said, 'you can bandage my head with fifty bandages and I will still be able to read you a book.'

He seemed perfectly serious. I felt my curiosity beginning to stir. 'Come here,' I said. He came over to me. 'Turn round.' He turned round. I placed my hands firmly over his eyes, holding the lids closed. 'Now,' I said. 'One of the other doctors in the room is going to hold up some fingers. Tell me how many he's holding up.'

Dr Marshall held up seven fingers.

'Seven,' the Indian said.

'Once more,' I said.

Dr Marshall clenched both fists and hid all his fingers.

'No fingers,' the Indian said.

I removed my hands from his eyes. 'Not bad,' I said.

'Hold on,' Dr Marshall said. 'Let's try this.' There was a white doctor's coat hanging from a peg on the door.

Dr Marshall took it down and rolled it into a sort of long scarf. He then wound it round the Indian's head and held the ends tight at the back. 'Try him now,' Dr Marshall said.

I took a key from my pocket. 'What is this?' I asked.

'A key,' he answered.

I put the key back and held up an empty hand. 'What is this object?' I asked him.

'There isn't any object,' the Indian said. 'Your hand is empty.'

Dr Marshall removed the covering from the man's eyes. 'How do you do it?' he asked. 'What's the trick?'

'There is no trick,' the Indian said. 'It is a genuine thing that I have managed after years of training.'

'What sort of training?' I asked.

'Forgive me, sir,' he said. 'But that is a private matter.'

'Then why did you come here?' I asked.

'I came to request a favour of you,' he said.

The Indian was a tall man of about thirty with light brown skin, the colour of a coconut. He had a small black moustache. Also, there was a curious matting of black hair growing all over the outsides of his ears. He wore a white cotton robe, and he had sandals on his bare feet.

'You see, gentlemen,' he went on, 'I am at present earning my living by working in a travelling theatre, and we have just arrived here in Bombay. Tonight we give our opening performance.'

'Where do you give it?' I asked.

'In the Royal Palace Hall,' he answered. 'In Acacia

Street. I am the star performer. I am billed on the pro-gramme as "Imhrat Khan, the man who sees without his eyes". And it is my duty to advertise the show in a big way. If we don't sell tickets, we don't eat.'

'What does this have to do with us?' I asked him.

'Very interesting for you,' he said. 'Lots of fun. Let me explain. You see, whenever our theatre arrives in a new town, I myself go straight to the largest hospital and I ask the doctors there to bandage my eyes. I ask them to do it in the most expert fashion. They must make sure my eyes are completely covered many times over. It is important that this job is done by doctors, otherwise people will think I am cheating. Then, when I am fully bandaged, I go out into the streets and I do a dangerous thing.'

'What do you mean by that?' I asked.

'What I mean is that I do something that is extremely dangerous for someone who cannot see.'

'What do you do?' I asked.

'It is very interesting,' he said. 'And you will see me do it if you will be so kind as to bandage me up first. It would be a great favour to me if you will do this little thing, sirs.'

I looked at the other three doctors. Dr Phillips said he had to go back to his patients. Dr Macfarlane said the same. Dr Marshall said, 'Well, why not? It might be amus-ing. It won't take a minute.'

'I'm with you,' I said. 'But let's do the job properly. Let's make absolutely sure he can't peep.'

'You are extremely kind,' the Indian said. 'Please do whatever you wish.'

Dr Phillips and Dr Macfarlane left the room.

'Before we bandage him,' I said to Dr Marshall, 'let's first of all seal down his eyelids. When we've done that, we'll fill his eye-sockets with something soft and solid and sticky.'

'Such as what?' Dr Marshall asked.

'What about dough?'

'Dough would be perfect,' Dr Marshall said.

'Right,' I said. 'If you will nip down to the hospital bakery and get some dough, I'll take him into the surgery and seal his lids.'

I led the Indian out of the Rest Room and down the long hospital corridor to the surgery. 'Lie down there,' I said, indicating the high bed. He lay down. I took a small bottle from the cupboard. It had an eyedropper in the top. 'This is something called collodion,' I told him. 'It will harden over your closed eyelids so that it is impossible for you to open them.'

'How do I get it off afterwards?' he asked me.

'Alcohol will dissolve it quite easily,' I said. 'It's perfectly harmless. Close your eyes now.'

The Indian closed his eyes. I applied collodion over both lids. 'Keep them closed,' I said. 'Wait for it to harden.'

In a couple of minutes, the collodion had made a hard film over the eyelids, sticking them down tight. 'Try to open them,' I said.

He tried but couldn't.

Dr Marshall came in with a basin of dough. It was the ordinary white dough used for baking bread. It was nice and soft. I took a lump of the dough and plastered it over one of the Indian's eyes. I filled the whole socket and let

93

the dough overlap on to the surrounding skin. Then I pressed the edges down hard. I did the same with the other eye.

'That isn't too uncomfortable, is it?' I asked.

'No,' the Indian said. 'It's fine.'

'You do the bandaging,' I said to Dr Marshall. 'My fingers are too sticky.'

'A pleasure,' Dr Marshall said. 'Watch this.' He took a thick wad of cotton-wool and laid it on top of the Indian's dough-filled eyes. The cotton-wool stuck to the dough and stayed in place. 'Sit up, please,' Dr Marshall said.

The Indian sat up on the bed.

Dr Marshall took a roll of three-inch bandage and proceeded to wrap it round and round the man's head. The bandage held the cotton-wool and the dough firmly in place. Dr Marshall pinned the bandage. After that, he took a second bandage and began to wrap that one not only around the man's eyes but around his entire face and head.

'Please to leave my nose free for breathing,' the Indian said.

'Of course,' Dr Marshall answered. He finished the job and pinned down the end of the bandage. 'How's that?' he asked.

'Splendid,' I said. 'There's no way he can possibly see through that.'

The whole of the Indian's head was now swathed in thick white bandage, and the only thing you could see was the end of his nose sticking out. He looked like a man who had had some terrible brain operation.

'How does that feel?' Dr Marshall asked him.

'It feels good,' the Indian said. 'I must compliment you gentlemen on doing such a fine job.'

'Off you go, then,' Mr Marshall said, grinning at me. 'Show us how clever you are at seeing things now.'

The Indian got off the bed and walked straight to the door. He opened the door and went out.

'Great Scott!' I said. 'Did you see that? He put his hand right on to the doorknob!'

Dr Marshall had stopped grinning. His face had suddenly gone white. 'I'm going after him,' he said, rushing for the door. I rushed for the door as well.

The Indian was walking quite normally along the hospital corridor. Dr Marshall and I were about five yards behind him. And very spooky it was to watch this man with the enormous white and totally bandaged head strolling casually along the corridor just like anyone else. It was especially spooky when you knew for a certainty that his eyelids were sealed, that his eye-sockets were filled with dough, and that there was a great wad of cotton-wool and bandages on top of that.

I saw a native orderly coming along the corridor towards the Indian. He was pushing a food-trolley. Suddenly the orderly caught sight of the man with the white head, and he froze. The bandaged Indian stepped casually to one side of the trolley and went on.

'He saw it!' I cried. 'He must have seen that trolley! He walked right round it! This is absolutely unbelievable!'

Dr Marshall didn't answer me. His cheeks were white, his whole face rigid with shocked disbelief.

The Indian came to the stairs and started to go down them.

He went down with no trouble at all. He didn't even put a hand on the stair-rail. Several people were coming up the stairs. Each one of them stopped, gasped, stared, and quickly got out of his way.

At the bottom of the stairs, the Indian turned right and headed for the doors that led out into the street. Dr Marshall and I kept close behind him.

The entrance to our hospital stands back a little from the street, and there is a rather grand series of steps leading down from the entrance into a small courtyard with acacia trees around it. Dr Marshall and I came out into the blazing sunshine and stood at the top of the steps. Below us, in the courtyard, we saw a crowd of maybe a hundred people. At least half of them were barefoot children, and as our white-headed Indian walked down the steps, they all cheered and shouted and surged towards him. He greeted them by holding both hands above his head.

Suddenly I saw the bicycle. It was over to one side at the bottom of the steps, and a small boy was holding it. The bicycle itself was quite ordinary, but on the back of it, fixed somehow to the rear wheel-frame, was a huge placard, about five feet square. On the placard were written the following words:

IMHRAT KHAN, THE MAN WHO SEES
WITHOUT HIS EYES!
TODAY MY EYES HAVE BEEN BANDAGED BY
HOSPITAL DOCTORS!

APPEARING TONIGHT AND
ALL THIS WEEK AT
THE ROYAL PALACE HALL
ACACIA STREET, AT 7 P.M.
DON'T MISS IT!
YOU WILL SEE MIRACLES PERFORMED

Our Indian had reached the bottom of the steps and now he walked straight over to the bicycle. He said something to the boy and the boy smiled. The Indian mounted the bicycle. The crowd made way for him. Then, lo and behold, this fellow with the blocked-up, bandaged eyes now proceeded to ride across the courtyard and straight out into the bustling honking traffic of the street beyond! The crowd cheered louder than ever. The barefoot children ran after him, squealing and laughing. For a minute or so, we were able to keep him in sight. We saw him ride superbly down the busy street with motor-cars whizzing past him and a bunch of children running in his wake. Then he turned a corner and was gone.

'I feel quite giddy,' Dr Marshall said. 'I can't bring myself to believe it.'

'We have to believe it,' I said. 'He couldn't possibly have removed the dough from under the bandages. We never let him out of our sight. And as for unsealing his eyelids, that job would take him five minutes with cotton-wool and alcohol.'

'Do you know what I think,' Dr Marshall said. 'I think we have witnessed a miracle.'

We turned and walked slowly back into the hospital.

*

For the rest of the day, I was kept busy with patients in the hospital. At six in the evening, I came off duty and drove back to my flat for a shower and a change of clothes. It was the hottest time of year in Bombay, and even after sundown the heat was like an open furnace. If you sat still in a chair and did nothing, the sweat would come seeping out of your skin. Your face glistened with dampness all day long and your shirt stuck to your chest. I took a long cool shower. I drank a whisky and soda sitting on the veranda, with only a towel round my waist. Then I put on some clean clothes.

At ten minutes to seven, I was outside the Royal Palace Hall in Acacia Street. It was not much of a place. It was one of those smallish seedy halls that can be hired inexpensively for meetings or dances. There was a fair-sized crowd of local Indians milling round outside the ticket office, and a large poster over the entrance proclaiming that THE INTERNATIONAL THEATRE COMPANY was performing every night that week. It said there would be jugglers and conjurers and acrobats and sword-swallowers and fire-eaters and snake-charmers and a one-act play entitled *The Rajah and the Tiger Lady*. But above all this and in far the largest letters, it said IMHRAT KHAN, THE MIRACLE MAN WHO SEES WITHOUT HIS EYES.

I bought a ticket and went in.

The show lasted two hours. To my surprise, I thoroughly enjoyed it. All the performers were excellent. I liked the man who juggled with cooking-utensils. He had a saucepan, a frying-pan, a baking tray, a huge plate and a casserole pot all flying through the air at the same time.

The snake-charmer had a big green snake that stood almost on the tip of its tail and swayed to the music of his flute. The fire-eater ate fire and the sword-swallower pushed a thin pointed rapier at least four feet down his throat and into his stomach. Last of all, to a great fanfare of trumpets, our friend Imhrat Khan came on to do his act. The bandages we had put on him at the hospital had now been removed.

Members of the audience were called on to the stage to blindfold him with sheets and scarves and turbans, and in the end there was so much material wrapped around his head he could hardly keep his balance. He was then given a revolver. A small boy came out and stood at the left of the stage. I recognized him as the one who had held the bicycle outside the hospital that morning. The boy placed a tin can on the top of his head and stood quite still. The audience became deathly silent as Imhrat Khan took aim. He fired. The bang made us all jump. The tin can flew off the boy's head and clattered to the floor. The boy picked it up and showed the bullet-hole to the audience. Everyone clapped and cheered. The boy smiled.

Then the boy stood against a wooden screen and Imhrat Khan threw knives all around his body, most of them going very close indeed. This was a splendid act. Not many people could have thrown knives with such accuracy even with their eyes uncovered, but here he was, this extraordinary fellow, with his head so swathed in sheets it looked like a great snowball on a stick, and he was flicking the sharp knives into the screen within a hair's breadth of the boy's head. The boy smiled all the way through the act, and when it was over the audience stamped its feet and screamed with excitement.

Imhrat Khan's last act, though not so spectacular, was even more impressive. A metal barrel was brought on stage. The audience was invited to examine it, to make sure there were no holes. There were no holes. The barrel was then placed over Imhrat Khan's already bandaged head. It came down over his shoulders and as far as his elbows, pinning the upper part of his arms to his sides. But he could still hold out his forearms and his hands. Someone put a needle in one of his hands and a length of cotton thread in the other. With no false moves, he neatly threaded the cotton through the eye of the needle. I was flabbergasted.

As soon as the show was over, I made my way backstage. I found Mr Imhrat Khan in a small but clean dressing-room, sitting quietly on a wooden stool. The little Indian boy was unwinding the masses of scarves and sheets from around his head.

'Ah,' he said. 'It is my friend the doctor from the hospital. Come in, sir, come in.'

'I saw the show,' I said.

'And what did you think?'

'I liked it very much. I thought you were wonderful.'

'Thank you,' he said. 'That is a high compliment.'

'I must congratulate your assistant as well,' I said, nodding to the small boy. 'He is very brave.'

'He cannot speak English,' the Indian said. 'But I will tell him what you said.' He spoke rapidly to the boy in Hindustani and the boy nodded solemnly but said nothing.

'Look,' I said. 'I did you a small favour this morning. Would you do me one in return? Would you consent to come out and have supper with me?'

All the wrappings were off his head now. He smiled at me and said, 'I think you are feeling curious, doctor. Am I not right?'

'Very curious,' I said. 'I'd like to talk to you.'

Once again, I was struck by the peculiarly thick matting of black hair growing on the outsides of his ears. I had not seen anything quite like it on another person. 'I have never been questioned by a doctor before,' he said. 'But I have no objection. It would be a pleasure to have supper with you.'

'Shall I wait in the car?'

'Yes, please,' he said. 'I must wash myself and get out of these dirty clothes.'

I told him what my car looked like and said I would be waiting outside.

He emerged fifteen minutes later, wearing a clean white cotton robe and the usual sandals on his bare feet. And soon the two of us were sitting comfortably in a small restaurant that I sometimes went to because it made the best curry in the city. I drank beer with my curry. Imhrat Khan drank lemonade.

'I am not a writer,' I said to him. 'I am a doctor. But if you will tell me your story from the beginning, if you will explain to me how you developed this magical power of being able to see without your eyes, I will write it down as faithfully as I can. And then, perhaps, I can get it published in the *British Medical Journal* or even in some famous magazine. And because I *am* a doctor and not just some writer trying to sell a story for money, people will be far more inclined to take seriously what I say. It would help you, wouldn't it, to become better known?'

'It would help me very much,' he said. 'But why should you want to do this?'

'Because I am madly curious,' I answered. 'That is the only reason.'

Imhrat Khan took a mouthful of curried rice and chewed it slowly. Then he said, 'Very well, my friend. I will do it.'

'Splendid!' I cried. 'Let's go back to my flat as soon as we've finished eating and then we can talk without anyone disturbing us.'

We finished our meal. I paid the bill. Then I drove Imhrat Khan back to my flat.

In the living-room, I got out paper and pencils so that I could make notes. I have a sort of private shorthand of my own that I use for taking down the medical history of patients, and with it I am able to record most of what a person says if he doesn't speak too quickly. I think I got just about everything Imhrat Khan said to me that evening, word for word, and here it is. I give it to you exactly as he spoke it:

'I am an Indian, a Hindu,' said Imhrat Khan, 'and I was born in Akhnur, in Kashmir State, in 1905. My family is poor and my father worked as a ticket inspector on the railway. When I was a small boy of thirteen, an Indian conjurer comes to our school and gives a performance. His name, I remember, is Professor Moor – all conjurers in India call themselves "professor" – and his tricks are very good. I am tremendously impressed. I think it is real magic. I feel – how shall I call it – I feel a powerful wish to learn about this magic myself, so two days later I run away from home, determined to find and to follow my new hero, Professor Moor. I take all my savings, fourteen rupees, and only the clothes I am wearing. I am wearing a white dhoti and sandals. This is in 1918 and I am thirteen years old.

'I find out that Professor Moor has gone to Lahore, two hundred miles away, so all alone, I take a ticket, third class, and I get on the train and follow him. In Lahore, I discover the Professor. He is working at his conjuring in a very cheap-type show. I tell him of my admiration and offer myself to him as assistant. He accepts me. My pay? Ah yes, my pay is eight annas a day.

'The Professor teaches me to do the linking-rings trick and my job is to stand in the street before the theatre doing this trick and calling to the people to come in and see the show.

'For six whole weeks this is very fine. It is much better than going to school. But then what a terrible bombshell I receive when suddenly it comes to me that there is no real magic in Professor Moor, that all is trickery and quickness of the hand. Immediately the Professor is no longer my hero. I lose every bit of interest in my job, but at the same time my whole mind becomes filled with a very strong longing. I long above all things to find out about the real magic and to discover something about the strange power which is called yoga.

'To do this, I must find a yogi who is willing to let me become his disciple. This is not going to be easy. True yogis do not grow on trees. There are very few of them in the whole of India. Also, they are fanatically religious people. Therefore, if I am to have success in finding a teacher, I too will have to pretend to be a very religious man.

'No, I am actually not religious. And because of that, I am what you would call a bit of a cheat. I wanted to acquire yoga powers purely for selfish reasons. I wanted to use these powers to get fame and fortune.

'Now this was something the true yogi would despise more than anything in the world. In fact, the true yogi believes that any yogi who misuses his powers will die an early and sudden death. A yogi must never perform in public. He must practise his art only in absolute privacy and as a religious service, otherwise he will be smitten to death. This I did not believe and I still don't.

'So now my search for a yogi instructor begins. I leave Professor Moor and go to a town called Amritsar in the Punjab, where I join a travelling theatre company. I have to make a living while I am searching for the secret, and already I have had success in amateur acting at my school. So for three years I travel with this theatre group all over the Punjab and by the end of it, when I am sixteen and a half years old, I am playing top of the bill. All the time I am saving money and now I have altogether a very great sum, two thousand rupees.

'It is at this moment that I hear news of a man called Banerjee. This Banerjee, it is said, is one of the truly great yogis of India, and he possesses extraordinary powers.

Above all, people are telling of how he has acquired the rare power of levitation, so that when he prays his whole body leaves the ground and becomes suspended in the air eighteen inches from the soil.

'Ah-ha, I think. This surely is the man for me. This Banerjee is the one that I must seek. So at once, I take my savings and leave the theatre company and make my way to Rishikesh, on the banks of the Ganges, where rumour says that Banerjee is living.

'For six months I search for Banerjee. Where is he? Where? Where is Banerjee? Ah yes, they say in Rishikesh, Banerjee has certainly been in the town, but that is a while ago, and even then no one saw him. And now? Now Banerjee has gone to another place. What other place? Ah well, they say, how can one know that. How indeed? How can one know about the movements of such a one as Banerjee. Does he not live a life of absolute seclusion? Does he not? And I say yes. Yes, yes, yes. Of course. That is obvious. Even to me.

'I spend all my savings trying to find this Banerjee, all except thirty-five rupees. But it is no good. However, I stay in Rishikesh and make a living by doing ordinary conjuring tricks for small groups and for suchlike. These are the tricks I have learned from Professor Moor and by nature my sleight of hand is very good.

'Then one day, there I am sitting in the small hotel in Rishikesh and again I hear talk of the yogi Banerjee. A traveller is saying how he has heard that Banerjee is now living in the jungle, not so very far away, but in the dense jungle and all alone.

'But where?

'The traveller is not sure where. "Possibly," he says, "it is over there, in that direction, north of the town," and he points with his finger.

'Well, that is enough for me. I go to the market and begin to bargain for hiring a tonga, which is a horse and cart, and the transaction is just being completed with the driver when up comes a man who has been standing listening nearby and he says that he too is going in that direction. He says can he come part of the way with me and share the cost. Of course I am delighted, and off we go, the man and me sitting in the cart, and the driver driving the horse. Off we go along a very small path which leads right through the jungle.

'And then what truly fantastic luck should happen! I am talking to my companion and I find that he is a disciple of none other than the great Banerjee himself and that he is going now on a visit to his master. So straight out I tell him that I too would like to become a disciple of the yogi.

'He turns and looks at me long and slow, and for perhaps three minutes he does not speak. Then he says, quietly, "No, that is impossible."

'All right, I say to myself, we shall see. Then I ask if it is really true that Banerjee levitates when he prays.

'"Yes," he says. "That is true. But no one is allowed to observe the thing happening. No one is ever allowed to come near Banerjee when he is praying."

'So we go on a little further in the tonga, talking all the

time about Banerjee, and I manage by very careful casual questioning to find out a number of small things about him, such as what time of day he commences with his praying. Then soon the man says, "I will leave you here. This is where I dismount."

'I drop him off and I pretend to drive on along my journey, but around a corner I tell the driver to stop and wait. Quickly I jump down and I sneak back along the road, looking for this man, the disciple of Banerjee. He is not on the road. Already he has disappeared into the jungle. But which way? Which side of the road? I stand very still and listen.

'I hear a sort of rustling in the undergrowth. That must be him, I tell myself. If it is not him, then it is a tiger. But it is him. I see him ahead. He is going forwards through thick jungle. There is not even a little path where he is walking, and he is having to push his way between tall bamboos and every kind of heavy vegetation. I creep after him. I keep about one hundred yards behind him because I am frightened he may hear me. I can certainly hear him. It is impossible to proceed in silence through very thick jungle, and when I lose sight of him, which is most of the time, I am able to follow his sound.

'For about half an hour this tense game of follow-the-leader goes on. Then suddenly, I can no longer hear the man in front of me. I stop and listen. The jungle is silent. I am terrified that I may have lost him. I creep on a little way, and all at once, through the thick undergrowth, I see before me a little clearing, and in the middle of the clearing are two huts. They are small huts built entirely of jungle leaves and branches. My heart jumps and I feel a great surging of excitement inside me because this, I know for certain, is the place of Banerjee, the yogi.

'The disciple has already disappeared. He must have gone into one of the huts. All is quiet. So now I proceed to make a most careful inspection of the trees and bushes and other things all around. There is a small water-hole beside the nearest hut, and I see a prayer-mat beside it, and that, I say to myself, is where Banerjee meditates and prays. Close to this water-hole, not thirty yards away, there is a large tree, a great spreading baobab tree with beautiful thick branches which spread in such a way you can put a bed on them and lie on the bed and still not be seen from underneath. That will be my tree, I say to myself. I shall hide in that tree, and wait until Banerjee comes out to pray. Then I will be able to see everything.

'But the disciple has told me that the time of prayer is not until five or six in the evening, so I have several hours to wait. Therefore I at once walk back through the jungle to the road and I speak to the tonga driver. I tell him he too must wait. For this, I have to pay him extra money, but it doesn't matter because now I am so excited I don't care about anything for the moment, not even money.

'And all through the great noontime heat of the jungle I wait beside the tonga, and on through the heavy wet heat of the afternoon, and then, as five o'clock approaches, I make my way quietly back through the jungle to the hut, my heart beating so fast I can feel it shaking my whole body. I climb up my tree and I hide among the leaves in such a way that I can see but cannot be seen. And I wait. I wait for forty-five minutes.

'A watch? Yes, I have on a wristwatch. I remember it clearly. It was a watch I won in a raffle and I was proud to own it. On the face of my watch it said the maker's name, The Islamia Watch Co., Ludhiana. And so with my watch I am careful to be timing everything that goes on because I want to remember every single detail of this experience.

'I sit up in the tree, waiting.

'Then, all at once, a man is coming out of the hut. The man is tall and thin. He is dressed in an orange-coloured dhoti and he carries before him a tray with brass pots and incense-burners. He goes over and sits down cross-legged on the mat by the water-hole, putting the tray on the ground before him, and all the movements that he makes seem somehow very calm and gentle. He leans forwards and scoops a handful of water from the pool and throws it over his shoulder. He takes the incense-burner and passes it back and forth across his chest, slowly, in a gentle, flowing manner. He puts his hands palm downwards on his knees. He pauses. He takes a long breath through his nostrils. I can see him take a long breath and suddenly I can see his face is changing, there is a sort of brightness coming over all his face, a sort of . . . well, a sort of brightness on his skin and I can see his face is changing.

'For fourteen minutes he remains quite still in that position, and then, as I look at him, I see, quite positively I see his body lifting slowly . . . slowly . . . slowly off the ground. He is still sitting cross-legged, the hands palm downwards on the knees, and his whole body is lifting slowly off the ground, up into the air. Now I can see daylight underneath him. Twelve inches above the ground he is sitting . . . fifteen inches . . . eighteen . . . twenty . . . and soon he is at least two feet above the prayer-mat.

'I stay quite still up there in the tree, watching, and I keep saying to myself, now look carefully. There before you, thirty yards away, is a man sitting in great serenity upon the air. Are you seeing him? Yes, I am seeing him. But are you sure there is no illusion? Are you sure there is no deception? Are you sure you are not imagining? Are you sure? Yes, I am sure, I say. I am sure. I stare at him, marvelling. For a long while I keep staring, and then the body is coming slowly down again towards the earth. I see it coming. I see it moving gently downwards, slowly downwards, lowering to the earth until again his buttocks rest upon the mat.

'Forty-six minutes by my watch the body has been suspended! I timed it.

'And then, for a long long while, for over two hours, the man remains sitting absolutely still, like a stone person, with not the slightest movement. To me, it does not seem that he is breathing. His eyes are closed, and still there is this brightness on his face and also this slightly smiling look, a thing I have not seen on any other face in all my life since then.

'At last he stirs. He moves his hands. He stands up. He bends down again. He picks up the tray and goes slowly back into the hut. I am wonderstruck. I feel exalted. I forget all caution and I climb down quickly from the tree and run straight over to the hut and rush in through the door.

Banerjee is bending over, washing his feet and hands in a basin. His back is towards me, but he hears me and he turns quickly and straightens up. There is great surprise on his face and the first thing he says is, "How long have you been here?" He says it sharply, as if he is not pleased.

'At once I tell the whole truth, the whole story about being up in the tree and watching him, and at the end I tell him there is nothing I want in life except to become his disciple. Please will he let me become his disciple?

'Suddenly he seems to explode. He becomes furious and he begins shouting at me: "Get out!" he shouts. "Get out of here! Get out! Get out! Get out!" and in his fury he picks up a small brick and flings it at me and it strikes my right leg just below the knee and tears the flesh. I have the scar still. I will show it to you. There, you see, just below the knee.

'Banerjee's anger is terrible and I am very frightened. I turn and run away. I run back through the jungle to where the tonga-driver is waiting, and we drive home to Rishikesh. But that night I regain my courage. I make for myself a decision and it is this: that I will return every day to the hut of Banerjee, and I will keep on and on at him until at last he *has* to take me on as a disciple, just to get himself some peace.

'This I do. Each day I go to see him and each day his anger pours out upon me like a volcano, him shouting and yelling and me standing there frightened but also obstinate and repeating always to him my wish to become a disciple. For five days it is like this. Then, all at once, on my sixth visit, Banerjee seems to become quite calm, quite polite. He explains he cannot himself take me on as a disciple. But he will give me a note, he says, to another man, a friend, a great yogi, who lives in Hardwar. I am to go there and I will receive help and instruction.'

Imhrat Khan paused and asked me if he might have a glass of water. I fetched it for him. He took a long slow drink, then he went on with his story:

'This is in 1922 and I am nearly seventeen years old. So I go to Hardwar. And there I find the yogi, and because I have a letter from the great Banerjee, he consents to give me instruction.

'Now what is this instruction?

'It is, of course, the critical part of the whole thing. It is what I have been yearning for and searching for, so you can be sure I am an eager pupil.

'The first instruction, the most elementary part, consists of having to practise the most difficult physical exercises, all of them concerned with muscle control and breathing. But after some weeks of this, even the eager pupil becomes impatient. I tell the yogi it is my mental powers I wish to develop, not my physical ones.

'He replies, "If you will develop control of your body, then the control of your mind will be an automatic thing." But I want both at once, and I keep asking him, and in the end he says, "Very well, I will give you some exercises to help you to concentrate the conscious mind."

'"*Conscious* mind?" I ask. "Why do you say *conscious* mind?"

'"Because each man has two minds, the conscious and

the sub-conscious. The sub-conscious mind is highly concentrated, but the conscious mind, the one everyone uses, is a scattered, unconcentrated thing. It is concerning itself with thousands of different items, the things you are seeing around you and the things you are thinking about. So you must learn to concentrate it in such a way that you can visualize at will *one item*, one item only, and absolutely nothing else. If you work hard at this, you should be able to concentrate your mind, your conscious mind, upon any one object you select for at least three and a half minutes. But that will take about fifteen years."

'"Fifteen years!" I cry.

'"It may take longer," he says. "Fifteen years is the usual time."

'"But I will be an old man by then!"

'"Do not despair," the yogi says. "The time varies with different people. Some take ten years, a few can take less, and on extremely rare occasions a special person comes along who is able to develop the power in only one or two years. But that is one in a million."

'"Who are these special people?" I ask. "Do they look different from other people?"

'"They look the same," he says. "A special person might be a humble roadsweeper or a factory worker. Or he might be a rajah. There is no way of telling until the training begins."

'"Is it really so difficult," I ask, "to concentrate the mind upon a single object for three and a half minutes?"

'"It is almost impossible," he answers. "Try it and see. Shut your eyes and think of something. Think of just one object. Visualize it. See it before you. And in a few seconds your mind will start wandering. Other little thoughts will creep in. Other visions will come to you. It is a very difficult thing.'

'Thus spoke the yogi of Hardwar.

'And so my real exercises begin. Each evening, I sit down and close my eyes and visualize the face of the person I love best, which is my brother. I concentrate upon visualizing his face. But the instant my mind begins to wander, I stop the exercise and rest for some minutes. Then I try again.

'After three years of daily practice, I am able to concentrate absolutely upon my brother's face for one and a half minutes. I am making progress. But an interesting thing happens. In doing these exercises, I lose my sense of smell absolutely. And never to this day does it come back to me.

'Then the necessity for earning my living to buy food forces me to leave Hardwar. I go to Calcutta where there are greater opportunities, and there I soon begin to make quite good money by giving conjuring performances. But always I continue with the exercises. Every evening, wherever I am, I settle myself down in a quiet corner and practise the concentrating of the mind upon my brother's face. Occasionally, I choose something not so personal, like for example an orange or a pair of spectacles, and that makes it even more difficult.

'One day, I travel from Calcutta to Dacca in East Bengal to give a conjuring show at a college there, and while in Dacca, I happen to be present at a demonstration of walking on fire. There are many people watching. There is a big trench dug at the bottom of a sloping lawn. The spectators are sitting in their hundreds upon the slopes of the lawn looking down upon the trench.

'The trench is about twenty-five feet long. It has been filled with logs and firewood and charcoal, and a lot of paraffin has been poured on it. The paraffin has been lit, and after a while the whole trench has become a smouldering red-hot furnace. It is so hot that the men who are stoking it are obliged to wear goggles. There is a high wind and the wind fans the charcoal almost to white heat.

'The Indian fire-walker then comes forwards. He is naked except for a small loincloth, and his feet are bare. The crowd becomes silent. The fire-walker enters the trench and walks the whole length of it, over the white-hot charcoal. He doesn't stop. Nor does he hurry. He simply walks over the white-hot coals and comes out at the other end, and his feet are not even singed. He shows the soles of his feet to the crowd. The crowd stares in amazement.

'Then the fire-walker walks the trench once more. This time he goes even slower, and as he does it, I can see on his face a look of pure and absolute concentration. This man, I tell myself, has practised yoga. He is a yogi.

'After the performance, the fire-walker calls out to the crowd, asking if there is anyone brave enough to come down and walk on the fire. There is a hush in the crowd. I feel a sudden surge of excitement in my chest. This is my chance. I must take it. I must have faith and courage. I *must* have a go. I have been doing my concentration exercises for over three years now and the time has come to give myself a severe test.

'While I am standing there thinking these thoughts, a volunteer comes forward from the crowd. It is a young Indian man. He announces that he would like to try the fire-walk. This decides me, and I also step forward and make my announcement. The crowd gives us both a cheer.

'Now the real fire-walker becomes the supervisor. He tells the other man he will go first. He makes him remove his dhoti, otherwise, he says, the hem will catch fire from the heat. And the sandals must be taken off.

'The young Indian does what he is told. But now that he is close to the trench and can feel the terrible heat coming from it, he begins to look frightened. He steps back a few paces, shielding his eyes from the heat with his hands.

'"You don't have to do it if you don't want to," the real fire-walker says.

'The crowd waits and watches, sensing a drama.

'The young man, though scared out of his wits, wishes to prove how brave he is, and he says, "Of course I'll do it."

'With that, he runs towards the trench. He steps into it with one foot, then the other. He gives a fearful scream and leaps out again and falls to the ground. The poor man lies there screaming in pain. The soles of his feet are badly burned and some of the skin has come right away. Two friends of his run forwards and carry him off.

'"Now it is your turn," says the fire-walker. "Are you ready?"

"'I am ready," I say. "But please be silent while I prepare myself."

'A great hush has come over the crowd. They have seen one man get badly burned. Is the second one going to be mad enough to do the same thing?

'Someone in the crowd shouts, "Don't do it! You must be mad!" Others take up the shout, all telling me to give up. I turn and face them and raise my hands for silence. They stop shouting and stare at me. Every eye in that place is upon me now.

'I feel extraordinarily calm.

'I pull my dhoti off over my head. I take off my sandals. I stand there naked except for my underpants. I stand very still and close my eyes. I begin to concentrate my mind. I concentrate on the fire. I see nothing but white-hot coals and I concentrate on them being not hot but cold. The coals are cold, I tell myself. They cannot burn me. It is impossible for them to burn me because there is no heat in them. I allow half a minute to go by. I know that I must not wait too long because I am only able to concentrate absolutely upon any one thing for a minute and a half.

'I keep concentrating. I concentrate so hard that I go into a sort of trance. I step out on the coals. I walk fairly fast the whole length of the trench. And behold, I am not burned!

'The crowd goes mad. They yell and cheer. The original fire-walker rushes up to me and examines the soles of my feet. He can't believe what he sees. There is not a burn mark on them.

'"Ayee!" he cries. "What is this? Are you a yogi?"

'"I am on the way, sir," I answer proudly. "I am well on the way."

'After that, I dress and leave quickly, avoiding the crowd.

'Of course I am excited. "It is coming to me," I say. "Now at last the power is beginning to come." And all the time I am remembering something else. I am remembering a thing that the old yogi of Hardwar said to me. He said, "Certain holy people have been known to develop so great a concentration that they could see without using their eyes." I keep remembering that saying and I keep longing for the power to do likewise myself. And after my success with the fire-walking, I decided that I will concentrate everything upon this single aim – to see without the eyes.'

For only the second time so far, Imhrat Khan broke off his story. He took another sip of water, then he leaned back in his chair and closed his eyes.

'I am trying to get everything in the correct order,' he said. 'I don't want to miss anything out.'

'You're doing fine,' I told him. 'Carry on.'

'Very well,' he said. 'So I am still in Calcutta and I have just had success with fire-walking. And now I have decided to concentrate all my energy on this one thing, which is to see without the eyes.

'The time has come, therefore, to make a slight change in the exercises. Each night now I light a candle and I begin by staring at the flame. A candle-flame, you know, has three separate parts, the yellow at the top, the mauve lower down, and the black right inside. I place the candle sixteen inches away from my face. The flame is absolutely level with my eyes. It must not be above or below. It must be dead level because then I do not have to make even the tiniest little adjustment of the eye muscles by looking up or down. I settle myself comfortably and I begin to stare at the black part of the flame, right in the centre. All this is merely to concentrate my conscious mind, to empty it of everything around me. So I stare at the black spot in the flame until everything around me has disappeared and I can see nothing else. Then slowly I shut my eyes and begin to concentrate as usual upon one single object of my choice, which as you know is usually my brother's face.

'I do this every night before bed and by 1929, when I am twenty-four years old, I can concentrate upon an object for three minutes without any wandering of my mind. So it is now, at this time, when I am twenty-four, that I begin to become aware of a slight ability to see an object with my eyes closed. It is a very slight ability, just a queer little feeling that when I close my eyes and look at something hard, with fierce concentration, then I can see the outline of the object I am looking at.

'Slowly I am beginning to develop my *inner* sense of sight.

'You ask me what I mean by that. I will explain it to you exactly as the yogi of Hardwar explained it to me.

'All of us, you see, have two senses of sight, just as we have two senses of smell and taste and hearing. There is the outer sense, the highly developed one which we all use, and there is the *inner* one also. If only we could develop these inner senses of ours, then we could smell without our noses, taste without our tongues, hear without our ears and see without our eyes. Do you not understand? Do you not see that our noses and tongues and ears and eyes are only . . . how shall I say it? . . . are only instruments which assist in conveying the sensation itself to the brain.

'And so it is that I am all the time striving to develop my inner senses of sight. Each night now I perform my usual exercises with the candle-flame and my brother's face. After that I rest a little while. I drink a cup of coffee. Then I blindfold myself and sit in my chair trying to visualize, trying to see, not just to imagine, but actually to *see* without my eyes every object in the room.

'And gradually success begins to come.

'Soon I am working with a pack of cards. I take a card from the top of the pack and hold it before me, back to front, trying to see through it. Then, with a pencil in my hand, I write down what I think it is. I take another card and do the same again. I go through the whole of the pack like that and when it is over I check what I have written down against the pile of cards beside me. Almost at once I have a sixty to seventy per cent success.

'I do other things. I buy maps and complicated navigating charts and pin them up all around my room. I spend hours looking at them blindfold, trying to see them, trying to read the small lettering of the place-names and the rivers. Every evening for the next four years, I proceed with this kind of practice.

'By the year 1933 – that is only last year – when I am twenty-eight years old, I can read a book. I can cover my eyes completely and I can read a book right through.

'So now at last I have it, this power. For certain I have it now, and at once, because I cannot wait with impatience, I include the blindfold act in my ordinary conjuring performance.

'The audience loves it. They applaud long and loud. But not one single person believes it to be genuine. Everyone thinks it is just another clever trick. And the fact that I am a conjurer makes them think more than ever that I am faking. Conjurers are men who trick you. They trick you with cleverness. And so no one believes me. Even the doctors who blindfold me in the most expert way refuse to believe that anyone can see without his eyes. They forget there may be other ways of sending the image to the brain.'

'What other ways?' I asked him.

'Quite honestly, I don't know exactly how it is I can see without my eyes. But what I do know is this; when my eyes are bandaged, I am not using the eyes at all. The seeing is done by another part of my body.'

'Which part?' I asked him.

'Any part at all so long as the skin is bare. For example, if you put a sheet of metal in front of me and put a book behind the metal, I cannot read the book. But if you allow me to put my hand around the sheet of metal so that the hand is seeing the book, then I can read it.'

'Would you mind if I tested you on that?' I asked.

'Not at all,' he answered.

'I don't have a sheet of metal,' I said. 'But the door will do just as well.'

I stood up and went to the bookshelf. I took down the first book that came to hand. It was *Alice in Wonderland*. I opened the door and asked my visitor to stand behind it, out of sight. I opened the book at random and propped it on a chair the other side of the door to him. Then I stationed myself in a position where I could see both him and the book.

'Can you read that book?' I asked him.

'No,' he answered. 'Of course not.'

'All right. You may now put your hand around the door, but only the hand.'

He slid his hand around the edge of the door until it was within sight of the book. Then I saw the fingers on the hand parting from one another, spreading wide, beginning to quiver slightly, feeling the air like the antennae of an insect. And the hand turned so that the back of it was facing the book.

'Try to read the left page from the top,' I said.

There was silence for perhaps ten seconds, then smoothly, without pause, he began to read: '*Have you guessed the riddle yet?*' *the Hatter said, turning to Alice again.* '*No, I give it up,*' *Alice replied:* '*What's the answer?*' '*I haven't the slightest idea,*' *said the Hatter.* '*Nor I,*' *said the Hare. Alice sighed wearily.* '*I think you might do something better with the time,*' *she said,* '*than waste it asking riddles with no answers . . .*'

'It's perfect!' I cried. 'Now I believe you! You are a miracle!' I was enormously excited.

'Thank you, doctor,' he said gravely. 'What you say gives me great pleasure.'

'One question,' I said. 'It's about the playing cards. When you held up the reverse side of one of them, did you put your hand around the other side to help you to read it?'

'You are very perceptive,' he said. 'No, I did not. In the case of the cards, I was actually able to *see through* them in some way.'

'How do you explain that?' I asked.

'I don't explain it,' he said. 'Except perhaps that a card is such a flimsy thing, it is so thin, and not solid like metal or thick like a door. That is all the explanation I can give. There are many things in this world, doctor, that we cannot explain.'

'Yes,' I said. 'There certainly are.'

'Would you be kind enough to take me home now,' he said. 'I feel very tired.'

I drove him home in my car.

That night I didn't go to bed. I was far too worked up to sleep. I had just witnessed a miracle. This man would have doctors all over the world turning somersaults in the air! He could change the whole course of medicine! From a doctor's point of view, he must be the most valuable man alive! We doctors must get hold of him and keep him safe. We must look after him. We mustn't let him go. We must find out exactly how it is that an image can be sent to the brain without using the eyes. And if we do that, then blind people might be able to see and deaf people might be able to hear. Above all, this incredible man must not be ignored and left to wander around India, living in cheap rooms and playing in second-rate theatres.

I got so steamed up thinking about this that after a while I grabbed a notebook and a pen and started writing down with great care everything that Imhrat Khan had told me that evening. I used the notes I had made while he was talking. I wrote for five hours without stopping. And at eight o'clock the next morning, when it was time to go to the hospital, I had finished the most important part, the pages you have just read.

At the hospital that morning, I didn't see Dr Marshall until we met in the Doctors' Rest Room in our tea-break.

I told him as much as I could in the ten minutes we had to spare. 'I'm going back to the theatre tonight,' I said. 'I *must* talk to him again. I must persuade him to stay here. We mustn't lose him now.'

'I'll come with you,' Dr Marshall said.

'Right,' I said. 'We'll watch the show first and then we'll take him out to supper.'

At a quarter to seven that evening, I drove Dr Marshall in my car to Acacia Road. I parked the car, and the two of us walked over to the Royal Palace Hall.

'There's something wrong,' I said. 'Where is everybody?'

There was no crowd outside the hall and the doors were closed. The poster advertising the show was still in place, but I now saw that someone had written across it in large printed letters, using black paint, the words TONIGHT'S PERFORMANCE CANCELLED. There was an old gatekeeper standing by the locked doors.

'What happened?' I asked him.

'Someone died,' he said.

'Who?' I asked, knowing already who it was.

'The man who sees without his eyes,' the gatekeeper answered.

'How did he die?' I cried. 'When? Where?'

'They say he died in his bed,' the gatekeeper said. 'He went to sleep and never woke up. These things happen.'

We walked slowly back to the car. I felt an overwhelming sense of grief and anger. I should never have allowed this precious man to go home last night. I should have kept him. I should have given him my bed and taken care of him. I shouldn't have let him out of my sight. Imhrat Khan was a maker of miracles. He had communicated with mysterious and dangerous forces that are beyond the reach of ordinary people. He had also broken all the rules. He had performed miracles in public. He had taken money for doing so. And, worst of all, he had told some of those secrets to an outsider – me. Now he was dead.

'So that's that,' Dr Marshall said.

'Yes,' I said. 'It's all over. Nobody will ever know how he did it.'

This is a true and accurate report of everything that took place concerning my two meetings with Imhrat Khan.

signed John F. Cartwright, M.D.

. . . .

Bombay, 4th December, 1934

'Well, well, well,' said Henry Sugar. 'Now *that* is extremely interesting.'

He closed the exercise-book and sat gazing at the rain splashing against the windows of the library.

'This,' Henry Sugar went on, talking aloud to himself, 'is a terrific piece of information. It could change my life.'

The piece of information Henry was referring to was that Imhrat Khan had trained himself to read the value of a playing-card from the reverse side. And Henry the gambler, the rather dishonest gambler, had realized at once that if only *he* could train himself to do the same thing, he could make a fortune.

For a few moments, Henry allowed his mind to dwell upon the marvellous things he would be able to do if he could read cards from the back. He would win every single time at canasta and bridge and poker. And better still, he would be able to go into any casino in the world and clean up at blackjack and all the other high-powered card games they played!

In gambling casinos, as Henry knew very well, nearly everything depended in the end upon the turn of a single card, and if you knew beforehand what the value of that card was, then you were home and dry!

But could he do it? Could he actually train himself to do this thing?

He didn't see why not. That stuff with the candle-flame didn't appear to be particularly hard work. And according to the book, that was really all there was to it – just staring into the middle of the flame and trying to concentrate upon the face of the person you loved best.

It would probably take him several years to bring it off, but then who in the world wouldn't be willing to train for a few years in order to beat the casinos every time he went in?

'By golly,' he said aloud, 'I'll do it! I'm going to do it!'

He sat very still in the armchair in the library, working out a plan of campaign. Above all, he would tell nobody what he was up to. He would steal the little book from the library so that none of his friends might come upon it by chance and learn the secret. He would carry the book with him wherever he went. It would be his bible. He couldn't possibly go out and find a real live yogi to instruct him, so the book would be his yogi instead. It would be his teacher.

Henry stood up and slipped the slim blue exercise-book under his jacket. He walked out of the library and went straight upstairs to the bedroom they had given him for the week-end. He got out his suitcase and hid the book underneath his clothes. He then went downstairs again and found his way to the butler's pantry.

'John,' he said, addressing the butler, 'can you find me a candle? Just an ordinary white candle.'

Butlers are trained never to ask reasons. They simply obey orders. 'Do you wish a candle-holder as well, sir?'

'Yes. A candle and a candle-holder.'

'Very good, sir. Shall I bring them to your room?'

'No. I'll hang around here till you find them.'

The butler soon found a candle and a candle-holder. Henry said, 'And now could you find me a ruler?' The butler found him a ruler. Henry thanked him and returned to his bedroom.

When he was inside the bedroom, he locked the door. He drew all the curtains so that the place was in twilight.

He put the candle-holder with the candle in it on the dressing-table and pulled up a chair. When he sat down, he noticed with satisfaction that his eyes were exactly level with the wick of the candle. Now, using the ruler, he positioned his face sixteen inches from the candle, which was what the book said must be done.

That Indian fellow had visualized the face of the person he loved best, which in his case was a brother. Henry didn't have a brother. He decided instead to visualize his own face. This was a good choice because when you are as selfish and self-centred as Henry was, then one's own face is certainly the face one loves best of all. Moreover, it was the face he *knew* best of all. He spent so much time looking at it in the mirror, he knew every twist and wrinkle.

With his cigarette-lighter, he lit the wick. A yellow flame appeared and burned steadily.

Henry sat quite still and stared into the candle-flame. The book had been quite right. The flame, when you looked into it closely, did have three separate parts. There was the yellow outside. Then there was the mauve inner sheath. And right in the middle was the tiny magic area of absolute blackness. He stared at the tiny black area. He focused his eyes upon it and kept staring at it, and as he did so, an extraordinary thing happened. His mind went absolutely blank, and his brain ceased fidgeting around, and all at once it felt as though he himself, his whole body, was actually encased within the flame, sitting snug and cosy within the little black area of nothingness.

With no trouble at all, Henry allowed the image of his

own face to swim into sight before him. He concentrated upon the face and nothing but the face. He blocked out all other thoughts. He succeeded completely in doing this, but only for about fifteen seconds. After that, his mind began to wander and he found himself thinking about gambling casinos and how much money he was going to win. At this point, he looked away from the candle and gave himself a rest.

This was his very first effort. He was thrilled. He had done it. Admittedly he hadn't kept it up for very long. But neither had that Indian fellow on the first attempt.

After a few minutes, he tried again. It went well. He had no stop-watch to time himself with, but he sensed that this was definitely a longer go than the first one.

'It's terrific!' he cried. 'I'm going to succeed! I'm going to do it!' He had never been so excited by anything in his life.

From that day on, no matter where he was or what he was doing, Henry made a point of practising with the candle every morning and every evening. Often he practised at midday as well. For the first time in his life he was throwing himself into something with genuine enthusiasm. And the progress he made was remarkable. After six months, he could concentrate absolutely upon his own face for no less than three minutes without a single outside thought entering his mind.

The yogi of Hardwar had told the Indian fellow that a man would have to practise for fifteen years to get that sort of result!

But wait! The yogi had also said something else. He had

said (and here Henry eagerly consulted the little blue exercise-book for the hundredth time), he had said that on extremely rare occasions a special person comes along who is able to develop the power in only one or two years.

'That's me!' Henry cried. 'It must be me! I am the one-in-a-million person who is gifted with the ability to acquire yoga powers at incredible speed! Whoopee and hurray! It won't be long now before I'm breaking the bank in every casino in Europe and America!'

But Henry at this point showed unusual patience and good sense. He didn't rush to get out a pack of cards to see if he could read them from the reverse side. In fact, he kept well away from card games of all kinds. He had given up bridge and canasta and poker as soon as he had started working with the candle. What's more, he had given up razzing around to parties and week-ends with his rich friends. He had become dedicated to this single aim of acquiring yoga powers, and everything else would have to wait until he had succeeded.

Some time during the tenth month, Henry became aware, just as Imhrat Khan had done before him, of a slight ability to see an object with his eyes closed. When he closed his eyes and stared at something hard, with fierce concentration, he could actually see the outline of the object he was looking at.

'It's coming to me!' he cried. 'I'm doing it! It's fantastic!'

Now he worked harder than ever at his exercises with the candle, and at the end of the first year he could actually concentrate upon the image of his own face for no less than five and a half minutes!

At this point, he decided the time had come to test himself with the cards. He was in the living-room of his London flat when he made this decision and it was near midnight. He got out a pack of cards and a pencil and paper. He was shaking with excitement. He placed the pack upside down before him and concentrated on the top card.

All he could see at first was the design on the back of the card. It was a very ordinary design of thin red lines, one of the commonest playing-card designs in the world. He now shifted his concentration from the pattern itself to the other side of the card. He concentrated with great intensity upon the invisible underneath of the card, and he allowed no other single thought to creep into his mind. Thirty seconds went by.

Then one minute . . .

Two minutes . . .

Three minutes . . .

Henry didn't move. His concentration was intense and absolute. He was visualizing the reverse side of the playing-card. No other thought of any kind was allowed to enter his head.

During the fourth minute, something began to happen. Slowly, magically, but very clearly, the black symbols became spades and alongside the spades appeared the figure five.

The five of spades!

Henry switched off his concentration. And now, with shaking fingers, he picked up the card and turned it over.

It *was* the five of spades!

'I've done it!' he cried aloud, leaping up from his chair. 'I've seen through it! I'm on my way!'

After resting for a while, he tried again, and this time he used a stop-watch to see how long it took him. After three minutes and fifty-eight seconds, he read the card as the king of diamonds. He was right!

The next time he was right again and it took him three minutes and fifty-four seconds. That was four seconds less.

He was sweating with excitement and exhaustion. 'That's enough for today,' he told himself. He got up and poured himself an enormous drink of whisky and sat down to rest and to gloat over his success.

His job now, he told himself, was to keep practising and practising with the cards until he could see through them instantly. He was convinced it could be done. Already, on the second go, he had knocked four seconds off his time. He would give up working with the candle and concentrate solely upon the cards. He would keep at it day and night.

And that is what he did. But now that he could smell real success in the offing, he became more fanatical than ever. He never left his flat except to buy food and drink. All day and often far into the night, he crouched over the cards with the stop-watch beside him, trying to reduce the time it took him to read from the reverse side.

Within a month, he was down to one and a half minutes.

And at the end of six months of fierce concentrated work, he could do it in twenty seconds. But even that was too long. When you are gambling in a casino and the dealer is waiting for you to say yes or no to the next card, you are not going to be allowed to stare at it for twenty seconds before making up your mind. Three or four seconds would be permissible. But no more.

Henry kept at it. But from now on, it became more and more difficult to improve his speed. To get down from twenty seconds to nineteen took him a week of very hard work. From nineteen to eighteen took him nearly two weeks. And seven more months went by before he could read through a card in ten seconds flat.

His target was four seconds. He knew that unless he could see through a card in a maximum of four seconds, he wouldn't be able to work the casinos successfully. Yet the nearer he got towards the target, the more difficult it became to reach it. It took four weeks to get his time down from ten seconds to nine, and five more weeks to go from nine to eight. But at this stage, hard work no longer bothered him. His powers of concentration had now developed to such a degree that he was able to work for twelve hours at a stretch with no trouble at all. And he knew with absolute certainty that he would get there in the end. He would not stop until he did. Day after day, night after night, he sat crouching over the cards with his stop-watch beside him, fighting with a terrible intensity to knock those last few stubborn seconds off his time.

The last three seconds were the worst of all. To get from seven seconds to his target of four took him exactly eleven months!

The great moment came on a Saturday evening. A card lay face down on the table in front of him. He clicked the stop-watch and began to concentrate. At once, he saw a blob of red. The blob swiftly took shape and became a diamond. And then, almost instantaneously, a figure six appeared in the top left-hand corner. He clicked the watch again. He checked the time. It was four seconds! He turned the card over. It was the six of diamonds! He had done it! He had read it in four seconds flat!

He tried again with another card. In four seconds he read it as the queen of spades. He went right through the pack, timing himself with every card. Four seconds! Four seconds! Four seconds! It was always the same. He had done it at last! It was all over. He was ready to go!

And how long had it taken him? It had taken him exactly three years and three months of concentrated work.

And now for the casinos!

When should he start?

Why not tonight?

Tonight was Saturday. All the casinos were crowded on Saturday nights. So much the better. There'd be less chance of becoming conspicuous. He went into his bedroom to change into his dinner-jacket and black tie. Saturday was a dressy night at the big London casinos.

He would go, he decided, to Lord's House. There are well over one hundred legitimate casinos in London, but none of them is open to the general public. You must become a member before you are allowed to walk in. Henry was a member of no less than ten of them. Lord's House was his favourite. It was the finest and most exclusive in the country.

*

Lord's House was a magnificent Georgian mansion in the centre of London, and for over two hundred years it had been the private residence of a Duke. Now it was taken over by the bookmakers, and the superb high-ceilinged rooms where the aristocracy and often royalty used to gather and play a gentle game of whist were today filled with a new kind of people who played a very different sort of game.

Henry drove to Lord's House and pulled up outside the great entrance. He got out of the car, but left the engine running. Immediately, an attendant in green uniform came forward to park it for him.

Along the kerb on both sides of the street stood perhaps a dozen Rolls-Royces. Only the very wealthy belonged to Lord's House.

'Why hello, Mr Sugar!' said the man behind the desk whose job it was never to forget a face. 'We haven't seen you for years!'

'I've been busy,' Henry answered.

He went upstairs, up the marvellous wide staircase with its carved mahogany banisters, and entered the cashier's office. There he wrote a cheque for one thousand pounds. The cashier gave him ten large pink rectangular plaques made of plastic. On each it said £100. Henry slipped them into his pocket and spent a few minutes sauntering through the various gaming-rooms to get the feel of things again after such a long absence. There was a big crowd here tonight. Well-fed women stood around the roulette wheel like plump hens around a feeding hopper. Jewels and gold were dripping over their bosoms and from their wrists. Many of them had blue hair. The men were in dinner-jackets and there wasn't a tall one among them. Why, Henry wondered, did this particular kind of rich man always have short legs? Their legs all seemed to stop at the knees with no thighs above. Most of them had bellies coming out a long way, and crimson faces, and cigars between their lips. Their eyes glittered with greed.

All this Henry noticed. It was the first time in his life that he had looked with distaste upon this type of wealthy gambling-casino person. Up until now, he had always regarded them as companions, as members of the same group and class as himself. Tonight they seemed vulgar.

Could it be, he wondered, that the yoga powers he had acquired over the last three years had altered him just a little bit?

He stood watching the roulette. Upon the long green table people were placing their money, trying to guess which little slot the small white ball would fall into on the next spin of the wheel. Henry looked at the wheel. And suddenly, perhaps more from habit than anything else, he found himself beginning to concentrate upon it. It was not difficult. He had been practising the art of total concentration for so long that it had become something of a routine. In a fraction of a second, his mind had become completely and absolutely concentrated upon the wheel. Everything else in the room, the noise, the people, the lights, the smell of cigar smoke, all this was wiped out of his mind, and he saw only the white numbers around the rim. The numbers went from 1 to 36, with an o between 1 and 36. Very quickly, all the numbers blurred and disappeared in front of his eyes. All except one, all except the number 18. It was the only number he could see. At first it was slightly muzzy and out of focus. Then the edges sharpened and the whiteness of it grew brighter, more brilliant, until it began to glow as though there was a bright light behind it. It grew bigger. It seemed to jump towards him. At that point, Henry switched off his concentration. The room swam back into vision.

'Have you all finished?' the croupier was saying.

Henry took a £100 plaque from his pocket and placed it on the square marked 18 on the green table. Although the table was covered all over with other people's bets, his was the only one on 18.

The croupier spun the wheel. The little white ball bounced and skittered around the rim. The people watched. All eyes were on the little ball. The wheel slowed. It came to rest. The ball jiggled a few more times, hesitated, then dropped neatly into slot 18.

'Eighteen!' called the croupier.

The crowd sighed. The croupier's assistant scooped up the piles of losing plaques with a long-handled wooden scooper. But he didn't take Henry's. They paid him thirty-six to one. Three thousand six hundred pounds for his hundred. They gave it to him in three one-thousand pound plaques and six hundreds.

Henry began to feel an extraordinary sense of power. He felt he could break this place if he wanted to. He could ruin this fancy high-powered expensive joint in a matter of hours. He could take a million off them and all the stony-faced sleek gentlemen who stood around watching the money rolling in would be scurrying about like panicky rats.

Should he do that?

It was a great temptation.

But it would be the end of everything. He would become famous and would never be allowed into a casino again anywhere in the world. He mustn't do it. He must be very careful not to draw attention to himself.

Henry moved casually out of the roulette room and passed into the room where they were playing blackjack. He stood in the doorway watching the action. There were four tables. They were oddly shaped, these blackjack tables, each one curved like a crescent moon, with the players sitting on high stools around the outside of the half-circle and the dealers standing inside.

The packs of cards (at Lord's House they used four packs shuffled together) lay in an open-ended box known as a shoe, and the dealer pulled the cards out of the shoe one by one with his fingers . . . The reverse side of the card in the shoe was always visible, but no others.

Blackjack, as the casinos call it, is a very simple game. You and I know it by one of three other names, pontoon, twenty-one or vingt-et-un. The player tries to get his cards to add up to as near twenty-one as possible, but if he goes over twenty-one, he's bust and the dealer takes the money. In nearly every hand, the player is faced with the problem of whether to draw another card and risk being bust, or whether to stick with what he's got. But Henry would not have that problem. In four seconds, he would have 'seen through' the card the dealer was offering him, and he would know whether to say yes or no. Henry could turn blackjack into a farce.

In all casinos, they have an awkward rule about blackjack betting which we do not have at home. At home, we look at our first card before we make a bet, and if it's a good one we bet high. The casinos don't allow you to do this. They insist that everyone at the table makes his bet *before* the first card of the hand is dealt. What's more, you are not allowed to increase your bet later on by buying a card.

None of this would disturb Henry either. So long as he sat on the dealer's immediate left, then he would always receive the first card in the shoe at the beginning of each deal. The reverse side of the card would be clearly visible to him, and he would 'read through' it before he made his bet.

Now, standing quietly just inside the doorway, Henry waited for a place to become vacant on the dealer's left at any of the four tables. He had to wait twenty minutes for this to happen, but he got what he wanted in the end.

He perched himself on the high stool and handed the dealer one of the £1,000 plaques he had won at roulette. 'All in twenty-fives, please,' he said.

The dealer was a youngish man with black eyes and grey skin. He never smiled and he spoke only when necessary. His hands were exceptionally slim and there was arithmetic in his fingers. He took Henry's plaque and dropped it in a slot in the table. Rows of different coloured circular chips lay neatly in a wooden tray in front of him, chips for £25, £10 and £5, maybe a hundred of each. With his thumb and forefinger, the dealer picked up a wedge of £25 chips and placed them in a tall pile on the table. He didn't have to count them. He knew there were exactly twenty chips in the pile. Those nimble fingers could pick up with absolute accuracy any number of chips from one to twenty and never be wrong. The dealer picked up a second lot of chips, making forty in all. He slid them over the table to Henry.

Henry stacked the chips in front of him, and as he did so, he glanced at the top card in the shoe. He switched on his concentration and in four seconds he read it as a ten. He pushed out eight of his chips, £200. This was the maximum stake allowed for blackjack at Lord's House.

He was dealt the ten, and for his second card he got a nine, nineteen altogether.

Everyone sticks on nineteen. You sit tight and hope the dealer won't get twenty or twenty-one.

So when the dealer came round again to Henry, he said, 'Nineteen,' and passed on to the next player.

'Wait,' Henry said.

The dealer paused and came back to Henry. He raised his brows and looked at him with those cool black eyes. 'You wish to draw to nineteen?' he asked somewhat sarcastically. He spoke with an Italian accent and there was scorn as well as sarcasm in his voice. There were only two cards in the pack that would not bust a nineteen, the ace (counting as a one) and the two. Only an idiot would risk drawing to nineteen, especially with £200 on the table.

The next card to be dealt lay clearly visible in the front of the shoe. At least, the reverse side of it was clearly visible. The dealer hadn't yet touched it.

'Yes,' Henry said. 'I think I'll have another card.'

The dealer shrugged and flipped the card out of the

shoe. The two of clubs landed neatly in front of Henry, alongside the ten and the nine.

'Thank you,' Henry said. 'That will do nicely.'

'Twenty-one,' the dealer said. His black eyes glanced up again into Henry's face, and they rested there, silent, watchful, puzzled. Henry had unbalanced him. He had never in his life seen anyone draw on nineteen. This fellow had drawn on nineteen with a calmness and a certainty that was quite staggering. And he had won.

Henry caught the look in the dealer's eyes, and he realized at once that he had made a silly mistake. He had been too clever. He had drawn attention to himself. He must never do that again. He must be very careful in future how he used his powers. He must even make himself lose occasionally, and every now and again he must do something a bit stupid.

The game went on. Henry's advantage was so enormous, he had difficulty keeping his winnings down to a reasonable sum. Every now and again, he would ask for a third card when he already knew it was going to bust him. And once, when he saw that his first card was going to be an ace, he put out his smallest stake, then made a great show of cursing himself aloud for not having made a bigger bet in the first place.

In an hour, he had won exactly three thousand pounds, and there he stopped. He pocketed his chips and made his way back to the cashier's office to turn them in for real money.

He had made £3,000 from blackjack and £3,600 from roulette, £6,600 in all. It could just as easily have been £660,000. As a matter of fact, he told himself he was now almost certainly able to make money faster than any other man in the entire world.

The cashier received Henry's pile of chips and plaques without twitching a muscle. He wore steel spectacles, and the pale eyes behind the spectacles were not interested in Henry. They looked only at the chips on the counter. This man also had arithmetic in his fingers. But he had more than that. He had arithmetic, trigonometry and calculus and algebra and Euclidean geometry in every nerve of his body. He was a human calculating-machine with a hundred thousand electric wires in his brain. It took him five seconds to count Henry's one hundred and twenty chips.

'Would you like a cheque for this, Mr Sugar?' he asked. The cashier, like the man at the desk downstairs, knew every member by name.

'No, thank you,' Henry said. 'I'll take it in cash.'

'As you wish,' said the voice behind the spectacles, and he turned away and went to a safe at the back of the office that must have contained millions.

By Lord's House standards, Henry's win was fairly small potatoes. The Arab oil boys were in London now and they liked to gamble. So did the shady diplomats from the Far East and the Japanese businessmen and the British tax-dodging real-estate operators. Staggering sums of money were being won and lost, mostly lost, in the large London casinos every day.

The cashier returned with Henry's money and dropped the bundle of notes on the counter. Although there was enough here to buy a small house or a large automobile, the chief cashier at Lord's House was not impressed. He might just as well have been passing Henry a pack of chewing-gum for all the notice he took of the money he was dishing out.

You wait, my friend, Henry thought to himself as he pocketed the money. You just wait. He walked away.

'Your car, sir?' said the man at the door in the green uniform.

'Not yet,' Henry told him. 'I think 'I'll take a bit of fresh air first.'

He strolled away down the street. It was nearly midnight. The evening was cool and pleasant. The great city was still wide awake. Henry could feel the bulge in the inside pocket of his jacket where the big wad of money was lying. He touched the bulge with one hand. He patted it gently. It was a lot of money for an hour's work.

And what of the future?

What was the next move going to be?

He could make a million in a month.

He could make more if he wanted to.

There was no limit to what he could make.

Walking through the streets of London in the cool of the evening, Henry began to think about the next move.

Now, had this been a made-up story instead of a true one, it would have been necessary to invent some sort of a surprising and exciting end for it. It would not be difficult to do that. Something dramatic and unusual. So before telling you what really *did* happen to Henry in real life, let us pause here for a moment to see what a competent fiction writer would have done to wrap this story up. His notes would read something like this:

1. Henry must die. Like Imhrat Khan before him, he had violated the code of the yogi and had used his powers for personal gain.

2. It will be best if he dies in some unusual and interesting manner that will surprise the reader.

3. For example, he could go home to his flat and start counting his money and gloating over it. While doing this, he might suddenly begin to feel unwell. He has a pain in his chest.

4. He becomes frightened. He decides to go to bed immediately and rest. He takes off his clothes. He walks naked to the cupboard to get his pyjamas. He passes the full-length mirror that stands against the wall. He stops. He stares at the reflection of his naked self in the mirror. Automatically, from force of habit he begins to concentrate. And then . . .

5. All at once, he is 'seeing through' his own skin. He 'sees through' it in the same way that he 'saw through' those playing-cards a while back. It is like an X-ray picture, only far better. An X-ray can see only the bones and the very dense areas. Henry can see everything. He sees his arteries and veins with the blood pumping through him. He can see his liver, his kidneys, his intestines and he can see his heart beating.

6. He looks at the place in his chest where the pain is coming from . . . and he sees . . . or thinks he sees . . . a small dark lump inside the big vein leading into the heart on the right-hand side.

What could a small dark lump be doing inside the vein? It must be a blockage of some kind. It must be a clot. A blood-clot!

7. At first, the clot seems to be stationary. Then it moves. The movement is very slight, no more than a millimetre or two. The blood inside the vein is pumping up behind the clot and pushing past it and the clot moves again. It jerks forward about half an inch. This time, up the vein, towards the heart. Henry watches in terror. He knows, as almost everyone else in the world knows, that a blood-clot which has broken free and is travelling in a vein will ultimately reach the heart. If the clot is a large one, it will stick in the heart and you will probably die . . .

That wouldn't be such a bad ending for a work of fiction, but this story is not fiction. It is true. The only untrue things about it are Henry's name and the name of the gambling casino. Henry's name was not Henry Sugar. His name has to be protected. It still must be protected. And for obvious reasons, one cannot call the casino by its real name. Apart from that, it is a true story.

And because it is a true story, it must have the true ending. The true one may not be quite so dramatic or spooky as a made-up one could be, but it is nonetheless interesting. Here is what actually happened.

After walking the London streets for about an hour, Henry returned to Lord's House and collected his car.

Then he drove back to his flat. He was a puzzled man. He couldn't understand why he felt so little excitement about his tremendous success. If this sort of thing had happened to him three years ago, before he'd started the yoga business, he'd have gone crazy with excitement. He'd have been dancing in the streets and rushing off to the nearest nightclub to celebrate with champagne.

The funny thing was that he didn't really feel excited at all. He felt melancholy. It had somehow all been too easy. Every time he'd made a bet, he'd been certain of winning. There was no thrill, no suspense, no danger of losing. He knew of course that from now on he could travel around the world and make millions. But was it going to be any fun doing it?

It was slowly beginning to dawn upon Henry that nothing is any fun if you can get as much of it as you want. Especially money.

Another thing. Was it not possible that the process he had gone through in order to acquire yoga powers had completely changed his outlook on life?

Certainly it was possible.

Henry drove home and went straight to bed.

The next morning he woke up late. But he didn't feel any more cheerful now than he had the night before. And when he got out of bed and saw the enormous bundle of money still lying on his dressing-table, he felt a sudden and very acute revulsion towards it. He didn't want it. For the life of him, he couldn't explain why this was so, but the fact remained that he simply did not want any part of it.

He picked up the bundle. It was all in twenty-pound notes, three hundred and thirty of them to be exact. He walked on to the balcony of his flat, and there he stood in his dark-red silk pyjamas looking down at the street below him.

Henry's flat was in Curzon Street, which is right in the middle of London's most fashionable and expensive district, known as Mayfair. One end of Curzon Street runs into Berkeley Square, the other into Park Lane. Henry lived three floors above street level, and outside his bedroom there was a small balcony with iron railings that overhung the street.

The month was June, the morning was full of sunshine, and the time was about eleven o'clock. Although it was a Sunday, there were quite a few people strolling about on the pavements.

Henry peeled off a single twenty-pound note from his wad and dropped it over the balcony. A breeze took hold of it and blew it sideways in the direction of Park Lane. Henry stood watching it. It fluttered and twisted in the air and eventually came to rest on the opposite side of the street, directly in front of an old man. The old man was wearing a long brown shabby overcoat and a floppy hat, and he was walking slowly, all by himself. He caught sight of the note as it fluttered past his face, and he stopped and picked it up. He held it with both hands and stared at it. He turned it over. He peered closer. Then he raised his head and looked up.

'Hey there!' Henry shouted, cupping a hand to his mouth. 'That's for you! It's a present!'

The old man stood quite still, holding the note in front of him and gazing up at the figure on the balcony above.

'Put it in your pocket!' Henry shouted. 'Take it home!' His voice carried far along the street, and many people stopped and looked up.

Henry peeled off another note and threw it down. The watchers below him didn't move. They simply watched. They had no idea what was going on. A man was up there on the balcony and he had shouted something, and now he had just thrown down what looked like a piece of paper. Everyone followed the piece of paper as it went fluttering down, and this one came to rest near a young couple who were standing arm in arm on the pavement across the street. The man unlinked his arm and tried to catch the paper as it went past him. He missed it but picked it up from the ground. He examined it closely. The watchers on both sides of the street all had their eyes on the young man. To many of them, the paper had looked very much like a bank-note of some kind, and they were waiting to find out.

'It's twenty pounds!' the man yelled, jumping up and down. 'It's a twenty-pound note!'

'Keep it!' Henry shouted at him. 'It's yours!'

'You mean it?' the man called back, holding the note out at arm's length. 'Can I really keep it?'

Suddenly there was a rustle of excitement along both sides of the street and everyone started moving at once. They ran out into the middle of the road and clustered underneath the balcony. They lifted their arms above their heads and started calling out, 'Me! How about one for me! Drop us another one, guv'nor! Send down a few more!'

Henry peeled off another five or six notes and threw them down.

There were screams and yells as the pieces of paper fanned out in the wind and floated downwards, and there was a good old-fashioned scrimmage in the streets as they reached the hands of the crowd. But it was all very good-natured. People were laughing. They thought it a fantastic joke. Here was a man standing three floors up in his pyjamas, slinging these enormously valuable notes into the air. Quite a few of those present had never seen a twenty-pound note in their lives until now.

But now something else was beginning to happen.

The speed with which news will spread along the streets of a city is phenomenal. The news of what Henry was doing flashed like lightning up and down the length of Curzon Street and into the smaller and larger streets beyond. From all sides, people came running. Within a few minutes, about a thousand men and women and children were blocking the road underneath Henry's balcony. Car-drivers who couldn't pass got out of their vehicles and joined the crowd. And all of a sudden, there was chaos in Curzon Street.

At this point, Henry simply raised his arm and swung it out and flung the entire bundle of notes into the air. More than six thousand pounds went fluttering down towards the screaming crowd below.

The scramble that followed was really something to see. People were jumping up to catch the notes before they reached the ground, and everyone was pushing and jostling and yelling and falling over, and soon the whole place was a mass of tangled, yelling, fighting human beings.

Above the noise and behind him in his own flat, Henry suddenly heard his doorbell ringing long and loud. He left the balcony and opened the front door. A large policeman with a black moustache stood outside with his hands on his hips. 'You!' he bellowed angrily. 'You're the one! What the devil d'you think you're doing?'

'Good morning, officer,' Henry said. 'I'm sorry about the crowd. I didn't think it would turn out like that. I was just giving away some money.'

'You are causing a nuisance!' the policeman bellowed. 'You are creating an obstruction! You are inciting a riot and you are blocking the *en*-tire street!'

'I said I was sorry,' Henry answered. 'I won't do it again, I promise. They'll soon go away.'

The policeman took one hand off his hip and from the inside of his palm he produced a twenty-pound note.

'Ah-ha!' Henry cried. 'You got one yourself! I'm so glad! I'm so happy for you!'

'Now you just stop that larking about!' the policeman said. 'Because I have a few serious questions to ask you about these here twenty-pound notes.' He took a note-book from his breast pocket. 'In the first place,' he went on, 'where exactly did you get them from?'

'I won them,' Henry said. 'I had a lucky night.' He went on to give the name of the club where he had won the money and the policeman wrote it down in his little book. 'Check it up,' Henry added. 'They'll tell you it's true.'

The policeman lowered the notebook, and looked Henry in the eye. 'As a matter of fact,' he said, 'I believe your story. I think you're telling the truth. But that doesn't excuse what you did one little bit.'

'I didn't do anything wrong,' Henry said.

'You're a blithering young idiot!' the policeman shouted, beginning to work himself up all over again. 'You're an ass and an imbecile! If you've been lucky enough to win yourself a tremendous big sum of money like that and you want to give it away, you don't throw it out the window!'

'Why not?' Henry asked, grinning. 'It's as good a way of getting rid of it as any.'

'It's a damned stupid silly way of getting rid of it!' the policeman cried. 'Why didn't you give it where it would do some good? To a hospital, for instance? Or an orphanage? There's orphanages all over the country that hardly have enough money to buy the kids a present even for Christmas! And then along comes a little twit like you who's never even known what it's like to be hard up and you throw the stuff out into the street! It makes me mad, it really does!'

'An orphanage?' Henry said.

'Yes, an *orphanage*!' the policeman cried. 'I was brought up in one so I ought to know what it's like!' With that, the policeman turned away and went quickly down the stairs towards the street.

Henry didn't move. The policeman's words, and more especially the genuine fury with which they had been spoken, smacked our hero right between the eyes.

'An orphanage?' he said aloud. 'That's quite a thought. But why only one orphanage? Why not lots of them?' And now, very quickly, there began to come to him the great and marvellous idea that was to change everything.

Henry shut the front door and went back into his flat. All at once, he felt a powerful excitement stirring in his belly. He started pacing up and down, ticking off the points that would make his marvellous idea possible.

'One,' he said, 'I can get hold of a very large sum of money each day of my life.

'Two. I must not go to the same casino more than once every twelve months.

'Three. I must not win too much from any one casino or somebody will get suspicious. I suggest I keep it down to twenty thousand pounds a night.

'Four. Twenty thousand pounds a night for three hundred and sixty-five days in the year comes to how much?'

Henry took a pencil and paper and worked this one out.

'It comes to seven million, three hundred thousand pounds,' he said aloud.

'Very well. Point number five. I shall have to keep moving. No more than two or three nights at a stretch in any one city or the word will get around. Go from London to Monte Carlo. Then to Cannes. To Biarritz. To Deauville. To Las Vegas. To Mexico City. To Buenos Aires. To Nassau. And so on.

'Six. With the money I make, I will set up an absolutely first-class orphanage in every country I visit. I will become a Robin Hood. I will take money from the bookmakers and the gambling proprietors and give it to the children. Does that sound corny and sentimental? As a dream, it does. But as a reality, if I can really make it work, it wouldn't be corny at all, or sentimental. It would be rather tremendous.

'Seven. I will need somebody to help me, a man who will sit at home and take care of all that money and buy the houses and organize the whole thing. A money man. Someone I can trust. What about John Winston?'

John Winston was Henry's accountant. He handled his income-tax affairs, his investments and all other problems that had to do with money. Henry had known him for eighteen years and a friendship had developed between the two men. Remember, though, that up until now, John Winston had known Henry only as the wealthy idle playboy who had never done a day's work in his life.

'You must be mad,' John Winston said when Henry told him his plan. 'Nobody has ever devised a system for beating the casinos.'

From his pocket, Henry produced a brand-new unopened pack of cards. 'Come on,' he said. 'We'll play a little blackjack. You're the dealer. And don't tell me those cards are marked. It's a new pack.'

Solemnly, for nearly an hour, sitting in Winston's office whose windows looked out over Berkeley Square, the two men played blackjack. They used matchsticks as counters, each match being worth twenty-five pounds. After fifty minutes, Henry was no less than thirty-four thousand pounds up!

John Winston couldn't believe it. 'How do you do it?' he said.

'Put the pack on the table,' Henry said. 'Face down.'

Winston obeyed.

Henry concentrated on the top card for four seconds. 'That's a knave of hearts,' he said. It was.

'The next one is . . . a three of hearts.' It was. He went right through the entire pack, naming every card.

'Go on,' John Winston said. 'Tell me how you do it.' This usually calm and mathematical man was leaning forward over his desk, staring at Henry with eyes as big and bright as two stars. 'You do realize you are doing something completely impossible?' he said.

'It's not impossible,' Henry said. 'It is only very difficult. I am the one man in the world who can do it.'

The telephone rang on John Winston's desk. He lifted the receiver and said to his secretary, 'No more calls please, Susan, until I tell you. Not even my wife.' He looked up, waiting for Henry to go on.

Henry then proceeded to explain to John Winston exactly how he had acquired the power. He told him how he had found the notebook and about Imhrat Khan and then he described how he had been working non-stop for the past three years, training his mind to concentrate.

When he had finished, John Winston said, 'Have you tried walking on fire?'

'No,' Henry said. 'And I'm not going to.'

'What makes you think you'll be able to do this thing with the cards in a casino?'

Henry then told him about his visit to Lord's House the night before.

'Six thousand, six hundred pounds!' John Winston cried. 'Did you honestly win that much in real money?'

'Listen,' Henry said. 'I just won thirty-four thousand from you in less than an hour!'

'So you did.'

'Six thousand was the very least I could win,' Henry said. 'It was a terrific effort not to win more.'

'You will be the richest man on earth.'

'I don't want to be the richest man on earth,' Henry said. 'Not any more.' He then told him about his plan for orphanages.

When he had finished, he said, 'Will you join me, John? Will you be my money man, my banker, my administrator and everything else? There will be millions coming in every year.'

John Winston, a cautious and prudent accountant, would not agree to anything at all on the spur of the moment. 'I want to see you in action first,' he said.

So that night, they went together to the Ritz Club on Curzon Street. 'Can't go to Lord's House again now for some time,' Henry said.

On the first spin of the roulette wheel, Henry staked £100 on number twenty-seven. It came up. The second time he put it on number four; that came up too. A total of £7,500 profit.

An Arab standing next to Henry said, 'I have just lost fifty-five thousand pounds. How do you do it?'

'Luck,' Henry said. 'Just luck.'

They moved into the Blackjack Room and there, in half an hour, Henry won a further £10,000. Then he stopped.

Outside in the street, John Winston said, 'I believe you now. I'll come in with you.'

'We start tomorrow,' Henry said.

'Do you really intend to do this every single night?'

'Yes,' Henry said. 'I shall move very fast from place to place, from country to country. And every day, I shall send the profits back to you through the banks.'

'Do you realize how much it will add up to in a year?'

'Millions,' Henry said cheerfully. 'About seven million a year.'

'In that case, I can't operate in this country,' John Winston said. 'The taxman will have it all.'

'Go anywhere you like,' Henry said. 'It makes no difference to me. I trust you completely.'

'I shall go to Switzerland,' John Winston said. 'But not tomorrow. I can't just pull up and fly away. I'm not an unattached bachelor like you with no responsibilities. I must talk to my wife and children. I must give notice to my partners in the firm. I must sell my house. I must find another house in Switzerland. I must take the kids out of school. My dear man, these things take time!'

Henry drew from his pocket the £17,500 he had just won and handed them to the other man. 'Here's some petty cash to tide you over until you get settled,' he said. 'But do hurry up. I want to get cracking.'

Within a week, John Winston was in Lausanne, with an office high up on the lovely hillside above Lake Geneva. His family would follow him as soon as possible.

And Henry went to work in the casinos.

One year later, he had sent a little over eight million pounds to John Winston in Lausanne. The money was sent five days a week to a Swiss company called ORPHAN-AGES S.A. Nobody except John Winston and Henry knew where the money came from or what was going to happen to it. As for the Swiss authorities, they never want to know where money comes from. Henry sent the money through the banks. The Monday remittance was always the biggest because it included Henry's take for Friday, Saturday and Sunday, when the banks were closed. He moved with astonishing speed, and often the only clue that John Winston had to his whereabouts was the address of the bank which had sent the money on a particular day. One day it would come perhaps from a bank in Manila. The next day from Bangkok. It came from Las Vegas, from Curaçao, from Freeport, from Grand Cayman, from San Juan, from Nassau, from London, from Biarritz. It came from anywhere and everywhere so long as there was a big casino in the city.

For seven years, all went well. Nearly fifty million pounds had arrived in Lausanne, and had been safely banked away. Already John Winston had got three orphanages established, one in France, one in England, and one in the United States. Five more were on the way.

Then came a bit of trouble. There is a grapevine among casino owners, and although Henry was always extraordinarily careful not to take too much from any one place on any one night, the news was bound to spread in the end.

They got wise to him one night in Las Vegas when Henry rather imprudently took one hundred thousand dollars from each of three separate casinos that all happened to be owned by the same mob.

What happened was this. The morning after, when Henry was in his hotel room packing to leave for the airport, there was a knock on his door. A bell-hop came in and whispered to Henry that two men were waiting for him in the lobby. Other men, the bell-hop said, were guarding the rear exit. These were very hard men, the bell-hop said, and he did not give much for Henry's chances of survival if he were to go downstairs at this moment.

'Why do you come and tell me?' Henry asked him. 'Why are you on my side?'

'I'm not on anyone's side,' the bell-hop said. 'But we all know you won a lot of money last night and I figured you might give me a nice present for tipping you off.'

'Thanks,' Henry said. 'But how do I get away? I'll give you a thousand dollars if you can get me out of here.'

'That's easy,' the bell-hop said. 'Take your own clothes off and put on my uniform. Then walk out through the lobby with your suitcase. But tie me up before you leave. I've gotta be lying here on the floor tied up hand and foot so they won't think I helped you. I'll say you had a gun and I couldn't do nothing.'

'Where's the cord to tie you up with?' Henry asked.

'Right here in my pocket,' the bell-hop said, grinning.

Henry put on the bell-hop's gold and green uniform, which wasn't too bad a fit. Then he tied the man up good and proper with the cord and stuffed a handkerchief in his mouth. Finally, he pushed ten one-hundred dollar bills under the carpet for the bell-hop to collect later.

Down in the lobby, two short, thick, black-haired thugs were watching the people as they came out of the elevators. But they hardly glanced at the man in the green and gold bell-hop's uniform who came out carrying a suitcase and who walked smartly across the lobby and out through the swing-doors that led to the street.

At the airport, Henry changed his flight and took the next plane to Los Angeles. Things were not going to be quite so easy from now on, he told himself. But that bell-hop had given him an idea.

In Los Angeles, and in nearby Hollywood and Beverly Hills, where the film people live, Henry sought out the very best make-up man in the business. This was Max Engelman. Henry called on him. He liked him immediately.

'How much do you earn?' Henry asked him.

'Oh, about forty thousand dollars a year,' Max told him.

'I'll give you a hundred thousand,' Henry said, 'if you will come with me and be my make-up artist.'

'What's the big idea?' Max asked him.

'I'll tell you,' Henry said. And he did.

Max was only the second person Henry had told. John Winston was the first. And when Henry showed Max how he could read the cards, Max was flabbergasted.

'Great heavens, man!' he cried. 'You could make a fortune!'

'I already have,' Henry told him. 'I've made ten fortunes. But I want to make ten more.' He told Max about the orphanages. With John Winston's help, he had already set up three of them, with more on the way.

Max was a small dark-skinned man who had escaped from Vienna when the Nazis went in. He had never married. He had no ties. He became wildly enthusiastic. 'It's crazy!' he cried. 'It's the craziest thing I've ever heard in my life! I'll join you, man! Let's go!'

From then on, Max Engelman travelled everywhere with Henry and he carried with him in a trunk such an assortment of wigs, false beards, sideburns, moustaches and make-up materials as you have never seen. He could turn his master into any one of thirty or forty unrecognizable people, and the casino managers, who were all watching for Henry now, never once saw him again as Mr Henry Sugar. As a matter of fact, only a year after the Las Vegas episode, Henry and Max actually went back to that dangerous city, and on a warm starry night Henry took a cool eighty thousand dollars from the first of the big casinos he had visited before. He went disguised as an elderly Brazilian diplomat, and they never knew what had hit them.

Now that Henry no longer appeared as himself in the casinos, there were, of course, a number of other details that had to be taken care of, such as false identity cards and passports. In Monte Carlo, for example, a visitor must always show his passport before being allowed to enter the casino. Henry visited Monte Carlo eleven more times with Max's assistance, every time with a different passport and in a different disguise.

Max adored the work. He loved creating new characters for Henry. 'I have an entirely fresh one for you today!' he would announce. 'Just wait till you see it! Today you will be an Arab sheikh from Kuwait!'

'Do we have an Arab passport?' Henry would ask. 'And Arab papers?'

'We have everything,' Max would answer. 'John Winston has sent me a lovely passport in the name of His Royal Highness Sheikh Abu Bin Bey!'

And so it went on. Over the years, Max and Henry became as close as brothers. They were crusading brothers, two men who moved swiftly through the skies, milking the casinos of the world and sending the money straight back to John Winston in Switzerland, where the company known as ORPHANAGES S.A. grew richer and richer.

Henry died last year, at the age of sixty-three; his work was completed. He had been at it for just on twenty years.

His personal reference book listed three hundred and seventy-one major casinos in twenty-one different countries or islands. He had visited them all many times and he had never lost.

According to John Winston's accounts, he had made altogether one hundred and forty-four million pounds.

He left twenty-one well-established well-run orphanages

scattered about the world, one in each country he visited. All these were administered and financed from Lausanne by John and his staff.

But how do I, who am neither Max Engelman nor John Winston, happen to know all this? And how did I come to write the story in the first place?

I will tell you.

Soon after Henry's death, John Winston telephoned me from Switzerland. He introduced himself simply as the head of a company calling itself ORPHANAGES S.A., and asked me if I would come out to Lausanne to see him with a view to writing a brief history of the organization. I don't know how he got hold of my name. He probably had a list of writers and stuck a pin into it. He would pay me well, he said. And he added, 'A remarkable man has died recently. His name was Henry Sugar. I think people ought to know a bit about what he has done.'

In my ignorance, I asked whether the story was really interesting enough to merit being put on paper.

'All right,' said the man who now controlled one hundred and forty-four million pounds. 'Forget it. I'll ask someone else. There are plenty of writers around.'

That needled me. 'No,' I said. 'Wait. Could you at least tell me who this Henry Sugar was and what he did? I've never even heard of him.'

In five minutes on the phone, John Winston told me something about Henry Sugar's secret career. It was secret no longer. Henry was dead and would never gamble again. I listened, enthralled.

'I'll be on the next plane,' I said.

'Thank you,' John Winston said. 'I would appreciate that.'

In Lausanne, I met John Winston, now over seventy, and also Max Engelman, who was about the same age. They were both still shattered by Henry's death. Max even more so than John Winston, for Max had been beside him constantly for over thirteen years. 'I loved him,' Max said, a shadow falling over his face. 'He was a great man. He never thought about himself. He never kept a penny of the money he won, except what he needed to travel and to eat. Listen, once we were in Biarritz and he had just been to the bank and given them half a million francs to send home to John. It was lunchtime. We went to a place and had a simple lunch, an omelette and a bottle of wine, and when the bill came, Henry hadn't got anything to pay it with. I hadn't either. He was a lovely man.'

John Winston told me everything he knew. He showed me the original dark-blue notebook written by Dr John Cartwright in Bombay in 1934, and I copied it out word for word.

'Henry always carried it with him,' John Winston said. 'In the end, he knew the whole thing by heart.'

He showed me the accounts books of ORPHANAGES S.A. with Henry's winnings recorded in them day by day over twenty years, and a truly staggering sight they were.

When he had finished, I said to him, 'There's a big gap in this story, Mr Winston. You've told me almost nothing about Henry's travels and about his adventures in the casinos of the world.'

'That's Max's story,' John Winston said. 'Max knows all

about that because he was with him. But he says he wants to have a shot at writing it himself. He's already started.'

'Then why not let Max write the whole thing?' I asked.

'He doesn't want to,' John Winston said. 'He only wants to write about Henry and Max. It should be a fantastic story if he ever gets it finished. But he is old now, like me, and I doubt he will manage it.'

'One last question,' I said. 'You keep calling him Henry Sugar. And yet you tell me that wasn't his name. Don't you want me to say who he really was when I do the story?'

'No,' John Winston said. 'Max and I promised never to reveal it. Oh, it'll probably leak out sooner or later. After all, he was from a fairly well-known English family. But I'd appreciate it if you don't try to find out. Just call him plain Mr Henry Sugar.'

And that is what I have done.

The Umbrella Man

First published in *More Tales of
the Unexpected* (1980)

I'm going to tell you about a funny thing that happened to
my mother and me yesterday evening. I am twelve years
old and I'm a girl. My mother is thirty-four but I am nearly
as tall as her already.

Yesterday afternoon, my mother took me up to London
to see the dentist. He found one hole. It was in a back
tooth and he filled it without hurting me too much. After
that, we went to a café. I had a banana split and my mother
had a cup of coffee. By the time we got up to leave, it was
about six o'clock.

When we came out of the café it had started to rain.
'We must get a taxi,' my mother said. We were wearing
ordinary hats and coats, and it was raining quite hard.

'Why don't we go back into the café and wait for it to
stop?' I said. I wanted another of those banana splits.
They were gorgeous.

'It isn't going to stop,' my mother said. 'We must get
home.'

We stood on the pavement in the rain, looking for a
taxi. Lots of them came by but they all had passengers
inside them. 'I wish we had a car with a chauffeur,' my
mother said.

Just then, a man came up to us. He was a small man and

he was pretty old, probably seventy or more. He raised his hat politely and said to my mother, 'Excuse me. I do hope you will excuse me . . .' He had a fine white moustache and bushy white eyebrows and a wrinkly pink face. He was sheltering under an umbrella, which he held high over his head.

'Yes?' my mother said, very cool and distant.

'I wonder if I could ask a small favour of you,' he said. 'It is only a very small favour.'

I saw my mother looking at him suspiciously. She is a suspicious person, my mother. She is especially suspicious of two things – strange men and boiled eggs. When she cuts the top off a boiled egg, she pokes around inside it with her spoon as though expecting to find a mouse or something. With strange men, she has a golden rule which says, 'The nicer the man seems to be, the more suspicious you must become.' This little old man was particularly nice. He was polite. He was well spoken. He was well dressed. He was a real gentleman. The reason I knew he was a gentleman was because of his shoes. 'You can always spot a gentleman by the shoes he wears,' was another of my mother's favourite sayings. This man had beautiful brown shoes.

'The truth of the matter is,' the little man was saying, 'I've got myself into a bit of a scrape. I need some help. Not much, I assure you. It's almost nothing, in fact, but I do need it. You see, madam, old people like me often become terribly forgetful . . .'

My mother's chin was up and she was staring down at him along the full length of her nose. It is a fearsome thing, this frosty-nosed stare of my mother's. Most people go to pieces completely when she gives it to them. I once saw my own headmistress begin to stammer and simper like an idiot when my mother gave her a really foul frosty-noser. But the little man on the pavement with the umbrella over his head didn't bat an eyelid. He gave a gentle smile and said, 'I beg you to believe, madam, that I am not in the habit of stopping ladies in the street and telling them my troubles.'

'I should hope not,' my mother said.

I felt quite embarrassed by my mother's sharpness. I wanted to say to her, 'Oh, Mummy, for heaven's sake, he's a very very old man, and he's sweet and polite, and he's in some sort of trouble, so don't be so beastly to him.' But I didn't say anything.

The little man shifted his umbrella from one hand to the other. 'I've never forgotten it before,' he said.

'You've never forgotten what?' my mother asked sternly.

'My wallet,' he said. 'I must have left it in my other jacket. Isn't that the silliest thing to do?'

'Are you asking me to give you money?' my mother said.

'Oh, good gracious me, no!' he cried. 'Heaven forbid I should ever do that!'

'Then what *are* you asking?' my mother said. 'Do hurry up. We're getting soaked to the skin standing here.'

'I know you are,' he said. 'And that is why I'm offering you this umbrella of mine to protect you, and to keep for ever, if . . . if only . . .'

'If only what?' my mother said.

'If only you would give me in return a pound for my taxi-fare just to get me home.'

My mother was still suspicious. 'If you had no money in the first place,' she said, 'then how did you get here?'

'I walked,' he answered. 'Every day I go for a lovely long walk and then I summon a taxi to take me home. I do it every day of the year.'

'Why don't you walk home now?' my mother asked.

'Oh, I wish I could,' he said. 'I do wish I could. But I don't think I could manage it on these silly old legs of mine. I've gone too far already.'

My mother stood there chewing her lower lip. She was beginning to melt a bit, I could see that. And the idea of getting an umbrella to shelter under must have tempted her a good deal.

'It's a lovely umbrella,' the little man said.

'So I've noticed,' my mother said.

'It's silk,' he said.

'I can see that.'

'Then why don't you take it, madam,' he said. 'It cost me over twenty pounds, I promise you. But that's of no importance so long as I can get home and rest these old legs of mine.'

I saw my mother's hand feeling for the clasp on her purse. She saw me watching her. I was giving her one of my *own* frosty-nosed looks this time and she knew exactly what I was telling her. Now listen, Mummy, I was telling her, you simply *mustn't* take advantage of a tired old man in this way. It's a rotten thing to do. My mother paused and looked back at me. Then she said to the little man,

'I don't think it's quite right that I should take a silk umbrella from you worth twenty pounds. I think I'd just better *give* you the taxi-fare and be done with it.'

'No, no, no!' he cried. 'It's out of the question! I wouldn't dream of it! Not in a million years! I would never accept money from you like that! Take the umbrella, dear lady, and keep the rain off your shoulders!'

My mother gave me a triumphant sideways look. There you are, she was telling me. You're wrong. He *wants* me to have it.

She fished into her purse and took out a pound note. She held it out to the little man. He took it and handed her the umbrella. He pocketed the pound, raised his hat, gave a quick bow from the waist, and said, 'Thank you, madam, thank you.' Then he was gone.

'Come under here and keep dry, darling,' my mother said. 'Aren't we lucky? I've never had a silk umbrella before. I couldn't afford it.'

'Why were you so horrid to him in the beginning?' I asked.

'I wanted to satisfy myself he wasn't a trickster,' she said. 'And I did. He was a gentleman. I'm very pleased I was able to help him.'

'Yes, Mummy,' I said.

'A *real* gentleman,' she went on. 'Wealthy, too, otherwise he wouldn't have had a silk umbrella. I shouldn't be surprised if he isn't a titled person. Sir Harry Goldsworthy or something like that.'

'Yes, Mummy.'

'This will be a good lesson to you,' she went on. 'Never

rush things. Always take your time when you are summing someone up. Then you'll never make mistakes.'

'There he goes,' I said. 'Look.'

'Where?'

'Over there. He's crossing the street. Goodness, Mummy, what a hurry he's in.'

We watched the little man as he dodged nimbly in and out of the traffic. When he reached the other side of the street, he turned left, walking very fast.

'He doesn't look very tired to me, does he to you, Mummy?'

My mother didn't answer.

'He doesn't look as though he's trying to get a taxi, either,' I said.

My mother was standing very still and stiff, staring across the street at the little man. We could see him clearly. He was in a terrific hurry. He was bustling along the pavement, sidestepping the other pedestrians and swinging his arms like a soldier on the march.

'He's up to something,' my mother said, stony-faced.

'But what?'

'I don't know,' my mother snapped. 'But I'm going to find out. Come with me.' She took my arm and we crossed the street together. Then we turned left.

'Can you see him?' my mother asked.

'Yes. There he is. He's turning right down the next street.'

We came to the corner and turned right. The little man was about twenty yards ahead of us. He was scuttling along like a rabbit and we had to walk fast to keep up with him. The rain was pelting down harder than ever now and I could see it dripping from the brim of his hat on to his shoulders. But we were snug and dry under our lovely big silk umbrella.

'What *is* he up to?' my mother said.

'What if he turns round and sees us?' I asked.

'I don't care if he does,' my mother said. 'He lied to us. He said he was too tired to walk any further and he's practically running us off our feet! He's a barefaced liar! He's a crook!'

'You mean he's *not* a titled gentleman?' I asked.

'Be quiet,' she said.

At the next crossing, the little man turned right again.

Then he turned left.

Then right.

'I'm not giving up now,' my mother said.

'He's disappeared!' I cried. 'Where's he gone?'

'He went in that door!' my mother said. 'I saw him! Into that house! Great heavens, it's a pub!'

It was a pub. In big letters right across the front it said THE RED LION.

'You're not going in, are you, Mummy?'

'No,' she said. 'We'll watch from outside.'

There was a big plate-glass window along the front of the pub, and although it was a bit steamy on the inside, we could see through it very well if we went close.

We stood huddled together outside the pub window. I was clutching my mother's arm. The big raindrops were making a loud noise on our umbrella. 'There he is,' I said. 'Over there.'

The room we were looking into was full of people and cigarette smoke, and our little man was in the middle of it all. He was now without his hat or coat, and he was edging his way through the crowd towards the bar. When he reached it, he placed both hands on the bar itself and spoke to the barman. I saw his lips moving as he gave his order. The barman turned away from him for a few seconds and came back with a smallish tumbler filled to the brim with light-brown liquid. The little man placed a pound note on the counter.

'That's my pound!' my mother hissed. 'By golly, he's got a nerve!'

'What's in the glass?' I asked.

'Whisky,' my mother said. 'Neat whisky.'

The barman didn't give him any change from the pound.

'That must be a treble whisky,' my mother said.

'What's a treble?' I asked.

'Three times the normal measure,' she answered.

The little man picked up the glass and put it to his lips. He tilted it gently. Then he tilted it higher . . . and higher . . . and higher . . . and very soon all the whisky had disappeared down his throat in one long pour.

'That was a jolly expensive drink,' I said.

'It's ridiculous!' my mother said. 'Fancy paying a pound for something you swallow in one go!'

'It cost him more than a pound,' I said. 'It cost him a twenty-pound silk umbrella.'

'So it did,' my mother said. 'He must be mad.'

The little man was standing by the bar with the empty glass in his hand. He was smiling now, and a sort of golden glow of pleasure was spreading over his round pink face. I saw his tongue come out to lick the white moustache, as though searching for the last drop of that precious whisky.

Slowly, he turned away from the bar and edged back through the crowd to where his hat and coat were hanging. He put on his hat. He put on his coat. Then, in a manner so superbly cool and casual that you hardly noticed anything at all, he lifted from the coat-rack one of the many wet umbrellas hanging there, and off he went.

'Did you see that!' my mother shrieked. 'Did you see what he did!'

'Ssshh!' I whispered. 'He's coming out!'

We lowered the umbrella to hide our faces, and peeped out from under it.

Out he came. But he never looked in our direction. He opened his new umbrella over his head and scurried off down the road the way he had come.

'So that's his little game!' my mother said.

'Neat,' I said. 'Super.'

We followed him back to the main street where we had first met him, and we watched him as he proceeded, with no trouble at all, to exchange his new umbrella for another pound note. This time it was with a tall thin fellow who didn't even have a coat or hat. And as soon as the transaction was completed, our little man trotted off down the street and was lost in the crowd. But this time he went in the opposite direction.

'You see how clever he is!' my mother said. 'He never goes to the same pub twice!'

'He could go on doing this all night,' I said.

'Yes,' my mother said. 'Of course. But I'll bet he prays like mad for rainy days.'

The Bookseller

First published in *Playboy*, January 1987

If, in those days, you walked up from Trafalgar Square into Charing Cross Road, you would come in a few minutes to a shop on the right-hand side that had above the window the words WILLIAM BUGGAGE - RARE BOOKS.

If you peered through the window itself you would see that the walls were lined with books from floor to ceiling, and if you then pushed open the door and went in, you would immediately be assailed by that subtle odour of old cardboard and tea leaves that pervades the interiors of every second-hand bookshop in London. Nearly always, you would find two or three customers in there, silent shadowy figures in overcoats and trilby hats rummaging among the sets of Jane Austen and Trollope and Dickens and George Eliot, hoping to find a first edition.

No shop-keeper ever seemed to be hovering around to keep an eye on the customers, and if somebody actually wanted to pay for a book instead of pinching it and walking out, then he or she would have to push through a door at the back of the shop on which it said OFFICE — PAY HERE. If you went into the office you would find both Mr William Buggage and his assistant, Miss Muriel Tottle, seated at their respective desks and very much preoccupied.

Mr Buggage would be sitting behind a valuable

eighteenth-century mahogany partners-desk, and Miss Tottle, a few feet away, would be using a somewhat smaller but
no less elegant piece of furniture, a Regency writing-table
with a top of faded green leather. On Mr Buggage's desk
there would invariably be one copy of the day's *London Times*,
as well as the *Daily Telegraph*, the *Manchester Guardian* the *Western Mail* and the *Glasgow Herald*. There would also be a current
edition of *Who's Who* close at hand, fat and red and well
thumbed. Miss Tottle's writing-table would have on it an
electric typewriter and a plain but very nice open box containing notepaper and envelopes, as well as a quantity of
paper-clips and staplers and other secretarial paraphernalia.

Now and again, but not very often, a customer would
enter the office from the shop and would hand his chosen
volume to Miss Tottle, who checked the price written in
pencil on the fly-leaf and accepted the money, giving
change when necessary from somewhere in the left-hand
drawer of her writing-table. Mr Buggage never bothered
even to glance up at those who came in and went out, and
if one of them asked a question, it would be Miss Tottle
who answered it.

Neither Mr Buggage nor Miss Tottle appeared to be in
the least concerned about what went on in the main shop.
In point of fact, Mr Buggage took the view that if someone was going to steal a book, then good luck to him. He
knew very well that there was not a single valuable first
edition out there on the shelves. There might be a moder-
ately rare volume of Galsworthy or an early Waugh that
had come in with a job lot bought at auction, and there
were certainly some good sets of Boswell and Walter

Scott and Robert Louis Stevenson and the rest, often very nicely bound in half or even whole calf. But those were not really the sort of things you could slip into your overcoat pocket. Even if a villain *did* walk out with half a dozen volumes, Mr Buggage wasn't going to lose any sleep over it. Why should he when he knew that the shop itself earned less money in a whole year than the back-room business grossed in a couple of days. It was what went on in the back room that counted.

One morning in February when the weather was foul and sleet was slanting white and wet on to the window panes of the office, Mr Buggage and Miss Tottle were in their respective places as usual and each was engrossed, one might even say fascinated, by his and her own work. Mr Buggage, with a gold Parker pen poised above a note-pad, was reading *The Times* and jotting things down as he went along. Every now and again, he would refer to *Who's Who* and make more jottings.

Miss Tottle, who had been opening the mail, was now examining some cheques and adding up totals.

'Three today,' she said.

'What's it come to?' Mr Buggage asked, not looking up.

'One thousand six hundred,' Miss Tottle said.

Mr Buggage said, 'I don't suppose we've 'eard anything yet from that bishop's 'ouse in Chester, 'ave we?'

'A bishop lives in a palace, Billy, not a house,' Miss Tottle said.

'I don't give a sod where 'ee lives,' Mr Buggage said. 'But I get just a little bit uneasy when there's no quick answer from somebody like that.'

'As a matter of fact, the reply came this morning,' Miss Tottle said.

'Coughed up all right?'

'The full amount.'

'That's a relief,' Mr Buggage said. 'We never done a bishop before and I'm not sure it was any too clever.'

'The cheque came from some solicitors.'

Mr Buggage looked up sharply. 'Was there a letter?' he asked.

'Yes.'

'Read it.'

Miss Tottle found the letter and began to read: 'Dear Sir, With reference to your communication of the 4th Instant, we enclose herewith a cheque for £537 in full settlement. Yours faithfully, Smithson, Briggs and Ellis.' Miss Tottle paused. 'That seems all right, doesn't it?'

'It's all right this time,' Mr Buggage said. 'But we don't want no more solicitors and let's not 'ave any more bishops either.'

'I agree about bishops,' Miss Tottle said. 'But you're not suddenly ruling out earls and lords and all that lot, I hope?'

'Lords is fine,' Mr Buggage said. 'We never 'ad no trouble with lords. Nor earls either. And didn't we do a duke once?'

'The Duke of Dorset,' Miss Tottle said. 'Did him last year. Over a thousand quid.'

'Very nice,' Mr Buggage said. 'I remember selectin' 'im myself straight off the front page.' He stopped talking while he prised a bit of food out from between two front teeth with the nail of his little finger. 'What I says is this,' he went on. 'The bigger the title, the bigger the twit. In fact, anyone's got a title on 'is name is almost certain to be a twit.'

'Now that's not quite true, Billy,' Miss Tottle said. 'Some people are given titles because they've done absolutely brilliant things, like inventing penicillin or climbing Mount Everest.'

'I'm talking about in'erited titles,' Mr Buggage said. 'Anyone gets born with a title, it's odds-on 'ee's a twit.'

'You're right there,' Miss Tottle said. 'We've never had the slightest trouble with the aristocracy.'

Mr Buggage leaned back in his chair and gazed solemnly at Miss Tottle. 'You know what?' he said. 'One of these days we might even 'ave a crack at royalty.'

'Ooh, I'd *love* it,' Miss Tottle said. 'Sock them for a fortune.'

Mr Buggage continued to gaze at Miss Tottle's profile, and as he did so, a slightly lascivious glint crept into his eye. One is forced to admit that Miss Tottle's appearance, when judged by the highest standards, was disappointing. To tell the truth when judged by *any* standards, it was still disappointing. Her face was long and horsey and her teeth, which were also rather long, had a sulphurous tinge about them. So did her skin. The best you could say about her was that she had a generous bosom, but even that had its faults. It was the kind that makes a single long tightly bound bulge from one side of the chest to the other, and at first glance one got the impression that there were not two individual breasts growing out of her body but simply one big long loaf of bread.

Then again, Mr Buggage himself was in no position to be overly finicky. When one saw him for the first time, the word that sprang instantly to mind was 'grubby'. He was squat, paunchy, bald and flaccid, and so far as his face was concerned, one could only make a guess at what it looked like because not much of it was visible to the eye. The major part was covered over by an immense thicket of black, bushy, slightly curly hair, a fashion, one fears, that is all too common these days, a foolish practice and incidentally a rather dirty habit. Why so many males wish to conceal their facial characteristics is beyond the comprehension of us ordinary mortals. One must presume that if it were possible for these people also to grow hair all over their noses and cheeks and eyes, then they would do so, ending up with no visible face at all but only an obscene and rather gamey ball of hair. The only possible conclusion one can arrive at when looking at one of these bearded males is that the vegetation is a kind of smoke-screen and is cultivated in order to conceal something unsightly or unsavoury.

This was almost certainly true in Mr Buggage's case, and it was therefore fortunate for all of us, and especially for Miss Tottle, that the beard was there. Mr Buggage continued to gaze wistfully at his assistant. Then he said, 'Now pet, why don't you 'urry up and get them cheques in the post because after you've done that I've got a little proposal to put to you.'

Miss Tottle looked back over her shoulder at the speaker and gave him a smirk that showed the cutting edges of her sulphur teeth. Whenever he called her 'pet', it was a sure sign that feelings of a carnal nature were beginning to stir within Mr Buggage's breast, and in other parts as well.

'Tell it to me now, lover,' she said.

'You get them cheques done first,' he said. He could be very commanding at times, and Miss Tottle thought it was wonderful.

Miss Tottle now began what she called her Daily Audit. This involved examining all of Mr Buggage's bank accounts and all of her own and then deciding into which of them the latest cheques should be paid. Mr Buggage, you see, at this particular moment, had exactly sixty-six different accounts in his own name and Miss Tottle had twenty-two. These were scattered around among various branches of the big three banks, Barclays, Lloyds and National Westminster, all over London and a few in the suburbs. There was nothing wrong with that. And it had not been difficult, as the business became more and more successful, for either of them to walk into any branch of these banks and open a Current Account, with an initial deposit of a few hundred pounds. They would then receive a cheque book, a paying-in book and the promise of a monthly statement.

Mr Buggage had discovered early on that if a person has an account with several or even many different branches of a bank, this will cause no comment by the staff. Each branch deals strictly with its own customers and their names are not circulated to other branches or to Head Office, not even in these computerized times.

On the other hand, banks are required by law to notify

the Inland Revenue of the names of all clients who have Deposit Accounts containing one thousand pounds or more. They must also report the amounts of interest earned. But no such law applies to Current Accounts because they earn no interest. Nobody takes any notice of a person's Current Account unless it is overdrawn or unless, and this seldom happens, the balance becomes ridiculously large. A Current Account containing let us say £100,000 might easily raise an eyebrow or two among the staff, and the client would almost certainly get a nice letter from the manager suggesting that some of the money be placed on deposit to earn interest. But Mr Buggage didn't give a fig for interest and he wanted no raised eyebrows either. That is why he and Miss Tottle had eighty-eight different bank accounts between them. It was Miss Tottle's job to see that the amounts in each of these accounts never exceeded £20,000. Anything more than that might, in Mr Buggage's opinion, cause an eyebrow to raise, especially if it were left lying untouched in a Current Account for months or years. The agreement between the two partners was seventy-five per cent of the profits of the business to Mr Buggage and twenty-five per cent to Miss Tottle.

Miss Tottle's Daily Audit involved examining a list she kept of all the balances in all those eighty-eight separate accounts and then deciding into which of them the daily cheque or cheques should be deposited. She had in her filing-cabinet eighty-eight different files, one for each bank account, and eighty-eight different cheque books and eighty-eight different paying-in books. Miss Tottle's task was not a complicated one but she had to keep her wits about her and not muddle things up. Only the previous week they had to open four new accounts at four new branches, three for Mr Buggage and one for Miss Tottle. 'Soon we're goin' to 'ave over a 'undred accounts in our names,' Mr Buggage had said to Miss Tottle at the time.

'Why not two hundred?' Miss Tottle had said.

'A day will come,' Mr Buggage said, 'when we'll 'ave used up all the banks in this part of the country and you and I is goin' to 'ave to travel all the way up to Sunderland or Newcastle to open new ones.'

But now Miss Tottle was busy with her Daily Audit. 'That's done,' she said, putting the last cheque and the paying-in slip into its envelope.

''Ow much we got in our accounts altogether at this very moment?' Mr Buggage asked her.

Miss Tottle unlocked the middle drawer of her writing-table and took out a plain school exercise book. On the cover she had written the words *My old arithmetic book from school*. She considered this a rather ingenious ploy designed to put people off the scent should the book ever fall into the wrong hands. 'Just let me add on today's deposit,' she said, finding the right page and beginning to write down figures. 'There we are. Counting today, *you* have got in all the sixty-six branches, one million, three hundred and twenty thousand, six hundred and forty-three pounds, unless you've been cashing any cheques in the last few days.'

'I 'aven't,' Mr Buggage said. 'And what've you got?'

'*I* have got . . . four hundred and thirty thousand, seven hundred and twenty-five pounds.'

'Very nice,' Mr Buggage said. 'And 'ow long's it taken us to gather in those tidy little sums?'

'Just eleven years,' Miss Tottle said. 'What was that teeny weeny proposal you were going to put to me, lover?'

'Ah,' Mr Buggage said, laying down his gold pencil and leaning back to gaze at her once again with that pale licentious eye. 'I was just thinkin' . . .'ere's exactly what I was thinkin' . . . why on earth should a millionaire like me be sittin' 'ere in this filthy freezin' weather when I could be reclinin' in the lap of luxury beside a swimmin' pool with a nice girl like you to keep me company and flunkeys bringin' us goblets of iced champagne every few minutes?'

'Why indeed?' Miss Tottle cried, grinning widely.

'Then get out the book and let's see where we 'aven't been?'

Miss Tottle walked over to a bookshelf on the opposite wall and took down a thickish paperback called *The 300 Best Hotels in the World chosen by Rene Lecler*. She returned to her chair and said, 'Where to this time, lover?'

'Somewhere in North Africa,' Mr Buggage said. 'This is February and you've got to go at least to North Africa to get it really warm. Italy's not 'ot enough yet, nor is Spain. And I don't want the flippin' West Indies. I've 'ad enough of them. Where 'aven't we been in North Africa?'

Miss Tottle was turning the pages of the book. 'That's not so easy,' she said. 'We've done the Palais Jamai in Fez . . . and the Gazelle d'Or in Taroudant . . . and the Tunis Hilton in Tunis. We didn't like that one . . .'

''Ow many we done so far altogether in that book?' Mr Buggage asked her.

'I think it was forty-eight the last time I counted.'

'And I 'as every intention of doin' all three 'undred of 'em before I'm finished,' Mr Buggage said. 'That's my big ambition and I'll bet nobody else 'as ever done it.'

'I think Mr Rene Lecler must have done it,' Miss Tottle said.

''Oo's 'ee?'

'The man who wrote the book.'

''Ee don't count,' Mr Buggage said. He leaned sideways in his chair and began to scratch the left cheek of his rump in a slow meditative manner. 'And I'll bet 'ee 'asn't anyway. These travel guides use any Tom, Dick and 'Arry to go round for 'em.'

'Here's one!' Miss Tottle cried. 'Hotel La Mamounia in Marrakech.'

'Where's that?'

'In Morocco. Just round the top corner of Africa on the left-hand side.'

'Go on then. What does it say about it?'

'It says,' Miss Tottle read, '*This was Winston Churchill's favourite haunt and from his balcony he painted the Atlas sunset time and again.*'

'I don't paint,' Mr Buggage said. 'What else does it say?'

Miss Tottle read on: '*As the liveried Moorish servant shows you into the tiled and latticed colonnaded court, you step decisively into an illustration of the 1001 Arabian nights . . .*'

'That's more like it,' Mr Buggage said. 'Go on.'

'*Your next contact with reality will come when you pay your bill on leaving.*'

'That don't worry us millionaires,' Mr Buggage said.

'Let's go. We'll leave tomorrow. Call that travel agent right away. First class. We'll shut the shop for ten days.'

'Don't you want to do today's letters?'

'Bugger today's letters,' Mr Buggage said. 'We're on 'oliday from now on. Get on to that travel agent quick.' He leaned the other way now and started scratching his right buttock with the fingers of his right hand. Miss Tottle watched him and Mr Buggage saw her watching him but he didn't care. 'Call that travel agent,' he said.

'And I'd better get us some Travellers' Cheques,' Miss Tottle said.

'Get five thousand quid's worth. I'll write the cheque. This one's on me. Give me a cheque book. Choose the nearest bank. And call that 'otel in wherever it was and ask for the biggest suite they're got. They're never booked up when you want the biggest suite.'

Twenty-four hours later, Mr Buggage and Miss Tottle were sunbathing beside the pool at La Mamounia in Marrakech and they were drinking champagne.

'This is the life,' Miss Tottle said. 'Why don't we retire altogether and buy a grand house in a climate like this?'

'What do we want to retire for?' Mr Buggage said. 'We got the best business in London goin' for us and personally I find that very enjoyable.'

On the other side of the pool a dozen Moroccan servants were laying out a splendid buffet lunch for the guests. There were enormous cold lobsters and large pink hams and very small roast chickens and several kinds of rice and about ten different salads. A chef was grilling steaks over a charcoal fire. Guests were beginning to get up from deck-chairs and mattresses to mill around the buffet with plates in their hands. Some were in swimsuits, some in light summer clothes, and most had straw hats on their heads. Mr Buggage was watching them. Almost without exception, they were English. They were the very rich English, smooth, well mannered, overweight, loud-voiced and infinitely dull. He had seen them before all around Jamaica and Barbados and places like that. It was evident that quite a few of them knew one another because at home, of course, they moved in the same circles. But whether they knew each other or not, they certainly *accepted* each other because all of them belonged to the same nameless and exclusive club. Any member of this club could always, by some subtle social alchemy, recognize a fellow member at a glance. Yes, they say to themselves, he's one of us. She's one of us. Mr Buggage was not one of them. He was not in the club and he never would be. He was a *nouveau* and that, regardless of how many millions he had, was unacceptable. He was also overtly vulgar and that was unacceptable, too. The very rich could be just as vulgar as Mr Buggage, or even more so, but they did it in a different way.

'There they are,' Mr Buggage said, looking across the pool at the guests. 'Them's our bread and butter. Every one of 'em's likely to be a future customer.'

'How right you are,' Miss Tottle said.

Mr Buggage, lying on a mattress that was striped in blue, red and green, was propped up on one elbow, staring at the guests. His stomach was bulging out in folds over his swimming-trunks and droplets of sweat were running out of the fatty crevices. Now he shifted his gaze to the recumbent figure of Miss Tottle lying beside him on her own mattress. Miss Tottle's loaf-of-bread bosom was encased in a strip of scarlet bikini. The bottom half of the bikini was daringly brief and possibly a shade too small and Mr Buggage could see traces of black hair high up on the inside of her thighs.

'We'll 'ave our lunch, pet, then we'll go to our room and take a little nap, right?'

Miss Tottle displayed her sulphurous teeth and nodded her head.

'And after that we'll do some letters.'

'Letters?' she cried. 'I don't want to do letters! I thought this was going to be a holiday!'

'It *is* a 'oliday, pet, but I don't like lettin' good business go to waste. The 'otel will lend you a typewriter. I already checked on that. And they're lendin' me their *'Oo's 'Oo*. Every good 'otel in the world keeps an English *'Oo's 'Oo*. The manager likes to know 'oo's important so 'ee can kiss their backsides.'

'They won't find *you* in it,' Miss Tottle said, a bit huffy now.

'No,' Mr Buggage said. 'I'll grant you that. But they won't find many in it that's got more money'n me neither. In this world, it's not 'oo you are, my girl. It's not even 'oo you know. It's what you *got* that counts.'

'We've never done letters on holiday before,' Miss Tottle said.

'There's a first time for everything, pet.'

'How can we do letters without newspapers?'

'You know very well English papers always go airmail to places like this. I bought a *Times* in the foyer when we arrived. It's actually the same as I was workin' on in the office yesterday so I done most of my 'omework already. I'm beginning to fancy a piece of that lobster over there. You ever seen bigger lobsters than that?'

'But you're surely not going to *post* the letters from here, are you?' Miss Tottle said.

'Certainly not. We'll leave 'em undated and date 'em and post 'em as soon as we return. That way we'll 'ave a nice backlog up our sleeves.'

Miss Tottle stared at the lobsters on the table across the pool, then at the people milling around, then she reached out and placed a hand on Mr Buggage's thigh, high up under the bathing-shorts. She began to stroke the hairy thigh. 'Come on, Billy,' she said, 'why don't we take a break from the letters same as we always do when we're on hols?'

'You surely don't want us throwing about a thousand quid away a day, do you?' Mr Buggage said. 'And quarter of it yours, don't forget that.'

'We don't have the firm's notepaper and we can't use hotel paper, for God's sake.'

'I brought the notepaper,' Mr Buggage said, triumphant. 'I got a 'ole box of it. *And* envelopes.'

'Oh, all *right*,' Miss Tottle said. 'Are you going to fetch me some of that lobster, lover?'

'We'll go together,' Mr Buggage said, and he stood up and started waddling round the pool in those almost knee-length bathing-trunks he had bought a couple of years back in Honolulu. They had a pattern of green and yellow and white flowers on them. Miss Tottle got to her feet and followed him.

Mr Buggage was busy helping himself at the buffet when he heard a man's voice behind him saying, 'Fiona, I don't think you've met Mrs Smith-Swithin . . . and this is Lady Hedgecock.'

'How d'you do' . . . 'How d'you do,' the voices said.

Mr Buggage glanced round at the speakers. There was a man and a woman in swimming-clothes and two elderly ladies wearing cotton dresses. Those names, he thought. I've heard those names before, I know I have . . . Smith-Swithin . . . Lady Hedgecock. He shrugged and continued to load food on to his plate.

A few minutes later, he was sitting with Miss Tottle at a small table under a sun-umbrella and each of them was tucking into an immense half lobster. 'Tell me, does the name Lady 'Edgecock mean anything to you?' Mr Buggage asked, talking with his mouth full.

'Lady Hedgecock? She's one of our clients. Or she was. I never forget names like that. Why?'

'And what about a Mrs Smith-Swithin? Does that also ring a bell?'

'It does, actually,' Miss Tottle said. 'Both of them do. Why do you ask that suddenly?'

'Because both of 'em's 'ere.'

'Good God! How d'you know?'

'And what's more, my girl, they're together! They're chums!'

'They're not!'

190

'Oh, yes they are!'

Mr Buggage told her how he knew. 'There they are,' he said, pointing with a fork whose prongs were yellow with mayonnaise. 'Those two fat old broads talkin' to the tall man and the woman.'

Miss Tottle stared, fascinated. 'You know,' she said, 'I've never actually seen a client of ours in the flesh before, not in all the years we've been in business.'

'Nor me,' Mr Buggage said. 'One thing's for sure. I picked 'em right, didn't I? They're rolling in it. That's obvious. And they're stupid. That's even more obvious.'

'Do you think it could be dangerous, Billy, the two of them knowing each other?'

'It's a bloody queer coincidence,' Mr Buggage said, 'but I don't think it's dangerous. Neither of 'em's ever goin' to say a word. That's the beauty of it.'

'I guess you're right.'

'The only possible danger,' Mr Buggage said, 'would be if they saw my name on the register. I got a very unusual name just like theirs. It would ring bells at once.'

'Guests don't see the register,' Miss Tottle said.

'No, they don't,' Mr Buggage said. 'No one's ever goin' to bother us. They never 'as and they never will.'

'Amazing lobster,' Miss Tottle said.

'Lobster is sex food,' Mr Buggage announced, eating more of it.

'You're thinking of oysters, lover.'

'I am not thinking of oysters. Oysters is sex food, too, but lobsters is stronger. A dish of lobsters can drive some people crazy.'

'Like you, perhaps?' she said, wriggling her rump in the chair.

'Maybe,' Mr Buggage said. 'We shall just 'ave to wait and see about that, won't we, pet?'

'Yes,' she said.

'It's a good thing they're so expensive,' Mr Buggage said. 'If every Tom, Dick and 'Arry could afford to buy 'em, the 'ole world would be full of *sex maniacs*.'

'Keep eating it,' she said.

After lunch, the two of them went upstairs to their suite, where they cavorted clumsily on the huge bed for a brief period. Then they took a nap.

And now they were in their private sitting-room and were wearing only dressing-gowns over their nakedness, Mr Buggage in a plum-coloured silk one, Miss Tottle in pastel pink and pale green. Mr Buggage was reclining on the sofa with a copy of yesterday's *Times* on his lap and a *Who's Who* on the coffee table.

Miss Tottle was at the writing-desk with a hotel type-writer before her and a notebook in her hand. Both were again drinking champagne.

'This is a prime one,' Mr Buggage was saying. 'Sir Edward Leishman. Got the lead obit. Chairman of Aerodynamics Engineering. *One of our major industrialists*, it says.'

'Nice,' Miss Tottle said. 'Make sure the wife's alive.'

'*Leaves a widow and three children*,' Mr Buggage read out. 'And . . . wait a minute . . . in *'Oo's 'Oo* it says, *Recreations, walkin' and fishin'. Clubs, White's and the Reform*.'

'Address?' Miss Tottle asked.

'The Red House, Andover, Wilts.'

'How d'you spell Leishman?' Miss Tottle asked. Mr Buggage spelled it.

'How much shall we go for?'

'A lot,' Mr Buggage said. 'He was loaded. Try around nine 'undred.'

'You want to slip in *The Compleat Angler*? It says he was a fisherman.'

'Yes. First edition. Four 'undred and twenty quid. You know the rest of it by 'eart. Bang it out quick. I got another good one to come.'

Miss Tottle put a sheet of notepaper into the typewriter and very rapidly she began to type. She had done so many thousands of these letters over the years that she never had to pause for one word. She even knew how to compile the list of books so that it came out to around nine hundred pounds or three hundred and fifty pounds or five hundred and twenty or whatever. She could make it come out to any sum Mr Buggage thought the client would stand. One of the secrets of this particular trade, as Mr Buggage knew, was never to be too greedy. Never go over a thousand quid with anyone, not even a famous millionaire.

The letter, as Miss Tottle typed it, went like this:

WILLIAM BUGGAGE — RARE BOOKS

27a Charing Cross Road,
London.

Dear Lady Leishman,

  It is with very great regret that I trouble you at this tragic time of your bereavement, but regretfully I am left with no alternative in the circumstances.

I had the pleasure of serving your late husband over a number of years and my invoices were always sent to him care of White's Club, as indeed were many of the little parcels of books that he collected with such enthusiasm.

He was always a prompt settler and a very pleasant gentleman to deal with. I am listing below his more recent purchases, those which, alas, he had ordered in more recent times before he passed away and which were delivered to him in the usual manner.

Perhaps I should explain to you that publications of this nature are often very rare and can therefore be rather costly. Some are privately printed, some are actually banned in this country and those are more costly still.

Rest assured, dear madam, that I always conduct business in the strictest confidence. My own reputation over many years in the trade is the best guarantee of my discretion. When the bill is paid, that is the last you will hear of the matter, unless of course you happen to be able to lay hands on your late husband's collection of erotica, in which case I should be happy to make you an offer for it.

To Books:

THE COMPLEAT ANGLER, Isaak Walton, First edition. Good clean copy. Some rubbing of edges. Rare.	£420
LOVE IN FURS, Leopold von Sacher-Masoch, 1920 edition. Slip cover.	75
SEXUAL SECRETS, Translation from Danish.	40
HOW TO PLEASURE YOUNG GIRLS WHEN YOU ARE OVER SIXTY, Illustrations. Private printing from Paris.	95

THE ART OF PUNISHMENT — THE CANE, THE WHIP AND THE LASH, Translated from German. Banned in UK.	115
THREE NAUGHTY NUNS, Good clean edition.	60
RESTRAINT — SHACKLES AND SILKEN CORDS, Illustrations.	80
WHY TEENAGERS PREFER OLD MEN, Illustrations. American.	90
THE LONDON DIRECTORY OF ESCORTS AND HOSTESSES, Current edition.	20

Total now due £995

Yours faithfully,
William Buggage

'Right,' Miss Tottle said, running the notepaper out of her typewriter. 'Done that one. But you realize I don't have my "Bible" here, so I'll have to check the names when I get home before posting the letters.'

'You do that,' Mr Buggage said.

Miss Tottle's Bible was a massive index-card file in which were recorded the names and addresses of every client they had written to since the beginning of the business. The purpose of this was to try as nearly as possible to ensure that no two members of the same family received a Buggage invoice. If this were to happen, there would always be the danger that they might compare notes. It also served to guard against a case where a widow who had received one invoice upon the death of her first husband might be sent another invoice on the death of the second husband. That, of course, would let the cat right out of the bag. There was no guaranteed way of avoiding this perilous mistake because the widow would have changed her name when she remarried, but Miss Tottle had developed an instinct for sniffing out such pitfalls, and the Bible helped her to do it.

'What's next?' Miss Tottle asked.

'The next is Major General Lionel Anstruther. Here 'ee is. Got about six inches in *'Oo's 'Oo. Clubs, Army and Navy. Recreations, Ridin' to 'Ounds.*'

'I suppose he fell off a horse and broke his flipping neck,' Miss Tottle said. 'I'll start with *Memoirs of a Fox-hunting Man, First edition*, right?'

'Right. Two 'undred and twenty quid,' Mr Buggage said. 'And make it between five and six 'undred altogether.'

'Okay.'

'And put in *The Sting of the Ridin' Crop*. Whips seem to come natural to these fox-huntin' folk.'

And so it went on.

The holiday in Marrakech continued pleasantly enough and nine days later Mr Buggage and Miss Tottle were back in the office in Charing Cross Road, both with sun-scorched skins as red as the shells of the many lobsters they had eaten. They quickly settled down again into their normal and stimulating routine. Day after day the letters went out and the cheques came in. It was remarkable how smoothly the business ran. The psychology behind it was, of course, very sound. Strike a widow at the height of her grief, strike her with something that is unbearably awful, something she wants to forget about and put behind her, something she wants nobody else to discover. What's more, the funeral is imminent. So she pays up fast to get the sordid little business out of the way. Mr Buggage knew his onions. In all the years he had been operating, he had never once had a protest or an angry reply. Just a cheque in an envelope. Now and again, but not often, there was no reply at all. The disbelieving widow had been brave enough to sling his letter into the waste-paper basket and that was the end of it. None of them quite dared to challenge the invoice because they could never be absolutely positive that the late husband had been as pure as the wife believed and hoped. Men never are. In many cases, of course, the widow knew very well that her beloved had been a lecherous old bird and Mr Buggage's invoice came as no surprise. So she paid up even faster.

About a month after their return from Marrakech, on a wet and rainy afternoon in March, Mr Buggage was reclining comfortably in his office with his feet up on the top of his fine partners' desk, dictating to Miss Tottle some details about a deceased and distinguished admiral. '*Recreations*,' he was saying, reading from *Who's Who*, '*Gardening, sailing and stamp-collecting* . . .' At that point, the door from the main shop opened and a young man came in with a book in his hand. 'Mr Buggage?' he said.

Mr Buggage looked up. 'Over there,' he said, waving towards Miss Tottle. 'She'll deal with you.'

The young man stood still. His navy-blue overcoat was wet from the weather and droplets of water were dripping from his hair. He didn't look at Miss Tottle. He kept his eyes on Mr Buggage. 'Don't you want the money?' he said, pleasantly enough.

'She'll take it.'

'Why won't you take it?'

'Because she's the cashier,' Mr Buggage said. 'You want to buy a book, go ahead. She'll deal with you.'

'I'd rather deal with *you*,' the young man said.

Mr Buggage looked up at him. 'Go on,' he said. 'Just do as you're told, there's a good lad.'

'You *are* the proprietor?' the young man said. 'You *are* Mr William Buggage?'

'What if I am?' Mr Buggage said, his feet still up on the desk.

'Are you or aren't you?'

'What's it to you?' Mr Buggage said.

'So that's settled,' the young man said. 'How d'you do, Mr Buggage.' There was a curious edge to his voice now, a mixture of scorn and mockery.

Mr Buggage took his feet down from the desk-top and sat up a trifle straighter. 'You're a bit of a cheeky young bugger, aren't you?' he said. 'If you want that book, I suggest you just pay your money over there and then you can 'op it. Right?'

The young man turned towards the still open door that led to the front of the shop. Just the other side of the door there were a couple of the usual kind of customers, men in raincoats, pulling out books and examining them.

'Mother,' the young man called softly. 'You can come in, Mother. Mr Buggage is here.'

A small woman of about sixty came in and stood beside the young man. She had a trim figure for her age and a face that must once have been ravishing, but now it showed traces of strain and exhaustion, and the pale blue eyes were dulled with grief. She was wearing a black coat and a simple black hat. She left the door open behind her.

'Mr Buggage,' the young man said. 'This is my mother, Mrs Northcote.'

Miss Tottle, the rememberer of names, turned round quick and looked at Mr Buggage and made little warning movements with her mouth. Mr Buggage got the message and said as politely as he could, 'And what can I do for you, madam?'

The woman opened her black handbag and took out a letter. She unfolded it carefully and held it out to Mr Buggage. 'Then it will be you who sent me this?' she said.

Mr Buggage took the letter and examined it at some length. Miss Tottle, who had turned right round in her chair now, was watching Mr Buggage.

'Yes,' Mr Buggage said. 'This is my letter and my invoice. All correct and in order. What is your problem, madam?'

'What I came here to ask you,' the woman said, 'is, are you sure it's right?'

'I'm afraid it is, madam.'

'But it is so unbelievable ... I find it impossible to believe that my husband bought those books.'

'Let's see now, your 'usband, Mr ... Mr ... er ...'

'Northcote,' Miss Tottle said.

'Yes, Mr Northcote, yes, of course, Mr Northcote. 'Ee wasn't in 'ere often, once or twice a year maybe, but a good customer and a very fine gentleman. May I offer you, madam, my sincere condolences on your sad loss.'

'Thank you, Mr Buggage. But are you really quite certain you haven't been mixing him up with somebody else?'

'Not a chance, madam. Not the slightest chance. My good secretary over there will confirm that there is no mistake.'

'May I see it?' Miss Tottle said, getting up and crossing to take the letter from Mr Buggage. 'Yes,' she said, examining it. 'I typed this myself. There is no mistake.'

'Miss Tottle's been with me a long time,' Mr Buggage said. 'She knows the business inside out. I can't remember 'er ever makin' a mistake.'

'I should hope not,' Miss Tottle said.

'So there you are, madam,' Mr Buggage said.

'It simply isn't *possible*,' the woman said.

'Ah, but men will be men,' Mr Buggage said. 'They all 'ave their little bit of fun now and again and there's no 'arm in that, is there, madam?' He sat confident and unmoved in his chair, waiting now to have done with it. He felt himself master of the situation.

The woman stood very straight and still, and she was looking Mr Buggage directly in the eyes. 'These curious books you list on your invoice,' she said, 'do they print them in Braille?'

'In what?'

'In Braille.'

'I don't know what you're talking about, madam.'

'I thought you wouldn't,' she said. 'That's the only way my husband could have read them. He lost his sight in the last war, in the Battle of Alamein more than forty years ago, and he was blind for ever after.'

The office became suddenly very quiet. The mother and her son stood motionless, watching Mr Buggage. Miss Tottle turned away and looked out of the window. Mr Buggage cleared his throat as though to say something, but thought better of it. The two men in raincoats, who were close enough to have heard every word through the open door, came quietly into the office. One of them held out a plastic card and said to Mr Buggage, 'Inspector Richards, Serious Crimes Division, Scotland Yard.' And to Miss Tottle, who was already moving back towards her desk, he said, 'Don't touch any of those papers, please, miss. Leave everything just where it is. You're both coming along with us.'

The son took his mother gently by the arm and led her out of the office, through the shop and on to the street.

Vengeance is Mine Inc.

First published in *More Tales of
the Unexpected* (1980)

It was snowing when I woke up.

I could tell that it was snowing because there was a kind of brightness in the room and it was quiet outside with no footstep-noises coming up from the street and no tyre-noises but only the engines of the cars. I looked up and I saw George over by the window in his green dressing-gown, bending over the paraffin-stove, making the coffee.

'Snowing,' I said.

'It's cold,' George answered. 'It's really cold.'

I got out of bed and fetched the morning paper from outside the door. It was cold all right and I ran back quickly and jumped into bed and lay still for a while under the bedclothes, holding my hands tight between my legs for warmth.

'No letters?' George said.

'No. No letters.'

'Doesn't look as if the old man's going to cough up.'

'Maybe he thinks four hundred and fifty is enough for one month,' I said.

'He's never been to New York. He doesn't know the cost of living here.'

'You shouldn't have spent it all in one week.'

George stood up and looked at me. '*We* shouldn't have spent it, you mean.'

'That's right,' I said. 'We.' I began reading the paper.

The coffee was ready now and George brought the pot over and put it on the table between our beds. 'A person can't live without money,' he said. 'The old man ought to know that.' He got back into his bed without taking off his green dressing-gown. I went on reading. I finished the racing page and the football page and then I started on Lionel Pantaloon, the great political and society columnist. I always read Pantaloon – same as the other twenty or thirty million people in the country. He's a habit with me; he's more than a habit; he's a part of my morning, like three cups of coffee, or shaving.

'This fellow's got a nerve,' I said.

'Who?'

'This Lionel Pantaloon.'

'What's he saying now?'

'Same sort of thing he's always saying. Same sort of scandal. Always about the rich. Listen to this: ". . . seen at the Penguin Club . . . banker William S. Womberg with beauteous starlet Theresa Williams . . . three nights running . . . Mrs Womberg at home with a headache . . . which is something anyone's wife would have if hubby was out squiring Miss Williams of an evening . . ."'

'That fixes Womberg,' George said.

'I think it's a shame,' I said. 'That sort of thing could cause a divorce. How can this Pantaloon get away with stuff like that?'

'He always does, they're all scared of him. But if I was William S. Womberg,' George said, 'you know what I'd do? I'd go right out and punch this Lionel Pantaloon right on the nose. Why, that's the only way to handle those guys.'

'Mr Womberg couldn't do that.'

'Why not?'

'Because he's an old man,' I said. 'Mr Womberg is a dignified and respectable old man. He's a very prominent banker in the town. He couldn't possibly . . .'

And then it happened. Suddenly, from nowhere, the idea came. It came to me right in the middle of what I was saying to George and I stopped short and I could feel the idea itself kind of flowing into my brain and I kept very quiet and let it come and it kept on coming and almost before I knew what had happened I had it all, the whole plan, the whole brilliant magnificent plan worked out clearly in my head; and right then I knew it was a beauty.

I turned and I saw George staring at me with a look of wonder on his face. 'What's wrong?' he said. 'What's the matter?'

I kept quite calm. I reached out and got some more coffee before I allowed myself to speak.

'George,' I said, and I still kept calm. 'I have an idea. Now listen very carefully because I have an idea which will make us both very rich. We are broke, are we not?'

'We are.'

'And this William S. Womberg,' I said; 'would you consider that he is angry with Lionel Pantaloon this morning?'

'Angry!' George shouted. 'Angry! Why, he'll be madder than hell!'

'Quite so. And do you think that he would like to see Lionel Pantaloon receive a good hard punch on the nose?'

'Damn right he would!'

'And now tell me, is it not possible that Mr Womberg would be prepared to pay a sum of money to someone who would undertake to perform this nose-punching operation efficiently and discreetly on his behalf?'

George turned and looked at me, and gently, carefully, he put down his coffee-cup on the table. A slowly widening smile began to spread across his face. 'I get you,' he said. 'I get the idea.'

'That's just a little part of the idea. If you read Pantaloon's column here you will see that there is another person who has been insulted today.' I picked up the paper. 'There is a Mrs Ella Gimple, a prominent socialite who has perhaps a million dollars in the bank . . .'

'What does Pantaloon say about her?'

I looked at the paper again. 'He hints,' I answered, 'at how she makes a stack of money out of her own friends by throwing roulette parties and acting as the bank.'

'That fixes Gimple,' George said. 'And Womberg. Gimple and Womberg.' He was sitting up straight in bed waiting for me to go on.

'Now,' I said, 'we have two different people both loathing Lionel Pantaloon's guts this morning, both wanting desperately to go out and punch him on the nose, and neither of them daring to do it. You understand that?'

'Absolutely.'

'So much then,' I said, 'for Lionel Pantaloon. But don't forget that there are others like him. There are dozens of other columnists who spend their time insulting wealthy and important people. There's Harry Weyman, Claude Taylor, Jacob Swinski, Walter Kennedy, and all the rest of them.'

'That's right,' George said. 'That's absolutely right.'

'I'm telling you, there's nothing that makes the rich so furious as being mocked and insulted in the newspapers.'

'Go on,' George said. 'Go on.'

'All right. Now this is the plan.' I was getting rather excited myself. I was leaning over the side of the bed, resting one hand on the little table, waving the other about in the air as I spoke. 'We will set up immediately an organization and we will call it . . . what shall we call it . . . we will call it . . . let me see . . . we will call it "Vengeance Is Mine Inc." . . . How about that?'

'Peculiar name.'

'It's biblical. It's good. I like it. "Vengeance Is Mine Inc." It sounds fine. And we will have little cards printed which we will send to all our clients reminding them that they have been insulted and mortified in public and offering to punish the offender in consideration of a sum of money. We will buy all the newspapers and read all the columnists and every day we will send out a dozen or more of our cards to prospective clients.'

'It's marvellous!' George shouted. 'It's terrific!'

'We shall be rich,' I told him. 'We shall be exceedingly wealthy in no time at all.'

'We must start at once!'

I jumped out of bed, fetched a writing-pad and a pencil and ran back to bed again. 'Now,' I said, pulling my knees under the blankets and propping the writing-pad against them, 'the first thing is to decide what we're going to say on the printed cards which we'll be sending to our clients,' and I wrote, 'VENGEANCE IS MINE INC.' as a heading on top of the sheet of paper. Then, with much care, I composed a finely phrased letter explaining the functions of the organization. It finished up with the following sentence: '*Therefore VENGEANCE IS MINE INC. will undertake, on your behalf and in absolute confidence, to administer suitable punishment to columnist .... and in this regard we respectfully submit to you a choice of methods (together with prices) for your consideration.*'

'What do you mean, "a choice of methods"?' George said.

'We must give them a choice. We must think up a number of things ... a number of different punishments. Number one will be ...' and I wrote down, '*1. Punch him on the nose, once, hard.* What shall we charge for that?'

'Five hundred dollars,' George said instantly.

I wrote it down. 'What's the next one?'

'Black his eye,' George said.

I wrote down, '*2. Black his eye ... $500.*'

'No!' George said. 'I disagree with the price. It definitely requires more skill and timing to black an eye nicely than to punch a nose. It is a skilled job. It should be six hundred.'

'OK,' I said. 'Six hundred. And what's the next one?'

'Both together, of course. The old one two.' We were in George's territory now. This was right up his street.

'Both together?'

'Absolutely. Punch his nose *and* black his eye. Eleven hundred dollars.'

'There should be a reduction for taking the two,' I said. 'We'll make it a thousand.'

'It's dirt cheap,' George said. 'They'll snap it up.'

'What's next?'

We were both silent now, concentrating fiercely. Three deep parallel grooves of wrinkled skin appeared upon George's rather low sloping forehead. He began to scratch his scalp, slowly but very strongly. I looked away and tried to think of all the terrible things which people had done to other people. Finally I got one, and with George watching the point of my pencil moving over the paper, I wrote: '*4. Put a rattlesnake (with venom extracted) on the floor of his car, by the pedals, when he parks it.*'

'Jesus Christ!' George whispered. 'You want to kill him with fright!'

'Sure,' I said.

'And where'd you get a rattlesnake, anyway?'

'Buy it. You can always buy them. How much shall we charge for that one?'

'Fifteen hundred dollars,' George said firmly. I wrote it down.

'Now we need one more.'

'Here it is,' George said. 'Kidnap him in a car, take all his clothes away except his underpants and his shoes and socks, then dump him out on Fifth Avenue in the rush hour.' He smiled, a broad triumphant smile.

'We can't do that.'

'Write it down. And charge two thousand five hundred

bucks. You'd do it all right if old Womberg were to offer you that much.'

'Yes,' I said. 'I suppose I would.' And I wrote it down. 'That's enough now,' I added. 'That gives them a wide choice.'

'And where will we get the cards printed?' George asked.

'George Karnoffsky,' I said. 'Another George. He's a friend of mine. Runs a small printing shop down on Third Avenue. Does wedding invitations and things like that for the big stores. He'll do it. I know he will.'

'Then what are we waiting for?'

We both leaped out of bed and began to dress. 'It's twelve o'clock,' I said. 'If we hurry we'll catch him before he goes to lunch.'

It was still snowing when we went out into the street and the snow was four or five inches thick on the side-walk, but we covered the fourteen blocks to Karnoffsky's shop at a tremendous pace and we arrived there just as he was putting on his coat to go out.

'Claude!' he shouted. 'Hi boy! How you been keeping?' and he pumped my hand. He had a fat friendly face and a terrible nose with great wide-open nose-wings which overlapped his cheeks by at least an inch on either side. I greeted him and told him that we had come to discuss some most urgent business. He took off his coat and led us back into the office; then I began to tell him about our plans and what we wanted him to do.

When I'd got about quarter way through my story, he started to roar with laughter and it was impossible for me to continue; so I cut it short and handed him the piece of paper with the stuff on it that we wanted him to print. And now, as he read it, his whole body began to shake with laughter and he kept slapping the desk with his hand and coughing and choking and roaring like someone crazy. We sat watching him. We didn't see anything particular to laugh about.

Finally he quietened down and he took out a handkerchief and made a great business about wiping his eyes. 'Never laughed so much,' he said weakly. 'That's a great joke, that is. It's worth a lunch. Come on out and I'll give you lunch.'

'Look,' I said severely, 'this isn't any joke. There is nothing to laugh at. You are witnessing the birth of a new and powerful organization . . .'

'Come on,' he said and he began to laugh again. 'Come on and have lunch.'

'When can you get those cards printed?' I said. My voice was stern and businesslike.

He paused and stared at us. 'You mean . . . you really mean . . . you're serious about this thing?'

'Absolutely. You are witnessing the birth . . .'

'All right,' he said, 'all right.' He stood up. 'I think you're crazy and you'll get in trouble. Sure as hell you'll get in trouble. Those boys like messing other people about, but they don't much fancy being messed about themselves.'

'When can you get them printed, and without any of your workers reading them?'

'For this,' he answered gravely, 'I will give up my lunch. I will set the type myself. It is the least I can do.' He laughed again and the rims of his huge nostrils twitched with pleasure. 'How many do you want?'

'A thousand – to start with, and envelopes.'

'Come back at two o'clock,' he said and I thanked him very much and as we went out we could hear his laughter rumbling down the passage into the back of the shop.

At exactly two o'clock we were back. George Karnoffsky was in his office and the first thing I saw as we went in was the high stack of printed cards on his desk in front of him. They were large cards, about twice the size of ordinary wedding or cocktail invitation-cards. 'There you are,' he said. 'All ready for you.' The fool was still laughing.

He handed us each a card and I examined mine carefully. It was a beautiful thing. He had obviously taken much trouble over it. The card itself was thick and stiff with narrow gold edging all the way around, and the letters of the heading were exceedingly elegant. I cannot reproduce it here in all its splendour, but I can at least show you how it read:

VENGEANCE IS MINE INC.

Dear ....

You have probably seen columnist ....'s slanderous and unprovoked attack upon your character in today's paper. It is an outrageous insinuation, a deliberate distortion of the truth.

Are you yourself prepared to allow this miserable malice-monger to insult you in this manner without doing anything about it?

The whole world knows that it is foreign to the nature of the American people to permit themselves to be insulted either in public or in private without rising up in righteous indignation and demanding – nay, exacting – a just measure of retribution.

On the other hand, it is only natural that a citizen of your standing and reputation will not wish *personally* to become further involved in this sordid petty affair, or indeed to have any *direct* contact whatsoever with this vile person.

How then are you to obtain satisfaction?

The answer is simple. VENGEANCE IS MINE INC. will obtain it for you. We will undertake, on your behalf and in absolute confidence, to administer individual punishment to columnist ...., and in this regard we respectfully submit to you a choice of methods (together with prices) for your consideration:

1. Punch him on the nose, once, hard $500
2. Black his eye $600
3. Punch him on the nose and black his eye $1000
4. Introduce a rattlesnake (with venom extracted) into his car, on the floor by the pedals, when he parks it $1500
5. Kidnap him, take all his clothes away except his underpants, his shoes and socks, then dump him out on Fifth Ave. in the rush hour $2500

This work executed by a professional.

If you desire to avail yourself of any of these offers, kindly reply to VENGEANCE IS MINE INC. at the address indicated upon the enclosed slip of paper. If it is practicable, you will be notified in advance of the place where the action will occur and of the time, so that you may, if you wish, watch the proceedings in person from a safe and anonymous distance.

No payment need be made until after your order has been satisfactorily executed, when an account will be rendered in the usual manner.

George Karnoffsky had done a beautiful job of printing. 'Claude,' he said, 'you like?'

'It's marvellous.'

'It's the best I could do for you. It's like in the war when I would see soldiers going off perhaps to get killed and all the time I would want to be giving them things and doing things for them.' He was beginning to laugh again, so I said, 'We'd better be going now. Have you got large envelopes for these cards?'

'Everything is here. And you can pay me when the money starts coming in.' That seemed to set him off worse than ever and he collapsed into his chair, giggling like a fool. George and I hurried out of the shop into the street, into the cold snow-falling afternoon.

We almost ran the distance back to our room and on the way up I borrowed a Manhattan telephone directory from the public telephone in the hall. We found 'Womberg, William S.' without any trouble and while I read out the address – somewhere up in the East Nineties – George wrote it on one of the envelopes.

'Gimple, Mrs Ella H.' was also in the book and we addressed an envelope to her as well. 'We'll just send to Womberg and Gimple today,' I said. 'We haven't really got started yet. Tomorrow we'll send a dozen.'

'We'd better catch the next post,' George said.

'We'll deliver them by hand,' I told him. 'Now, at once. The sooner they get them the better. Tomorrow might be too late. They won't be half so angry tomorrow as they are today. People are apt to cool off through the night. See here,' I said, 'you go ahead and deliver those two cards right away. While you're doing that I'm going to snoop around the town and try to find out something about the habits of Lionel Pantaloon. See you back here later in the evening . . .'

At about nine o'clock that evening I returned and found George lying on his bed smoking cigarettes and drinking coffee.

'I delivered them both,' he said. 'Just slipped them through the letter-boxes and rang the bells and beat it up the street. Womberg had a huge house, a huge white house. How did you get on?'

'I went to see a man I know who works in the sports section of the *Daily Mirror*. He told me all.'

'What did he tell you?'

'He said Pantaloon's movements are more or less routine. He operates at night, but wherever he goes earlier in the evening, he *always* – and this is the important point – he *always* finishes up at the Penguin Club. He gets there round about midnight and stays until two or two thirty. That's when his legmen bring him all the dope.'

'That's all we want to know,' George said happily.

'It's too easy.'

'Money for old rope.'

There was a full bottle of blended whisky in the cupboard and George fetched it out. For the next two hours we sat upon our beds drinking the whisky and making wonderful and complicated plans for the development of our organization. By eleven o'clock we were employing a staff of fifty, including twelve famous pugilists, and our offices were in the Rockefeller Center. Towards midnight we had obtained control over all columnists and were dictating their daily columns to them by telephone from our headquarters, taking care to insult and infuriate at least twenty rich persons in one part of the country or another every day. We were immensely wealthy and George had a British Bentley, I had five Cadillacs. George kept practising telephone talks with Lionel Pantaloon. 'That you, Pantaloon?' 'Yes, sir.' 'Well, listen here. I think your column stinks today. It's lousy.' 'I'm very sorry, sir. I'll try to do better tomorrow.' 'Damn right you'll do better, Pantaloon. Matter of fact we've been thinking about getting someone else to take over.' 'But please, please sir, just give me another chance.' 'OK, Pantaloon, but this is the last. And by the way, the boys are putting a rattlesnake in your car tonight, on behalf of Mr Hiram C. King, the soap manufacturer. Mr King will be watching from across the street so don't forget to act scared when you see it.' 'Yes, sir, of course, sir. I won't forget, sir . . .'

When we finally went to bed and the light was out, I could still hear George giving hell to Pantaloon on the telephone.

The next morning we were both woken up by the church clock on the corner striking nine. George got up and went to the door to get the papers and when he came back he was holding a letter in his hand.

'Open it!' I said.

He opened it and carefully he unfolded a single sheet of thin notepaper.

'Read it!' I shouted.

He began to read it aloud, his voice low and serious at first but rising gradually to a high, almost hysterical shout of triumph as the full meaning of the letter was revealed to him. It said:

'Your methods appear curiously unorthodox. At the same time anything you do to that scoundrel has my approval. So go ahead. Start with Item I, and if you are successful I'll be only too glad to give you an order to work right on through the list. Send the bill to me, William S. Womberg.'

I recollect that in the excitement of the moment we did a kind of dance around the room in our pyjamas, praising Mr Womberg in loud voices and singing that we were rich. George turned somersaults on his bed and it is possible that I did the same.

'When shall we do it?' he said. 'Tonight?'

I paused before replying. I refused to be rushed. The pages of history are filled with the names of great men who have come to grief by permitting themselves to make hasty decisions in the excitement of a moment. I put on my dressing-gown, lit a cigarette and began to pace up and down the room. 'There is no hurry,' I said. 'Womberg's order can be dealt with in due course. But first of all we must send out today's cards.'

I dressed quickly, went out to the newsstand across the street, bought one copy of every daily paper there was and returned to our room. The next two hours were spent in reading the columnists' columns, and in the end we had a list of eleven people – eight men and three women – all of whom had been insulted in one way or another by one of the columnists that morning. Things were going well. We were working smoothly. It took us only another half-hour to look up the addresses of the insulted ones – two we couldn't find – and to address the envelopes.

In the afternoon we delivered them, and at about six in the evening we got back to our room, tired but triumphant. We made coffee and we fried hamburgers and we had supper in bed. Then we re-read Womberg's letter aloud to each other many many times.

'What he's doing he's giving us an order for six thousand one hundred dollars,' George said. 'Items 1 to 5 inclusive.'

'It's not a bad beginning. Not bad for the first day. Six thousand a day works out at . . . let me see . . . it's nearly two million dollars a year, not counting Sundays. A million each. It's more than Betty Grable.'

'We are very wealthy people,' George said. He smiled, a slow and wondrous smile of pure contentment.

'In a day or two we will move to a suite of rooms at the St Regis.'

'I think the Waldorf,' George said.

'All right, the Waldorf. And later on we might as well take a house.'

'One like Womberg's?'

'All right. One like Womberg's. But first,' I said, 'we have work to do. Tomorrow we shall deal with Pantaloon. We will catch him as he comes out of the Penguin Club. At 2.30 a.m. we will be waiting for him, and when he comes out into the street you will step forward and you will punch him once, hard, right upon the point of the nose as per contract.'

'It will be a pleasure,' George said. 'It will be a real pleasure. But how do we get away? Do we run?'

'We shall hire a car for an hour. We have just enough money left for that, and I shall be sitting at the wheel with the engine running, not ten yards away, and the door will be open and when you've punched him you'll just jump back into the car and we'll be gone.'

'It is perfect. I shall punch him very hard.' George paused. He clenched his right fist and examined his knuckles. Then he smiled again and he said slowly, 'This nose of his, is it not possible that it will afterwards be so much blunted that it will no longer poke well into other people's business?'

'It is quite possible,' I answered, and with that happy thought in our minds we switched out the light and went early to sleep.

The next morning I was woken by a shout and I sat up and saw George standing at the foot of my bed in his pyjamas, waving his arms. 'Look!' he shouted. 'There are four! There are four!' I looked, and indeed there were four letters in his hand.

'Open them. Quickly, open them.'

The first one he read aloud: '"*Dear Vengeance Is Mine Inc., That's the best proposition I've had in years. Go right ahead and give Mr Jacob Swinski the rattlesnake treatment (Item 4). But I'll be glad to pay double if you'll forget to extract the poison from its fangs. Yours Gertrude Porter-Vandervelt. P.S. You'd better insure the snake. That guy's bite carries more poison than any rattler's."*'

George read the second one aloud: '"*My cheque for $500 is made out and lies before me on my desk. The moment I receive proof that you have punched Lionel Pantaloon hard on the nose, it will be posted to you. I should prefer a fracture, if possible. Yours etc. Wilbur H. Gollogly.*'"

George read the third one aloud: '"*In my present frame of mind and against my better judgement, I am tempted to reply to your card and to request that you deposit that scoundrel Walter Kennedy upon Fifth Avenue dressed only in his underwear. I make the proviso that there shall be snow upon the ground at the time and that the temperature shall be sub-zero. H. Gresham.*"'

The fourth one also he read aloud: '"*A good hard sock on the nose for Pantaloon is worth five hundred of mine or anyone else's money. I should like to watch. Yours sincerely, Claudia Calthorpe Hines.*"'

George laid the letters down gently, carefully, upon the bed. For a while there was silence. We stared at each other, too astonished, too happy to speak. I began to calculate the value of those four orders in terms of money.

'That's five thousand dollars' worth,' I said softly.

Upon George's face there was a huge bright grin. 'Claude,' he said, 'should we not move now to the Waldorf?'

'Soon,' I answered, 'but at the moment we have no time for moving. We have not even time to send out any fresh cards today. We must start to execute the orders we have in hand. We are overwhelmed with work.'

'Should we not engage extra staff and enlarge our organization?'

'Later,' I said. 'Even for that there is no time today. Just think what we have to do. We have to put a rattlesnake in Jacob Swinski's car . . . we have to dump Walter Kennedy on Fifth Avenue in his underpants . . . we have to punch Pantaloon on the nose . . . let me see . . . yes, for three different people we have to punch Pantaloon . . .'

I stopped. I closed my eyes. I sat still. Again I became conscious of a small clear stream of inspiration flowing into the tissues of my brain. 'I have it!' I shouted. 'I have it! I have it! Three birds with one stone! Three customers with one punch!'

'How?'

'Don't you see? We only need to punch Pantaloon once and each of the three customers . . . Womberg, Gollogly and Claudia Hines . . . will think it's being done specially for him or her.'

'Say it again.' I said it again.

'It's brilliant.'

'It's common sense. And the same principle will apply to the others. The rattlesnake treatment and the other one can wait until we have more orders. Perhaps in a few days we shall have ten orders for rattlesnakes in Swinski's car. Then we will do them all in one go.'

'It's wonderful.'

'This evening then,' I said, 'we will handle Pantaloon. But first we must hire a car. Also we must send telegrams, one to Womberg, one to Gollogly and one to Claudia Hines, telling them where and when the punching will take place.'

We dressed rapidly and went out.

In a dirty silent little garage down on East 9th Street we managed to hire a car, a 1934 Chevrolet, eight dollars for the evening. We then sent three telegrams, each one identical and cunningly worded to conceal its true meaning from inquisitive people: '*Hope to see you outside Penguin Club 2.30 a.m. Regards V.I. Mine.*'

'There is one thing more,' I said. 'It is essential that you should be disguised. Pantaloon, or the doorman, for example, must not be able to identify you afterwards. You must wear a false moustache.'

'What about you?'

'Not necessary. I'll be sitting in the car. They won't see me.'

We went to a children's toy-shop and we bought for George a magnificent black moustache, a thing with long pointed ends, waxed and stiff and shining, and when he held it up against his face he looked exactly like the Kaiser of Germany. The man in the shop also sold us a tube of glue and he showed us how the moustache should be attached to the upper lip. 'Going to have fun with the kids?' he asked, and George said, 'Absolutely.'

All was now ready; but there was a long time to wait. We had three dollars left between us and with this we bought a sandwich each and then went to a movie. Then, at eleven o'clock that evening, we collected our car and in it we began to cruise slowly through the streets of New York waiting for the time to pass.

'You'd better put on your moustache so as you get used to it.'

We pulled up under a street-lamp and I squeezed some glue on to George's upper lip and fixed on the huge black hairy thing with its pointed ends. Then we drove on. It was cold in the car and outside it was beginning to snow again. I could see a few small snowflakes falling through the beams of the car-lights. George kept saying, 'How hard shall I hit him?' and I kept answering, 'Hit him as hard as you can, and on the nose. It must be on the nose because that is a part of the contract. Everything must be done right. Our clients may be watching.'

At two in the morning we drove slowly past the entrance to the Penguin Club in order to survey the situation. 'I will park there,' I said, 'just past the entrance in that patch of dark. But I will leave the door open for you.'

We drove on. Then George said, 'What does he look like? How do I know it's him?'

'Don't worry,' I answered. 'I've thought of that,' and I took from my pocket a piece of paper and handed it to him. 'You take this and fold it up small and give it to the doorman and tell him to see it gets to Pantaloon quickly. Act as though you are scared to death and in an awful hurry. It's a hundred to one Pantaloon will come out. No columnist could resist that message.'

On the paper I had written: *'I am a worker in Soviet Con-*

sulate. Come to the door very quickly please I have something to tell but come quickly as I am in danger. I cannot come in to you.'

'You see,' I said, 'your moustache will make you look like a Russian. All Russians have big moustaches.'

George took the paper and folded it up very small and held it in his fingers. It was nearly half past two in the morning now and we began to drive towards the Penguin Club.

'You all set?' I said.

'Yes.'

'We're going in now. Here we come. I'll park just past the entrance . . . here. Hit him hard,' I said, and George opened the door and got out of the car. I closed the door behind him but I leaned over and kept my hand on the handle so I could open it again quick, and I let down the window so I could watch. I kept the engine ticking over.

I saw George walk swiftly up to the doorman who stood under the red and white canopy which stretched out over the sidewalk. I saw the doorman turn and look down at George and I didn't like the way he did it. He was a tall proud man dressed in a fine magenta-coloured uniform with gold buttons and gold shoulders and a broad white stripe down each magenta trouser-leg. Also he wore white gloves and he stood there looking proudly down at George, frowning, pressing his lips together hard. He was looking at George's moustache and I thought, Oh my God, we have overdone it. We have overdisguised him. He's going to know it's false and he's going to take one of the long pointed ends in his fingers and then he'll give it a tweak and it'll come off. But he didn't. He was distracted by George's acting, for George was acting well. I could see him hopping about, clasping and unclasping his hands, swaying his body and shaking his head, and I could hear him saying, 'Plees plees plees you must hurry. It is life and teth. Plees plees take it kvick to Mr Pantaloon.' His Russian accent was not like any accent I had heard before, but all the same there was a quality of real despair in his voice.

Finally, gravely, proudly, the doorman said, 'Give me the note.' George gave it to him and said, 'Tank you, tank you, but say it is urgent,' and the doorman disappeared inside. In a few moments he returned and said, 'It's being delivered now.' George paced nervously up and down. I waited, watching the door. Three or four minutes elapsed. George wrung his hands and said, 'Vere is he? Vere is he? Plees to go see if he is not coming!'

'What's the matter with you?' the doorman said. Now he was looking at George's moustache again.

'It is life and teth! Mr Pantaloon can help! He must come!'

'Why don't you shut up?' the doorman said, but he opened the door again and he poked his head inside and I heard him saying something to someone.

To George he said, 'They say he's coming now.'

A moment later the door opened and Pantaloon himself, small and dapper, stepped out. He paused by the door, looking quickly from side to side like a nervous inquisitive ferret. The doorman touched his cap and pointed at George. I heard Pantaloon say, 'Yes, what did you want?'

George said, 'Plees, dis vay a leetle so as novone can hear,' and he led Pantaloon along the pavement, away from the doorman and towards the car.

'Come on, now,' Pantaloon said. 'What is it you want?'

Suddenly George shouted 'Look!' and he pointed up the street. Pantaloon turned his head and as he did so George swung his right arm and he hit Pantaloon plumb on the point of the nose. I saw George leaning forward on the punch, all his weight behind it, and the whole of Pantaloon appeared somehow to lift slightly off the ground and to float backwards for two or three feet until the façade of the Penguin Club stopped him. All this happened very quickly, and then George was in the car beside me and we were off and I could hear the doorman blowing a whistle behind us.

'We've done it!' George gasped. He was excited and out of breath. 'I hit him good! Did you see how good I hit him!'

It was snowing hard now and I drove fast and made many sudden turnings and I knew no one would catch us in this snowstorm.

'Son of a bitch almost went through the wall I hit him so hard.'

'Well done, George,' I said. 'Nice work, George.'

'And did you see him lift? Did you see him lift right up off the ground?'

'Womberg will be pleased,' I said.

'And Gollogly, and the Hines woman.'

'They'll all be pleased,' I said. 'Watch the money coming in.'

'There's a car behind us!' George shouted. 'It's following us! It's right on our tail! Drive like mad!'

'Impossible!' I said. 'They couldn't have picked us up already. It's just another car going somewhere.' I turned sharply to the right.

'He's still with us,' George said. 'Keep turning. We'll lose him soon.'

'How the hell can we lose a police-car in a 1934 Chev,' I said. 'I'm going to stop.'

'Keep going!' George shouted. 'You're doing fine.'

'I'm going to stop,' I said. 'It'll only make them mad if we go on.'

George protested fiercely but I knew it was no good and I pulled in to the side of the road. The other car swerved out and went past us and skidded to a standstill in front of us.

'Quick,' George said. 'Let's beat it.' He had the door open and he was ready to run.

'Don't be a fool,' I said. 'Stay where you are. You can't get away now.'

A voice from outside said, 'All right, boys, what's the hurry?'

'No hurry,' I answered. 'We're just going home.'

'Yea?'

'Oh yes, we're just on our way home now.'

The man poked his head in through the window on my side, and he looked at me, then at George, then at me again.

'It's a nasty night,' George said. 'We're just trying to reach home before the streets get all snowed up.'

'Well,' the man said, 'you can take it easy. I just thought I'd like to give you this right away.' He dropped a wad of banknotes on to my lap. 'I'm Gollogly,' he added, 'Wilbur H. Gollogly,' and he stood out there in the snow grinning at us, stamping his feet and rubbing his hands to keep them warm. 'I got your wire and I watched the whole thing from across the street. You did a fine job. I'm paying you double. It was worth it. Funniest thing I ever seen. Goodbye, boys. Watch your steps. They'll be after you now. Get out of town if I were you. Goodbye.' And before we could say anything, he was gone.

When finally we got back to our room I started packing at once.

'You crazy?' George said. 'We've only got to wait a few hours and we receive five hundred dollars each from Womberg and the Hines woman. Then we'll have two thousand altogether and we can go anywhere we want.'

So we spent the next day waiting in our room and reading the papers, one of which had a whole column on the front page headed, 'Brutal assault on famous columnist'. But sure enough the late afternoon post brought us two letters and there was five hundred dollars in each.

And right now, at this moment, we are sitting in a Pullman car, drinking Scotch whisky and heading south for a place where there is always sunshine and where the horses are running every day. We are immensely wealthy and George keeps saying that if we put the whole of our two thousand dollars on a horse at ten to one we shall make another twenty thousand and we will be able to retire. 'We will have a house at Palm Beach,' he says, 'and we will entertain upon a lavish scale. Beautiful socialites will loll around the edge of our swimming pool sipping cool drinks, and after a while we will perhaps put another large sum of money upon another horse and we shall become wealthier still. Possibly we will become tired of Palm Beach and then we will move around in a leisurely manner among the playgrounds of the rich. Monte Carlo and places like that. Like the Ali Khan and the Duke of Windsor. We will become prominent members of the international set and film stars will smile at us and head-waiters will bow to us and perhaps, in time to come, perhaps we might even get ourselves mentioned in Lionel Pantaloon's column.'

'That would be something,' I said.

'Wouldn't it just,' he answered happily. 'Wouldn't that just be something.'

Lamb to the Slaughter

First published in *Harper's* (September 1953)

The room was warm and clean, the curtains drawn, the two table lamps alight – hers and the one by the empty chair opposite. On the sideboard behind her, two tall glasses, soda water, whisky. Fresh ice cubes in the Thermos bucket.

Mary Maloney was waiting for her husband to come home from work.

Now and again she would glance up at the clock, but without anxiety, merely to please herself with the thought that each minute gone by made it nearer the time when he would come. There was a slow smiling air about her, and about everything she did. The drop of the head as she bent over her sewing was curiously tranquil. Her skin – for this was her sixth month with child – had acquired a wonderful translucent quality, the mouth was soft, and the eyes, with their new placid look, seemed larger, darker than before.

When the clock said ten minutes to five, she began to listen, and a few moments later, punctually as always, she heard the tyres on the gravel outside, and the car door slamming, the footsteps passing the window, the key turning in the lock. She laid aside her sewing, stood up and went forward to kiss him as he came in.

'Hullo darling,' she said.

'Hullo,' he answered.

She took his coat and hung it in the closet. Then she walked over and made the drinks, a strongish one for him, a weak one for herself; and soon she was back again in her chair with the sewing, and he in the other, opposite, holding the tall glass with both his hands, rocking it so the ice cubes tinkled against the side.

For her, this was always a blissful time of day. She knew he didn't want to speak much until the first drink was finished, and she, on her side, was content to sit quietly, enjoying his company after the long hours alone in the house. She loved to luxuriate in the presence of this man, and to feel – almost as a sunbather feels the sun – that warm male glow that came out of him to her when they were alone together. She loved him for the way he sat loosely in a chair, for the way he came in a door, or moved slowly across the room with long strides. She loved the intent, far look in his eyes when they rested on her, the funny shape of the mouth, and especially the way he remained silent about his tiredness, sitting still with himself until the whisky had taken some of it away.

'Tired, darling?'

'Yes,' he said. 'I'm tired.' And as he spoke, he did an unusual thing. He lifted his glass and drained it in one swallow although there was still half of it, at least half of it, left. She wasn't really watching him, but she knew what he had done because she heard the ice cubes falling back against the bottom of the empty glass when he lowered his arm. He paused a moment, leaning forward in the chair, then he got up and went slowly over to fetch himself another.

'I'll get it!' she cried, jumping up.

'Sit down,' he said.

When he came back, she noticed that the new drink was dark amber with the quantity of whisky in it.

'Darling, shall I get your slippers?'

'No.'

She watched him as he began to sip the dark-yellow drink, and she could see little oily swirls in the liquid because it was so strong.

'I think it's a shame,' she said, 'that when a policeman gets to be as senior as you, they keep him walking about on his feet all day long.'

He didn't answer, so she bent her head again and went on with her sewing; but each time he lifted the drink to his lips, she heard the ice cubes clinking against the side of the glass.

'Darling,' she said. 'Would you like me to get you some cheese? I haven't made any supper because it's Thursday.'

'No,' he said.

'If you're too tired to eat out,' she went on, 'it's still not too late. There's plenty of meat and stuff in the freezer, and you can have it right here and not even move out of the chair.'

Her eyes waited on him for an answer, a smile, a little nod, but he made no sign.

'Anyway,' she went on, 'I'll get you some cheese and crackers first.'

'I don't want it,' he said.

She moved uneasily in her chair, the large eyes still watching his face. 'But you *must* have supper. I can easily do it here. I'd like to do it. We can have lamb chops. Or pork. Anything you want. Everything's in the freezer.'

'Forget it,' he said.

'But darling, you *must* eat! I'll fix it anyway, and then you can have it or not, as you like.'

She stood up and placed her sewing on the table by the lamp.

'Sit down,' he said. 'Just for a minute, sit down.'

It wasn't till then that she began to get frightened.

'Go on,' he said. 'Sit down.'

She lowered herself back slowly into the chair, watching him all the time with those large, bewildered eyes. He had finished the second drink and was staring down into the glass, frowning.

'Listen,' he said. 'I've got something to tell you.'

'What is it, darling? What's the matter?'

He had now become absolutely motionless, and he kept his head down so that the light from the lamp beside him fell across the upper part of his face, leaving the chin and mouth in shadow. She noticed there was a little muscle moving near the corner of his left eye.

'This is going to be a bit of a shock to you, I'm afraid,' he said. 'But I've thought about it a good deal and I've decided the only thing to do is tell you right away. I hope you won't blame me too much.'

And he told her. It didn't take long, four or five minutes at most, and she sat very still through it all, watching him with a kind of dazed horror as he went farther and farther away from her with each word.

'So there it is,' he added. 'And I know it's kind of a bad time to be telling you, but there simply wasn't any other way. Of course I'll give you money and see you're looked after. But there needn't really be any fuss. I hope not anyway. It wouldn't be very good for my job.'

Her first instinct was not to believe any of it, to reject it all. It occurred to her that perhaps he hadn't even spoken, that she herself had imagined the whole thing. Maybe, if she went about her business and acted as though she hadn't been listening, then later, when she sort of woke up again, she might find none of it had ever happened.

'I'll get the supper,' she managed to whisper, and this time he didn't stop her.

When she walked across the room she couldn't feel her feet touching the floor. She couldn't feel anything at all – except a slight nausea and a desire to vomit. Everything was automatic now – down the steps to the cellar, the light switch, the deep-freeze, the hand inside the cabinet taking hold of the first object it met. She lifted it out, and looked at it. It was wrapped in paper, so she took off the paper and looked at it again.

A leg of lamb.

All right then, they would have lamb for supper. She carried it upstairs, holding the thin bone-end of it with both her hands, and as she went through the living-room, she saw him standing over by the window with his back to her, and she stopped.

'For God's sake,' he said, hearing her, but not turning round. 'Don't make supper for me. I'm going out.'

At that point, Mary Maloney simply walked up behind him and without any pause she swung the big frozen leg of lamb high in the air and brought it down as hard as she could on the back of his head.

She might just as well have hit him with a steel club.

She stepped back a pace, waiting, and the funny thing was that he remained standing there for at least four or five seconds, gently swaying. Then he crashed to the carpet.

The violence of the crash, the noise, the small table overturning, helped bring her out of the shock. She came out slowly, feeling cold and surprised, and she stood for a while blinking at the body, still holding the ridiculous piece of meat tight with both hands.

All right, she told herself. So I've killed him.

It was extraordinary, now, how clear her mind became all of a sudden. She began thinking very fast. As the wife of a detective, she knew quite well what the penalty would be. That was fine. It made no difference to her. In fact, it would be a relief. On the other hand, what about the child? What were the laws about murderers with unborn children? Did they kill them both – mother and child? Or did they wait until the tenth month? What did they do?

Mary Maloney didn't know. And she certainly wasn't prepared to take a chance.

She carried the meat into the kitchen, placed it in a pan, turned the oven on high, and shoved it inside. Then she washed her hands and ran upstairs to the bedroom. She sat down before the mirror, tidied her hair, touched up her lips and face. She tried a smile. It came out rather peculiar. She tried again.

'Hullo, Sam,' she said brightly, aloud.

The voice sounded peculiar too.

'I want some potatoes please, Sam. Yes, and I think a can of peas.'

That was better. Both the smile and the voice were coming out better now. She rehearsed it several times more. Then she ran downstairs, took her coat, went out the back door, down the garden, into the street.

It wasn't six o'clock yet and the lights were still on in the grocery shop.

'Hullo, Sam,' she said brightly, smiling at the man behind the counter.

'Why, good evening, Mrs Maloney. How're *you*?'

'I want some potatoes please, Sam. Yes, and I think a can of peas.'

The man turned and reached up behind him on the shelf for the peas.

'Patrick's decided he's tired and doesn't want to eat out tonight,' she told him. 'We usually go out Thursdays, you know, and now he's caught me without any vegetables in the house.'

'Then how about meat, Mrs Maloney?'

'No, I've got meat, thanks. I got a nice leg of lamb from the freezer.'

'Oh.'

'I don't much like cooking it frozen, Sam, but I'm taking a chance on it this time. You think it'll be all right?'

'Personally,' the grocer said, 'I don't believe it makes any difference. You want these Idaho potatoes?'

'Oh yes, that'll be fine. Two of those.'

'Anything else?' The grocer cocked his head on one side, looking at her pleasantly. 'How about afterwards? What you going to give him for afterwards?'

'Well – what would you suggest, Sam?'

The man glanced around his shop. 'How about a nice big slice of cheesecake? I know he likes that.'

'Perfect,' she said. 'He loves it.'

And when it was all wrapped and she had paid, she put on her brightest smile and said, 'Thank you, Sam. Good night.'

'Good night, Mrs Maloney. And thank *you*.'

And now, she told herself as she hurried back, all she was doing now, she was returning home to her husband and he was waiting for his supper; and she must cook it good, and make it as tasty as possible because the poor man was tired; and if, when she entered the house, she happened to find anything unusual, or tragic, or terrible, then naturally it would be a shock and she'd become frantic with grief and horror. Mind you, she wasn't *expecting* to find anything. She was just going home with the vegetables. Mrs Patrick Maloney going home with the vegetables on Thursday evening to cook supper for her husband.

That's the way, she told herself. Do everything right and natural. Keep things absolutely natural and there'll be no need for any acting at all.

Therefore, when she entered the kitchen by the back door, she was humming a little tune to herself and smiling.

'Patrick!' she called. 'How are you, darling?'

She put the parcel down on the table and went through into the living-room; and when she saw him lying there on the floor with his legs doubled up and one arm twisted back underneath his body, it really was rather a shock. All the old love and longing for him welled up inside her, and she ran over to him, knelt down beside him, and began to cry her heart out. It was easy. No acting was necessary.

A few minutes later she got up and went to the phone. She knew the number of the police station, and when the man at the other end answered, she cried to him, 'Quick! Come quick! Patrick's dead!'

'Who's speaking?'

'Mrs Maloney. Mrs Patrick Maloney.'

'You mean Patrick Maloney's dead?'

'I think so,' she sobbed. 'He's lying on the floor and I think he's dead.'

'Be right over,' the man said.

The car came very quickly, and when she opened the front door, two policemen walked in. She knew them both – she knew nearly all the men at that precinct – and she fell right into Jack Noonan's arms, weeping hysterically. He put her gently in a chair, then went over to join the other one, who was called O'Malley, kneeling by the body.

'Is he dead?' she cried.

'I'm afraid he is. What happened?'

Briefly, she told her story about going out to the grocer's and coming back to find him on the floor. While she was talking, crying and talking, Noonan discovered a small patch of congealed blood on the dead man's head. He showed it to O'Malley, who got up at once and hurried to the phone.

Soon, other men began to come into the house. First a doctor, then two detectives, one of whom she knew by name. Later, a police photographer arrived and took pictures, and a man who knew about fingerprints. There was a great deal of whispering and muttering beside the corpse, and the detectives kept asking her a lot of questions. But they always treated her kindly. She told her story again, this time right from the beginning, when Patrick had come in, and she was sewing, and he was tired, so tired he hadn't wanted to go out for supper. She told how she'd put the meat in the oven – 'It's there now, cooking' – and how she'd slipped out to the grocer's for vegetables, and come back to find him lying on the floor.

'Which grocer?' one of the detectives asked.

She told him, and he turned and whispered something to the other detective, who immediately went outside into the street.

In fifteen minutes he was back with a page of notes, and there was more whispering, and through her sobbing she heard a few of the whispered phrases – '. . . acted quite normal . . . very cheerful . . . wanted to give him a good supper . . . peas . . . cheesecake . . . impossible that she . . .'

After a while, the photographer and the doctor departed and two other men came in and took the corpse away on a stretcher. Then the fingerprint man went away.

The two detectives remained, and so did the two police-men. They were exceptionally nice to her and Jack Noonan asked if she wouldn't rather go somewhere else, to her sister's house perhaps, or to his own wife, who would take care of her and put her up for the night.

No, she said. She didn't feel she could move even a yard at the moment. Would they mind awfully if she stayed just where she was until she felt better? She didn't feel too good at the moment, she really didn't.

Then hadn't she better lie down on the bed? Jack Noo-nan asked.

No, she said. She'd like to stay right where she was, in this chair. A little later perhaps, when she felt better, she would move.

So they left her there while they went about their busi-ness, searching the house. Occasionally one of the detectives asked her another question. Sometimes Jack Noonan spoke at her gently as he passed by. Her husband, he told her, had been killed by a blow on the back of the head administered with a heavy blunt instrument, almost certainly a large piece of metal. They were looking for the weapon. The murderer may have taken it with him, but on the other hand he may've thrown it away or hidden it somewhere on the premises.

'It's the old story,' he said. 'Get the weapon, and you've got the man.'

Later, one of the detectives came up and sat beside her. Did she know, he asked, of anything in the house that could've been used as the weapon? Would she mind having a look around to see if anything was missing – a very big spanner, for example, or a heavy metal vase.

They didn't have any heavy metal vases, she said.

Or a big spanner?

She didn't think they had a big spanner. But there might be some things like that in the garage.

The search went on. She knew that there were other policemen in the garden all around the house. She could hear their footsteps on the gravel outside, and sometimes she saw the flash of a torch through a chink in the curtains. It began to get late, nearly nine, she noticed, by the clock on the mantel. The four men searching the rooms seemed to be growing weary, a trifle exasperated.

'Jack,' she said, the next time Sergeant Noonan went by. 'Would you mind giving me a drink?'

'Sure I'll give you a drink. You mean this whisky?'

'Yes, please. But just a small one. It might make me feel better.'

He handed her the glass.

'Why don't you have one yourself?' she said. 'You must be awfully tired. Please do. You've been very good to me.'

'Well,' he answered. 'It's not strictly allowed, but I might take just a drop to keep me going.'

One by one the others came in and were persuaded to take a little nip of whisky. They stood around rather awkwardly with the drinks in their hands, uncomfortable in her presence, trying to say consoling things to her. Sergeant Noonan wandered into the kitchen, came out quickly and said, 'Look, Mrs Maloney. You know that oven of yours is still on, and the meat still inside.'

'Oh *dear* me!' she cried. 'So it is!'

'I better turn it off for you, hadn't I?'

'Will you do that, Jack? Thank you so much.'

When the sergeant returned the second time, she looked at him with her large, dark, tearful eyes. 'Jack Noonan,' she said.

'Yes?'

'Would you do me a small favour – you and these others?'

'We can try, Mrs Maloney.'

'Well,' she said. 'Here you all are, and good friends of dear Patrick's too, and helping to catch the man who killed him. You must be terribly hungry by now because it's long past your suppertime, and I know Patrick would never forgive me, God bless his soul, if I allowed you to remain in his house without offering you decent hospitality. Why don't you eat up that lamb that's in the oven. It'll be cooked just right by now.'

'Wouldn't dream of it,' Sergeant Noonan said.

'Please,' she begged. 'Please eat it. Personally, I couldn't touch a thing, certainly not what's been in the house when he was here. But it's all right for you. It'd be a favour to me if you'd eat it up. Then you can go on with your work again afterwards.'

There was a good deal of hesitating among the four policemen, but they were clearly hungry, and in the end they were persuaded to go into the kitchen and help themselves. The woman stayed where she was, listening to them through the open door, and she could hear them speaking among themselves, their voices thick and sloppy because their mouths were full of meat.

'Have some more, Charlie?'

'No. Better not finish it.'

'She *wants* us to finish it. She said so. Be doing her a favour.'

'OK then. Give me some more.'

'That's a hell of a big club the guy must've used to hit poor Patrick,' one of them was saying. 'The doc says his skull was smashed all to pieces just like from a sledge-hammer.'

'That's why it ought to be easy to find.'

'Exactly what I say.'

'Whoever done it, they're not going to be carrying a thing like that around with them longer than they need.'

One of them belched.

'Personally, I think it's right here on the premises.'

'Probably right under our very noses. What you think, Jack?'

And in the other room, Mary Maloney began to giggle.

Mr Botibol

First published in *More Tales of
the Unexpected* (1980)

Mr Botibol pushed his way through the revolving doors and emerged into the large foyer of the hotel. He took off his hat, and holding it in front of him with both hands, he advanced nervously a few paces, paused and stood looking around him, searching the faces of the lunchtime crowd. Several people turned and stared at him in mild astonishment, and he heard – or he thought he heard – at least one woman's voice saying, 'My dear, *do* look what's just come in!'

At last he spotted Mr Clements sitting at a small table in the far corner, and he hurried over to him. Clements had seen him coming, and now, as he watched Mr Botibol threading his way cautiously between the tables and the people, walking on his toes in such a meek and self-effacing manner and clutching his hat before him with both hands, he thought how wretched it must be for any man to look as conspicuous and as odd as this Botibol. He resembled, to an extraordinary degree, an asparagus. His long narrow stalk did not appear to have any shoulders at all; it merely tapered upwards, growing gradually narrower and narrower until it came to a kind of point at the top of the small bald head. He was tightly encased in a shiny blue double-breasted suit, and this, for some curious reason, accentuated the illusion of a vegetable to a preposterous degree.

Clements stood up, they shook hands, and then at once, even before they had sat down again, Mr Botibol said, 'I have decided, yes I have decided to accept the offer which you made to me before you left my office last night.'

For some days Clements had been negotiating, on behalf of clients, for the purchase of the firm known as Botibol & Co., of which Mr Botibol was sole owner, and the night before, Clements had made his first offer. This was merely an exploratory, much-too-low bid, a kind of signal to the seller that the buyers were seriously interested. And by God, thought Clements, the poor fool has gone and accepted it. He nodded gravely many times in an effort to hide his astonishment, and he said, 'Good, good. I'm so glad to hear that, Mr Botibol.' Then he signalled a waiter and said, 'Two large martinis.'

'No, please!' Mr Botibol lifted both hands in horrified protest.

'Come on,' Clements said. 'This is an occasion.'

'I drink very little, and never, no, never during the middle of the day.'

But Clements was in a gay mood now and he took no notice. He ordered the martinis and when they came along Mr Botibol was forced, by the banter and good humour of the other, to drink to the deal which had just been concluded. Clements then spoke briefly about the drawing up and signing of documents, and when all that had been arranged, he called for two more cocktails. Again Mr Botibol protested, but not quite so vigorously this time, and

Clements ordered the drinks and then he turned and smiled at the other man in a friendly way. 'Well, Mr Botibol,' he said, 'now that it's all over, I suggest we have a pleasant non-business lunch together. What d'you say to that? And it's on me.'

'As you wish, as you wish,' Mr Botibol answered without any enthusiasm. He had a small melancholy voice and a way of pronouncing each word separately and slowly, as though he was explaining something to a child.

When they went into the dining-room Clements ordered a bottle of Lafite 1912 and a couple of plump roast partridges to go with it. He had already calculated in his head the amount of his commission and he was feeling fine. He began to make bright conversation, switching smoothly from one subject to another in the hope of touching on something that might interest his guest. But it was no good. Mr Botibol appeared to be only half listening. Every now and then he inclined his small bald head a little to one side or the other and said, 'Indeed.' When the wine came along Clements tried to have a talk about that.

'I am sure it is excellent,' Mr Botibol said, 'but please give me only a drop.'

Clements told a funny story. When it was over, Mr Botibol regarded him solemnly for a few moments, then he said, 'How amusing.' After that Clements kept his mouth shut and they ate in silence. Mr Botibol was drinking his wine and he didn't seem to object when his host reached over and refilled his glass. By the time they had finished eating, Clements estimated privately that his guest had consumed at least three-quarters of the bottle.

'A cigar, Mr Botibol?'

'Oh no, thank you.'

'A little brandy?'

'No, really, I am not accustomed . . .' Clements noticed that the man's cheeks were slightly flushed and that his eyes had become bright and watery. Might as well get the old boy properly drunk while I'm about it, he thought, and to the waiter he said, 'Two brandies.'

When the brandies arrived, Mr Botibol looked at his large glass suspiciously for a while, then he picked it up, took one quick birdlike sip and put it down again. 'Mr Clements,' he said suddenly, 'how I envy you.'

'Me? But why?'

'I will tell you, Mr Clements, I will tell you, if I may make so bold.' There was a nervous, mouselike quality in his voice which made it seem he was apologizing for everything he said.

'Please tell me,' Clements said.

'It is because to me you appear to have made such a success of your life.'

He's going to get melancholy drunk, Clements thought. He's one of the ones that gets melancholy and I can't stand it. 'Success,' he said. 'I don't see anything especially successful about me.'

'Oh yes, indeed. Your whole life, if I may say so, Mr Clements, appears to be such a pleasant and successful thing.'

'I'm a very ordinary person,' Clements said. He was trying to figure just how drunk the other really was.

'I believe,' said Mr Botibol, speaking slowly, separating each word carefully from the other, 'I believe that the wine has gone a little to my head, but . . .' He paused, searching for words. '. . . But I do want to ask you just one question.' He had poured some salt on to the tablecloth and he was shaping it into a little mountain with the tip of one finger.

'Mr Clements,' he said without looking up, 'do you think that it is possible for a man to live to the age of fifty-two without ever during his whole life having experienced one single small success in anything that he has done?'

'My dear Mr Botibol,' Clements laughed, 'everyone has his little successes from time to time, however small they may be.'

'Oh no,' Mr Botibol said gently. 'You are wrong. I, for example, cannot remember having had a single success of any sort during my whole life.'

'Now come!' Clements said, smiling. 'That can't be true. Why only this morning you sold your business for a hundred thousand. I call that one hell of a success.'

'The business was left me by my father. When he died nine years ago, it was worth four times as much. Under my direction it has lost three-quarters of its value. You can hardly call that a success.'

Clements knew this was true. 'Yes, yes, all right,' he said. 'That may be so, but all the same you know as well as I do that every man alive has his quota of little successes. Not big ones maybe. But lots of little ones. I mean, after all, goddammit, even scoring a goal at school was a little success, a little triumph, at the time, or making some runs or learning to swim. One forgets about them, that's all. One just forgets.'

'I never scored a goal,' Mr Botibol said. 'And I never learned to swim.'

Clements threw up his hands and made exasperated noises. 'Yes, yes, I know, but don't you see, don't you see there are thousands, literally thousands of other things, things like . . . well . . . like catching a good fish, or fixing the motor of the car, or pleasing someone with a present, or growing a decent row of French beans, or winning a little bet or . . . or . . . why hell, one can go on listing them for ever!'

'Perhaps *you* can, Mr Clements, but to the best of my knowledge, I have never done any of those things. That is what I am trying to tell you.'

Clements put down his brandy glass and stared with new interest at the remarkable shoulderless person who sat facing him. He was annoyed and he didn't feel in the least sympathetic. The man didn't inspire sympathy. He was a fool. He must be a fool. A tremendous and absolute fool. Clements had a sudden desire to embarrass the man as much as he could. 'What about women, Mr Botibol?' There was no apology for the question in the tone of his voice.

'Women?'

'Yes, women! Every man under the sun, even the most wretched filthy down-and-out tramp has some time or other had some sort of silly little success with . . .'

'Never!' cried Mr Botibol with sudden vigour. 'No, sir, never!'

I'm going to hit him, Clements told himself. I can't stand this any longer and if I'm not careful I'm going to jump right up and hit him. 'You mean you don't like them?' he said.

'Oh dear me yes, of course I like them. As a matter of fact I admire them very much, very much indeed. But I'm afraid . . . oh dear me . . . I do not know quite how to say it . . . I am afraid that I do not seem to get along with them very well. I never have. Never. You see, Mr Clements, I *look* so queer. I know I do. They stare at me, and often I see them laughing at me. I have never been able to get within . . . well, within striking distance of them, as you might say.' The trace of a smile, weak and infinitely sad, flickered around the corners of his mouth.

Clements had had enough. He mumbled something about how he was sure Mr Botibol was exaggerating the situation, then he glanced at his watch, called for the bill, and said he was sorry but he would have to get back to the office.

They parted in the street outside the hotel and Mr Botibol took a cab back to his house. He opened the front door, went into the living-room and switched on the radio; then he sat down in a large leather chair, leaned back and closed his eyes. He didn't feel exactly giddy, but there was a singing in his ears and his thoughts were coming and going more quickly than usual. That solicitor gave me too much wine, he told himself. I'll stay here for a while and listen to some music and I expect I'll go to sleep and after that I'll feel better.

They were playing a symphony on the radio. Mr Botibol had always been a casual listener to symphony concerts and he knew enough to identify this as one of Beethoven's.

But now, as he lay back in his chair listening to the marvellous music, a new thought began to expand slowly within his tipsy mind. It wasn't a dream because he was not asleep. It was a clear conscious thought and it was this: I am the composer of this music. I am a great composer. This is my latest symphony and this is the first performance. The huge hall is packed with people – critics, musicians and music-lovers from all over the country – and I am up there in front of the orchestra, conducting.

Mr Botibol could see the whole thing. He could see himself up on the rostrum dressed in a white tie and tails, and before him was the orchestra, the massed violins on his left, the violas in front, the cellos on his right, and back of them were all the woodwinds and bassoons and drums and cymbals, the players watching every movement of his baton with an intense, almost a fanatical reverence. Behind him, in the half-darkness of the huge hall, was row upon row of white enraptured faces, looking up towards him, listening with growing excitement as yet another new symphony by the greatest composer the world had ever seen unfolded itself majestically before them. Some of the audience were clenching their fists and digging their nails into the palms of their hands because the music was so beautiful that they could hardly stand it. Mr Botibol became so carried away by this exciting vision that he began to swing his arms in time with the music in the manner of a conductor. He found it was such fun doing this that he decided to stand up, facing the radio, in order to give himself more freedom of movement.

He stood there in the middle of the room, tall, thin and

shoulderless, dressed in his tight blue double-breasted suit, his small bald head jerking from side to side as he waved his arms in the air. He knew the symphony well enough to be able occasionally to anticipate changes in tempo or volume, and when the music became loud and fast he beat the air so vigorously that he nearly knocked himself over, when it was soft and hushed, he leaned forward to quieten the players with gentle movements of his outstretched hands, and all the time he could feel the presence of the huge audience behind him, tense, immobile, listening. When at last the symphony swelled to its tremendous conclusion, Mr Botibol became more frenzied than ever and his face seemed to thrust itself round to one side in an agony of effort as he tried to force more and still more power from his orchestra during those final mighty chords.

Then it was over. The announcer was saying something, but Mr Botibol quickly switched off the radio and collapsed into his chair, blowing heavily.

'Phew!' he said aloud. 'My goodness gracious me, what *have* I been doing!' Small globules of sweat were oozing out all over his face and forehead, trickling down his neck inside his collar. He pulled out a handkerchief and wiped them away, and he lay there for a while, panting, exhausted, but exceedingly exhilarated.

'Well, I must say,' he gasped, still speaking aloud, 'that *was* fun. I don't know that I have ever had such fun before in all my life. My goodness, it *was* fun, it really *was*!' Almost at once he began to play with the idea of doing it again. But should he? Should he allow himself to do it again?

There was no denying that now, in retrospect, he felt a little guilty about the whole business, and soon he began to wonder whether there wasn't something downright immoral about it all. Letting himself go like that! And imagining he was a genius! It was wrong. He was sure other people didn't do it. And what if Mason had come in the middle and seen him at it! That would have been terrible!

He reached for the paper and pretended to read it, but soon he was searching furtively among the radio programmes for the evening. He put his finger under a line which said '8.30 Symphony Concert. Brahms Symphony No. 2'. He stared at it for a long time. The letters in the word 'Brahms' began to blur and recede, and gradually they disappeared altogether and were replaced by letters which spelled 'Botibol'. Botibol's Symphony No. 2. It was printed quite clearly. He was reading it now, this moment. 'Yes, yes,' he whispered. 'First performance. The world is waiting to hear it. Will it be as great, they are asking, will it perhaps be greater than his earlier work? And the composer himself has been persuaded to conduct. He is shy and retiring, hardly ever appears in public, but on this occasion he has been persuaded . . .'

Mr Botibol leaned forward in his chair and pressed the bell beside the fireplace. Mason, the butler, the only other person in the house, ancient, small and grave, appeared at the door.

'Er . . . Mason, have we any wine in the house?'

'Wine, sir?'

'Yes, wine.'

'Oh no, sir. We haven't had any wine this fifteen or sixteen years. Your father, sir . . .'

'I know, Mason, I know, but will you get some, please. I want a bottle with my dinner.'

The butler was shaken. 'Very well, sir, and what shall it be?'

'Claret, Mason. The best you can obtain. Get a case. Tell them to send it round at once.'

When he was alone again, he was momentarily appalled by the simple manner in which he had made this decision. Wine for dinner! Just like that! Well, yes, why not? Why ever not now he came to think of it? He was his own master. And anyway it was essential that he have wine. It seemed to have a good effect, a very good effect indeed. He wanted it and he was going to have it and to hell with Mason.

He rested for the remainder of the afternoon, and at seven thirty Mason announced dinner. The bottle of wine was on the table and he began to drink it. He didn't give a damn about the way Mason watched him as he refilled his glass. Three times he refilled it; then he left the table saying that he was not to be disturbed and returned to the living-room. There was quarter of an hour to wait. He could think of nothing now except the coming concert. He lay back in the chair and allowed his thoughts to wander deliciously towards eight thirty. He was the great composer waiting impatiently in his dressing-room in the concert-hall. He could hear in the distance the murmur of excitement from the crowd as they settled themselves in their seats. He knew what they were saying to each other.

Same sort of thing the newspapers had been saying for months, Botibol is a genius; greater, far greater than Beethoven or Bach or Brahms or Mozart or any of them. Each new work of his is more magnificent than the last. What will the next one be like? We can hardly wait to hear it! Oh yes, he knew what they were saying. He stood up and began to pace the room. It was nearly time now. He seized a pencil from the table to use as a baton, then he switched on the radio. The announcer had just finished the preliminaries and suddenly there was a burst of applause, which meant that the conductor was coming on to the platform. The previous concert in the afternoon had been from gramophone records, but this one was the real thing. Mr Botibol turned around, faced the fireplace and bowed graciously from the waist. Then he turned back to the radio and lifted his baton. The clapping stopped. There was a moment's silence. Someone in the audience coughed. Mr Botibol waited. The symphony began.

Once again, as he began to conduct, he could see clearly before him the whole orchestra and the faces of the players and even the expressions on their faces. Three of the violinists had grey hair. One of the cellists was very fat, another wore heavy brown-rimmed glasses, and there was a man in the second row playing a horn who had a twitch on one side of his face, but they were all magnificent. And so was the music. During certain impressive passages Mr Botibol experienced a feeling of exultation so powerful that it made him cry out for joy, and once during the Third Movement, a little shiver of ecstasy radiated spontaneously from his solar plexus and moved downwards over the skin of his stomach like needles. But the thunderous applause and the cheering which came at the end of the symphony was the most splendid thing of all. He turned slowly towards the fireplace and bowed. The clapping continued and he went on bowing until at last the noise died away and the announcer's voice jerked him suddenly back into the living-room. He switched off the radio and collapsed into his chair, exhausted but very happy.

As he lay there, smiling with pleasure, wiping his wet face, panting for breath, he was already making plans for his next performance. But why not do it properly? Why not convert one of the rooms into a sort of concert-hall and have a stage and rows of chairs and do the thing properly? And have a gramophone so that one could perform at any time without having to rely on the radio programme. Yes, by heavens, he would do it!

The next morning Mr Botibol arranged with a firm of decorators that the largest room in the house be converted into a miniature concert-hall. There was to be a raised stage at one end and the rest of the floor-space was to be filled with rows of red plush seats. 'I'm going to have some little concerts here,' he told the man from the firm, and the man nodded and said that would be very nice. At the same time he ordered a radio shop to install an expensive self-changing gramophone with two powerful amplifiers, one on the stage, the other at the back of the auditorium. When he had done this, he went off and bought all of Beethoven's nine symphonies on gramophone records; and from a place which specialized in recorded sound effects he ordered several records of clapping and applauding by enthusiastic audiences. Finally he bought himself a conductor's baton, a slim ivory stick which lay in a case lined with blue silk.

In eight days the room was ready. Everything was perfect: the red chairs, the aisle down the centre and even a little dais on the platform with a brass rail running round it for the conductor. Mr Botibol decided to give the first concert that evening after dinner.

At seven o'clock he went up to his bedroom and changed into white tie and tails. He felt marvellous. When he looked at himself in the mirror, the sight of his own grotesque shoulderless figure didn't worry him in the least. A great composer, he thought, smiling, can look as he damn well pleases. People *expect* him to look peculiar. All the same he wished he had some hair on his head. He would have liked to let it grow rather long. He went downstairs to dinner, ate his food rapidly, drank half a bottle of wine and felt better still. 'Don't worry about me, Mason,' he said. 'I'm not mad. I'm just enjoying myself.'

'Yes, sir.'

'I shan't want you any more. Please see that I'm not disturbed.' Mr Botibol went from the dining-room into the miniature concert-hall. He took out the records of Beethoven's First Symphony, but before putting them on the gramophone, he placed two other records with them. The one, which was to be played first of all, before the music began, was labelled 'prolonged enthusiastic applause'. The other, which would come at the end of the symphony, was labelled 'Sustained applause, clapping, cheering, shouts of encore'. By a simple mechanical device on the record changer, the gramophone people had arranged that the sound from the first and the last records – the applause – would come only from the loud-speaker in the auditorium. The sound from all the others – the music – would come from the speaker hidden among the chairs of the orchestra. When he had arranged the records in the correct order, he placed them on the machine but he didn't switch on at once. Instead he turned out all the lights in the room except one small one which lit up the conductor's dais and he sat down in a chair up on the stage, closed his eyes and allowed his thoughts to wander into the usual delicious regions: the great com-poser, nervous, impatient, waiting to present his latest masterpiece, the audience assembling, the murmur of their excited talk, and so on. Having dreamed himself right into the part, he stood up, picked up his baton and switched on the gramophone.

A tremendous wave of clapping filled the room. Mr Botibol walked across the stage, mounted the dais, faced the audience and bowed. In the darkness he could just make out the faint outline of the seats on either side of the centre aisle, but he couldn't see the faces of the people. They were making enough noise. What an ovation! Mr Botibol turned and faced the orchestra. The applause behind him died down. The next record dropped. The symphony began.

This time it was more thrilling than ever, and during the performance he registered any number of prickly sensa-tions around his solar plexus. Once, when it suddenly occurred to him that this music was being broadcast all over the world, a sort of shiver ran right down the length of his spine. But by far the most exciting part was the applause which came at the end. They cheered and clapped and stamped and shouted, 'Encore! encore! encore!' and he turned towards the darkened auditorium and bowed gravely to the left and right. Then he went off the stage, but they called him back. He bowed several more times and went off again, and again they called him back. The audience had gone mad. They simply wouldn't let him go. It was terrific. It was truly a terrific ovation.

Later, when he was resting in his chair in the other room, he was still enjoying it. He closed his eyes because he didn't want anything to break the spell. He lay there and he felt like he was floating. It was really a most marvellous floating feeling, and when he went upstairs and undressed and got into bed, it was still with him.

The following evening he conducted Beethoven's – or rather Botibol's – Second Symphony, and they were just as mad about that one as the first. The next few nights he played one symphony a night, and at the end of nine evenings he had worked through all nine of Beethoven's symphonies. It got more exciting every time because before each concert the audience kept saying, 'He can't do it again, not another masterpiece. It's not humanly possible.' But he did. They were all of them equally magnificent. The last symphony, the Ninth, was especially exciting because here the composer surprised and delighted everyone by suddenly providing a choral masterpiece. He had to conduct a huge choir as well as the orchestra itself, and Benjamino Gigli had flown over from Italy to take the tenor part. Enrico Pinza sang bass. At the end of it the audience shouted themselves hoarse. The whole musical world was on its feet cheering, and on all sides they were saying how you never could tell what wonderful things to expect next from this amazing person.

The composing, presenting and conducting of nine great symphonies in as many days is a fair achievement for any man, and it was not astonishing that it went a little to Mr Botibol's head. He decided now that he would once again surprise his public. He would compose a mass of marvellous piano music and he himself would give the recitals. So early the next morning he set out for the show-room of the people who sold Bechsteins and Steinways. He felt so brisk and fit that he walked all the way, and as he walked he hummed little snatches of new and lovely tunes for the piano. His head was full of them. All the time they kept coming to him and once, suddenly, he had the feeling that thousands of small notes, some white, some black, were cascading down a chute into his head through a hole in his head, and that his brain, his amazing musical brain, was receiving them as fast as they could come and unscrambling them and arranging them neatly in a certain order so that they made wondrous melodies. There were Nocturnes, there were Études and there were Waltzes, and soon, he told himself, soon he would give them all to a grateful and admiring world.

When he arrived at the piano-shop, he pushed the door open and walked in with an air almost of confidence. He had changed much in the last few days. Some of his nervousness had left him and he was no longer wholly preoccupied with what others thought of his appearance. 'I want,' he said to the salesman, 'a concert grand, but you must arrange it so that when the notes are struck, no sound is produced.'

The salesman leaned forward and raised his eyebrows.

'Could that be arranged?' Mr Botibol asked.

'Yes, sir, I think so, if you desire it. But might I inquire what you intend to use the instrument for?'

'If you want to know, I'm going to pretend I'm Chopin. I'm going to sit and play while a gramophone makes the music. It gives me a kick.' It came out, just like that, and Mr Botibol didn't know what had made him say it. But it was done now and he had said it and that was that. In a way he felt relieved, because he had proved he didn't mind telling people what he was doing. The man would probably answer what a jolly good idea. Or he might not. He might say, Well you ought to be locked up.

'So now you know,' Mr Botibol said.

The salesman laughed out loud. 'Ha ha! Ha ha ha! That's very good, sir. Very good indeed. Serves me right for asking silly questions.' He stopped suddenly in the middle of the laugh and looked hard at Mr Botibol. 'Of course, sir, you probably know that we sell a simple noiseless keyboard specially for silent practising.'

'I want a concert grand,' Mr Botibol said. The salesman looked at him again.

Mr Botibol chose his piano and got out of the shop as quickly as possible. He went on to the store that sold gramophone records and there he ordered a quantity of albums containing recordings of all Chopin's Nocturnes, Études and Waltzes, played by Arthur Rubinstein.

'My goodness, you *are* going to have a lovely time!'

Mr Botibol turned and saw standing beside him at the counter a squat, short-legged girl with a face as plain as a pudding.

'Yes,' he answered. 'Oh yes, I am.' Normally he was strict about not speaking to females in public places, but this one had taken him by surprise.

'I love Chopin,' the girl said. She was holding a slim brown paper bag with string handles containing a single record she had just bought. 'I like him better than any of the others.'

It was comforting to hear the voice of this girl after the way the piano salesman had laughed. Mr Botibol wanted to talk to her but he didn't know what to say.

The girl said, 'I like the Nocturnes best, they're so soothing. Which are your favourites?'

Mr Botibol said, 'Well . . .' The girl looked up at him and she smiled pleasantly, trying to assist him with his embarrassment. It was the smile that did it. He suddenly found himself saying, 'Well now, perhaps, would you, I wonder . . . I mean I was wondering . . .' She smiled again; she couldn't help it this time. 'What I mean is I would be glad if you would care to come along some time and listen to these records.'

'Why, how nice of you.' She paused, wondering whether it was all right. 'You really mean it?'

'Yes, I should be glad.'

She had lived long enough in the city to discover that

old men, if they are dirty old men, do not bother about trying to pick up a girl as unattractive as herself. Only twice in her life had she been accosted in public and each time the man had been drunk. But this one wasn't drunk. He was nervous and he was peculiar-looking, but he wasn't drunk. Come to think of it, it was she who had started the conversation in the first place. 'It would be lovely,' she said. 'It really would. When could I come?'

Oh dear, Mr Botibol thought. Oh dear, oh dear, oh dear, oh dear.

'I could come tomorrow,' she went on. 'It's my afternoon off.'

'Well, yes, certainly,' he answered slowly. 'Yes, of course. I'll give you my card. Here it is.'

'A. W. Botibol,' she read aloud. 'What a funny name. Mine's Darlington. Miss L. Darlington. How d'you do, Mr Botibol.' She put out her hand for him to shake. 'Oh I *am* looking forward to this! What time shall I come?'

'Any time,' he said. 'Please come any time.'

'Three o'clock?'

'Yes. Three o'clock.'

'Lovely! I'll be there.'

He watched her walk out of the shop, a squat, stumpy, thick-legged little person and, My word, he thought, what have I done! He was amazed at himself. But he was not displeased. Then at once he started to worry about whether or not he should let her see his concert-hall. He worried still more when he realized that it was the only place in the house where there was a gramophone.

That evening he had no concert. Instead he sat in his

chair brooding about Miss Darlington and what he should do when she arrived. The next morning they brought the piano, a fine Bechstein in dark mahogany which was carried in minus its legs and later assembled on the platform in the concert-hall. It was an imposing instrument and when Mr Botibol opened it and pressed a note with his finger, it made no sound at all. He had originally intended to astonish the world with a recital of his first piano compositions – a set of Études – as soon as the piano arrived, but it was no good now. He was too worried about Miss Darlington and three o'clock. At lunchtime his trepidation had increased and he couldn't eat. 'Mason,' he said, 'I'm, I'm expecting a young lady to call at three o'clock.'

'A what, sir?' the butler said.

'A young lady, Mason.'

'Very good, sir.'

'Show her into the sitting-room.'

'Yes, sir.'

Precisely at three he heard the bell ring. A few moments later Mason was showing her into the room. She came in, smiling, and Mr Botibol stood up and shook her hand. 'My!' she exclaimed. 'What a lovely house! I didn't know I was calling on a millionaire!'

She settled her small plump body into a large armchair and Mr Botibol sat opposite. He didn't know what to say. He felt terrible. But almost at once she began to talk and she chattered away gaily about this and that for a long time without stopping. Mostly it was about his house and the furniture and the carpets and about how nice it was of him to invite her because she didn't have such an awful lot of excitement in her life. She worked hard all day and she shared a room with two other girls in a boarding-house and he could have no idea how thrilling it was for her to be here. Gradually Mr Botibol began to feel better. He sat there listening to the girl, rather liking her, nodding his bald head slowly up and down, and the more she talked, the more he liked her. She was gay and chatty, but underneath all that any fool could see that she was a lonely tired little thing. Even Mr Botibol could see that. He could see it very clearly indeed. It was at this point that he began to play with a daring and risky idea.

'Miss Darlington,' he said. 'I'd like to show you something.' He led her out of the room straight into the little concert-hall. 'Look,' he said.

She stopped just inside the door. 'My goodness! Just look at that! A theatre! A real little theatre!' Then she saw the piano on the platform and the conductor's dais with the brass rail running round it. 'It's for concerts!' she cried. 'Do you really have concerts here? Oh, Mr Botibol, how exciting!'

'Do you like it?'

'Oh yes!'

'Come back into the other room and I'll tell you about it.' Her enthusiasm had given him confidence and he wanted to get going. 'Come back and listen while I tell you something funny.' And when they were seated in the sitting-room again, he began at once to tell her his story. He told the whole thing, right from the beginning, how one day, listening to a symphony, he had imagined himself to be the composer, how he had stood up and started to conduct, how he had got an immense pleasure out of it, how he had done it again with similar results and how finally he had built himself the concert-hall where already he had conducted nine symphonies. But he cheated a little bit in the telling. He said that the only real reason he did it was in order to obtain the maximum appreciation from the music. There was only one way to listen to music, he told her, only one way to make yourself listen to every single note and chord. You had to do two things at once. You had to imagine that you had composed it, and at the same time you had to imagine that the public were hearing it for the first time. 'Do you think,' he said, 'do you really think that any outsider has ever got half as great a thrill from a symphony as the composer himself when he first heard his work played by a full orchestra?'

'No,' she answered timidly. 'Of course not.'

'Then become the composer! Steal his music! Take it away from him and give it to yourself!' He leaned back in his chair and for the first time she saw him smile. He had only just thought of this new complex explanation of his conduct, but to him it seemed a very good one and he smiled. 'Well, what do you think, Miss Darlington?'

'I must say it's very very interesting.' She was polite and puzzled but she was a long way away from him now.

'Would you like to try?'

'Oh no. Please.'

'I wish you would.'

'I'm afraid I don't think I should be able to feel the same way as you do about it, Mr Botibol. I don't think I have a strong enough imagination.'

She could see from his eyes he was disappointed. 'But I'd love to sit in the audience and listen while you do it,' she added.

Then he leaped up from his chair. 'I've got it!' he cried. 'A piano concerto! You play the piano, I conduct. You the greatest pianist, the greatest in the world. First performance of my Piano Concerto No. 1. You playing, me conducting. The greatest pianist and the greatest composer together for the first time. A tremendous occasion! The audience will go mad! They'll be queueing all night outside the hall to get in. It'll be broadcast around the world. It'll, it'll . . .' Mr Botibol stopped. He stood behind the chair with both hands resting on the back of the chair and suddenly he looked embarrassed and a trifle sheepish. 'I'm sorry,' he said. 'I get worked up. You see how it is. Even the thought of another performance gets me worked up.' And then plaintively, 'Would you, Miss Darlington, would you play a piano concerto with me?'

'It's like children,' she said, but she smiled.

'No one will know. No one but us will know anything about it.'

'All right,' she said at last. 'I'll do it. I think I'm daft but just the same I'll do it. It'll be a bit of a lark.'

'Good!' Mr Botibol cried. 'When? Tonight?'

'Oh well, I don't . . .'

'Yes,' he said eagerly. 'Please. Make it tonight. Come back and have dinner here with me and we'll give the concert afterwards.' Mr Botibol was excited again now. 'We must make a few plans. Which is your favourite piano concerto, Miss Darlington?'

'Oh well, I should say Beethoven's Emperor.'

'The Emperor it shall be. You will play it tonight. Come to dinner at seven. Evening dress. You must have evening dress for the concert.'

'I've got a dancing dress but I haven't worn it for years.'

'You shall wear it tonight.' He paused and looked at her in silence for a moment, then quite gently, he said, 'You're not worried, Miss Darlington? Perhaps you would rather not do it. I'm afraid, I'm afraid I've let myself get rather carried away. I seem to have pushed you into this. And I know how stupid it must seem to you.'

That's better, she thought. That's much better. Now I know it's all right. 'Oh no,' she said. 'I'm really looking forward to it. But you frightened me a bit, taking it all so seriously.'

When she had gone, he waited for five minutes, then went out into the town to the gramophone shop and bought the records of the Emperor Concerto, conductor, Toscanini – soloist, Horowitz. He returned at once, told his astonished butler that there would be a guest for dinner, then went upstairs and changed into his tails.

She arrived at seven. She was wearing a long sleeveless dress made of some shiny green material and to Mr Botibol she did not look quite so plump or quite so plain as before. He took her straight in to dinner and in spite of the silent disapproving manner in which Mason prowled around the table, the meal went well. She protested gaily when Mr Botibol gave her a second glass of wine, but she didn't refuse it. She chattered away almost without a stop throughout the three courses and Mr Botibol listened and nodded and kept refilling her glass as soon as it was half empty.

Afterwards, when they were seated in the living-room, Mr Botibol said, 'Now Miss Darlington, now we begin to fall into our parts.' The wine, as usual, had made him happy, and the girl, who was even less used to it than the man, was not feeling so bad either. 'You, Miss Darlington, are the great pianist. What is your first name, Miss Darlington?'

'Lucille,' she said.

'The great pianist Lucille Darlington. I am the composer Botibol. We must talk and act and think as though we are pianist and composer.'

'What is *your* first name, Mr Botibol. What does the A stand for?'

'Angel,' he answered.

'Not Angel.'

'Yes,' he said irritably.

'Angel Botibol,' she murmured and she began to giggle. But she checked herself and said, 'I think it's a most unusual and distinguished name.'

'Are you ready, Miss Darlington?'

'Yes.'

Mr Botibol stood up and began pacing nervously up and down the room. He looked at his watch. 'It's nearly time to go on,' he said. 'They tell me the place is packed. Not an empty seat anywhere. I always get nervous before a concert. Do you get nervous, Miss Darlington?'

'Oh yes, I do, always. Especially playing with you.'

'I think they'll like it. I put everything I've got into this concerto, Miss Darlington. It nearly killed me composing it. I was ill for weeks afterwards.'

'Poor thing,' she said.

'It's time now,' he said. 'The orchestra are all in their places. Come on.' He led her out and down the passage, then he made her wait outside the door of the concert-hall while he nipped in, arranged the lighting and switched on the gramophone. He came back and fetched her and as they walked on to the stage, the applause broke out. They both stood and bowed towards the darkened auditorium and the applause was vigorous and it went on for a long time. Then Mr Botibol mounted the dais and Miss Darlington took her seat at the piano. The applause died down. Mr Botibol held up his baton. The next record dropped and the Emperor Concerto began.

It was an astonishing affair. The thin stalk-like Mr Botibol, who had no shoulders, standing on the dais in his evening clothes, waving his arms about in approximate time to the music; and the plump Miss Darlington in her shiny green dress seated at the keyboard of the enormous piano thumping the silent keys with both hands for all she was worth. She recognized the passages where the piano was meant to be silent, and on these occasions she folded her hands primly on her lap and stared straight ahead with a dreamy and enraptured expression on her face. Watching her, Mr Botibol thought that she was particularly wonderful in the slow solo passages of the Second Movement. She allowed her hands to drift smoothly and gently up and down the keys and she inclined her head first to one side, then to the other, and once she closed her eyes for a long time while she played. During the exciting last movement, Mr Botibol himself lost his balance and would have fallen off the platform had he not saved himself by clutching the brass rail. But in spite of everything, the concerto moved on majestically to its mighty conclusion. Then the real clapping came. Mr Botibol walked over and took Miss Darlington by the hand and led her to the edge of the platform, and there they stood, the two of them, bowing, and bowing, and bowing again as the clapping and the shouting of 'Encore' continued. Four times they left the stage and came back, and then, the fifth time, Mr Botibol whispered, 'It's you they want. You take this one alone.' 'No,' she said. 'It's you. It's you. Please.' But he pushed her forward and she took her call, and came back and said, 'Now you. They want you. Can't you hear them shouting for you?' So Mr Botibol walked alone on to the stage, bowed gravely to right, left and centre and came off just as the clapping stopped altogether.

He led her straight back to the living-room. He was breathing fast and the sweat was pouring down all over his face. She too was a little breathless, and her cheeks were shining red.

'A tremendous performance, Miss Darlington. Allow me to congratulate you.'

'But what a concerto, Mr Botibol! What a superb concerto!'

'You played it perfectly, Miss Darlington. You have a real feeling for my music.' He was wiping the sweat from his face with a handkerchief. 'And tomorrow we perform my Second Concerto.'

'Tomorrow?'

'Of course. Had you forgotten, Miss Darlington? We are booked to appear together for a whole week.'

'Oh . . . oh yes . . . I'm afraid I had forgotten that.'

'But it's all right, isn't it?' he asked anxiously. 'After hearing you tonight I could not bear to have anyone else play my music.'

'I think it's all right,' she said. 'Yes, I think that'll be all right.' She looked at the clock on the mantelpiece. 'My heavens, it's late! I must go! I'll never get up in the morning to get to work!'

'To work?' Mr Botibol said. 'To work?' Then slowly, reluctantly, he forced himself back to reality. 'Ah yes, to work. Of course, you have to get to work.'

'I certainly do.'

'Where do you work, Miss Darlington?'

'Me? Well,' and now she hesitated a moment, looking at Mr Botibol. 'As a matter of fact I work at the old Academy.'

'I hope it is pleasant work,' he said. 'What Academy is that?'

'I teach the piano.'

Mr Botibol jumped as though someone had stuck him from behind with a hatpin. His mouth opened very wide.

'It's quite all right,' she said, smiling. 'I've always wanted to be Horowitz. And could I, do you think could I please be Schnabel tomorrow?'

Man from the South

First published in *Collier's* (4 September 1948)
as 'Collector's Item'; also known
as 'The Smoker'

It was getting on towards six o'clock so I thought I'd buy myself a beer and go out and sit in a deck-chair by the swimming-pool and have a little evening sun.

I went to the bar and got the beer and carried it outside and wandered down the garden towards the pool.

It was a fine garden with lawns and beds of azaleas and tall coconut palms, and the wind was blowing strongly through the tops of the palm trees, making the leaves hiss and crackle as though they were on fire. I could see the clusters of big brown nuts hanging down underneath the leaves.

There were plenty of deck-chairs around the swimming-pool and there were white tables and huge brightly coloured umbrellas and sunburned men and women sitting around in bathing suits. In the pool itself there were three or four girls and about a dozen boys, all splashing about and making a lot of noise and throwing a large rubber ball at one another.

I stood watching them. The girls were English girls from the hotel. The boys I didn't know about, but they sounded American and I thought they were probably naval cadets who'd come ashore from the US naval training vessel which had arrived in harbour that morning.

I went over and sat down under a yellow umbrella where there were four empty seats, and I poured my beer and settled back comfortably with a cigarette.

It was very pleasant sitting there in the sunshine with beer and cigarette. It was pleasant to sit and watch the bathers splashing about in the green water.

The American sailors were getting on nicely with the English girls. They'd reached the stage where they were diving under the water and tipping them up by their legs.

Just then I noticed a small, oldish man walking briskly around the edge of the pool. He was immaculately dressed in a white suit and he walked very quickly with little bouncing strides, pushing himself high up on to his toes with each step. He had on a large creamy Panama hat, and he came bouncing along the side of the pool, looking at the people and the chairs.

He stopped beside me and smiled, showing two rows of very small, uneven teeth, slightly tarnished. I smiled back.

'Excuse pleess, but may I sit here?'

'Certainly,' I said. 'Go ahead.'

He bobbed around to the back of the chair and inspected it for safety, then he sat down and crossed his legs. His white buckskin shoes had little holes punched all over them for ventilation.

'A fine evening,' he said. 'They are all evenings fine here in Jamaica.' I couldn't tell if the accent was Italian or Spanish, but I felt fairly sure he was some sort of a South American. And old too, when you saw him close. Probably around sixty-eight or seventy.

'Yes,' I said. 'It is wonderful here, isn't it?'

'And who, might I ask, are all dese? Dese is no hotel people.' He was pointing at the bathers in the pool.

'I think they're American sailors,' I told him. 'They're Americans who are learning to be sailors.'

'Of course dey are Americans. Who else in de world is going to make as much noise as dat? You are not American, no?'

'No,' I said. 'I am not.'

Suddenly one of the American cadets was standing in front of us. He was dripping wet from the pool and one of the English girls was standing there with him.

'Are these chairs taken?' he said.

'No,' I answered.

'Mind if I sit down?'

'Go ahead.'

'Thanks,' he said. He had a towel in his hand and when he sat down he unrolled it and produced a pack of cigarettes and a lighter. He offered the cigarettes to the girl and she refused; then he offered them to me and I took one. The little man said. 'Tank you, no, but I tink I have a cigar.' He pulled out a crocodile case and got himself a cigar, then he produced a knife which had a small scissors in it and he snipped the end off the cigar.

'Here, let me give you a light.' The American boy held up his lighter.

'Dat will not work in dis wind.'

'Sure, it'll work. It always works.'

The little man removed his unlighted cigar from his mouth, cocked his head on one side and looked at the boy.

'*All*-ways?' he said slowly.

'Sure, it never fails. Not with me anyway.'

The little man's head was still cocked over on one side and he was still watching the boy. 'Well, well. So you say dis famous lighter it never fails. Iss dat you say?'

'Sure,' the boy said. 'That's right.' He was about nineteen or twenty, with a long freckled face and a rather sharp birdlike nose. His chest was not very sunburned and there were freckles there too, and a few wisps of pale-reddish hair. He was holding the lighter in his right hand, ready to flip the wheel. 'It never fails,' he said, smiling now because he was purposely exaggerating his little boast. 'I promise you it never fails.'

'One momint, pleess.' The hand that held the cigar came up high, palm outward, as though it were stopping traffic. 'Now juss one momint.' He had a curiously soft, toneless voice and he kept looking at the boy all the time.

'Shall we not perhaps make a little bet on dat?' He smiled at the boy. 'Shall we not make a little bet on whether your lighter lights?'

'Sure, I'll bet,' the boy said. 'Why not?'

'You like to bet?'

'Sure, I'll always bet.'

The man paused and examined his cigar, and I must say I didn't much like the way he was behaving. It seemed he was already trying to make something out of this, and to embarrass the boy, and at the same time I had the feeling he was relishing a private little secret all his own.

He looked up again at the boy and said slowly, 'I like to

bet, too. Why we don't have a good bet on dis ting? A good big bet.'

'Now wait a minute,' the boy said. 'I can't do that. But I'll bet you a quarter. I'll even bet you a dollar, or whatever it is over here – some shillings, I guess.'

The little man waved his hand again. 'Listen to me. Now we have some fun. We make a bet. Den we go up to my room here in de hotel where iss no wind and I bet you you cannot light dis famous lighter of yours ten times running without missing once.'

'I'll bet I can,' the boy said.

'All right. Good. We make a bet, yes?'

'Sure. I'll bet you a buck.'

'No, no. I make you very good bet. I am rich man and I am sporting man also. Listen to me. Outside de hotel iss my car. Iss very fine car. American car from your country. Cadillac –'

'Hey, now. Wait a minute.' The boy leaned back in his deck-chair and he laughed. 'I can't put up that sort of property. This is crazy.'

'Not crazy at all. You strike lighter successfully ten times running and Cadillac is yours. You like to have dis Cadillac, yes?'

'Sure, I'd like to have a Cadillac.' The boy was still grinning.

'All right. Fine. We make a bet and I put up my Cadillac.'

'And what do I put up?'

The little man carefully removed the red band from his still-unlighted cigar. 'I never ask you, my friend, to bet something you cannot afford. You understand?'

'Then what do I bet?'

'I make it very easy for you, yes?'

'OK. You make it easy.'

'Some small ting you can afford to give away, and if you did happen to lose it you would not feel too bad. Right?'

'Such as what?'

'Such as, perhaps, de little finger of your left hand.'

'My *what*!' The boy stopped grinning.

'Yes. Why not? You win, you take de car. You looss, I take de finger.'

'I don't get it. How d'you mean, you take the finger?'

'I chop it off.'

'Jumping jeepers! That's a crazy bet. I think I'll just make it a dollar.'

The little man leaned back, spread out his hands palms upward and gave a tiny contemptuous shrug of the shoulders. 'Well, well, well,' he said. 'I do not understand. You say it lights but you will not bet. Den we forget it, yes?'

The boy sat quite still, staring at the bathers in the pool. Then he remembered suddenly he hadn't lighted his cigarette. He put it between his lips, cupped his hands around the lighter and flipped the wheel. The wick lighted and burned with a small, steady, yellow flame and the way he held his hands the wind didn't get to it at all.

'Could I have a light, too?' I said.

'Gee, I'm sorry. I forgot you didn't have one.'

I held out my hand for the lighter, but he stood up and came over to do it for me.

'Thank you,' I said, and he returned to his seat.

'You having a good time?' I asked.

'Fine,' he answered. 'It's pretty nice here.'

There was silence then, and I could see that the little man had succeeded in disturbing the boy with his absurd proposal. He was sitting there very still, and it was obvious that a small tension was beginning to build up inside him. Then he started shifting about in his seat, and rubbing his chest, and stroking the back of his neck, and finally he placed both hands on his knees and began tap-tapping with his fingers against the knee-caps. Soon he was tapping with one of his feet as well.

'Now just let me check up on this bet of yours,' he said at last. 'You say we go up to your room and if I make this lighter light ten times running I win a Cadillac. If it misses just once then I forfeit the little finger of my left hand. Is that right?'

'Certainly. Dat is de bet. But I think you are afraid.'

'What do we do if I lose? Do I have to hold my finger out while you chop it off?'

'Oh no! Dat would be no good. And you might be tempted to refuse to hold it out. What I should do I should tie one of your hands to de table before we started and I should stand dere with a knife ready to go *chop* de momint your lighter missed.'

'What year is the Cadillac?' the boy asked.

'Excuse. I not understand.'

'What year – how old is the Cadillac?'

'Ah! How old? Yes. It is last year. Quite new car. But I see you are not betting man. Americans never are.'

The boy paused for just a moment and he glanced first at the English girl, then at me. 'Yes,' he said sharply. 'I'll bet you.'

'Good!' The little man clapped his hands together quietly, once. 'Fine,' he said. 'We do it now. And you, sir,' he turned to me, 'you would perhaps be good enough to, what you call it, to – to referee.' He had pale, almost colourless eyes with tiny bright black pupils.

'Well,' I said. 'I think it's a crazy bet. I don't think I like it very much.'

'Nor do I,' said the English girl. It was the first time she'd spoken. 'I think it's a stupid, ridiculous bet.'

'Are you serious about cutting off this boy's finger if he loses?' I said.

'Certainly I am. Also about giving him Cadillac if he win. Come now. We go to my room.'

He stood up. 'You like to put on some clothes first?' he said.

'No,' the boy answered. 'I'll come like this.' Then he turned to me. 'I'd consider it a favour if you'd come along and referee.'

'All right,' I said. 'I'll come along, but I don't like the bet.'

'You come too,' he said to the girl. 'You come and watch.'

The little man led the way back through the garden to the hotel. He was animated now, and excited, and that seemed to make him bounce up higher than ever on his toes as he walked along.

'I live in annexe,' he said. 'You like to see car first? Iss just here.'

He took us to where we could see the front driveway of

the hotel and he stopped and pointed to a sleek pale-green Cadillac parked close by.

'Dere she iss. De green one. You like?'

'Say, that's a nice car,' the boy said.

'All right. Now we go up and see if you can win her.'

We followed him into the annexe and up one flight of stairs. He unlocked his door and we all trooped into what was a large pleasant double bedroom. There was a woman's dressing-gown lying across the bottom of one of the beds.

'First,' he said, 'we 'ave a little Martini.'

The drinks were on a small table in the far corner, all ready to be mixed, and there was a shaker and ice and plenty of glasses. He began to make the Martini, but meanwhile he'd rung the bell and now there was a knock on the door and a coloured maid came in.

'Ah!' he said, putting down the bottle of gin, taking a wallet from his pocket and pulling out a pound note. 'You will do something for me now, pleess.' He gave the maid the pound.

'You keep dat,' he said. 'And now we are going to play a little game in here and I want you to go off and find for me two – no tree tings. I want some nails; I want a hammer, and I want a chopping knife, a butcher's chopping knife which you can borrow from de kitchen. You can get, yes?'

'A *chopping knife*!' The maid opened her eyes wide and clasped her hands in front of her. 'You mean a *real* chopping knife?'

'Yes, yes, of course. Come on now, pleess. You can find dose tings surely for me.'

'Yes, sir, I'll try, sir. Surely I'll try to get them.' And she went.

The little man handed round the Martinis. We stood there and sipped them, the boy with the long freckled face and the pointed nose, bare-bodied except for a pair of faded brown bathing shorts; the English girl, a large-boned, fair-haired girl wearing a pale-blue bathing suit, who watched the boy over the top of her glass all the time; the little man with the colourless eyes standing there in his immaculate white suit drinking his Martini and looking at the girl in her pale-blue bathing dress. I didn't know what to make of it all. The man seemed serious about the bet and he seemed serious about the business of cutting off the finger. But hell, what if the boy lost? Then we'd have to rush him to the hospital in the Cadillac that he hadn't won. That would be a fine thing. Now wouldn't that be a really fine thing? It would be a damn silly unnecessary thing so far as I could see.

'Don't you think this is rather a silly bet?' I said.

'I think it's a fine bet,' the boy answered. He had already downed one large Martini.

'I think it's a stupid, ridiculous bet,' the girl said. 'What'll happen if you lose?'

'It won't matter. Come to think of it, I can't remember ever in my life having had any use for the little finger on my left hand. Here he is.' The boy took hold of the finger. 'Here he is and he hasn't ever done a thing for me yet. So why shouldn't I bet him. I think it's a fine bet.'

The little man smiled and picked up the shaker and refilled our glasses.

'Before we begin,' he said, 'I will present to de – to de referee de key of de car.' He produced a car key from his pocket and gave it to me. 'De papers,' he said, 'de owning papers and insurance are in de pocket of de car.'

Then the coloured maid came in again. In one hand she carried a small chopper, the kind used by butchers for chopping meat bones, and in the other a hammer and a bag of nails.

'Good! You get dem all. Tank you, tank you. Now you can go.' He waited until the maid had closed the door, then he put the implements on one of the beds and said, 'Now we prepare ourselves, yes?' And to the boy, 'Help me, pleess, with dis table. We carry it out a little.'

It was the usual kind of hotel writing desk, just a plain rectangular table about four feet by three with a blotting pad, inks, pens and paper. They carried it out into the room away from the wall, and removed the writing things.

'And now,' he said, 'a chair.' He picked up a chair and placed it beside the table. He was very brisk and very animated, like a person organizing games at a children's party. 'And now de nails. I must put in de nails.' He fetched the nails and began to hammer them into the top of the table.

We stood there, the boy, the girl and I, holding Martinis in our hands, watching the little man at work. We watched him hammer two nails into the table, about six inches apart. He didn't hammer them right home; he allowed a small part of each one to stick up. Then he tested them for firmness with his fingers.

Anyone would think the son of a bitch had done this before, I told myself. He never hesitates. Table, nails, hammer, kitchen chopper. He knows exactly what he needs and how to arrange it.

'And now,' he said, 'all we want is some string.' He found some string. 'All right, at last we are ready. Will you pleess to sit here at de table,' he said to the boy.

The boy put his glass away and sat down.

'Now place de left hand between dese two nails. De nails are only so I can tie your hand in place. All right, good. Now I tie your hand secure to de table – so.'

He wound the string around the boy's wrist, then several times around the wide part of the hand, then he fastened it tight to the nails. He made a good job of it and when he'd finished there wasn't any question about the boy being able to draw his hand away. But he could move his fingers.

'Now pleess, clench de fist, all except for de little finger. You must leave de little finger out, lying on de table.

'*Ex*-cellent! *Ex*-cellent! Now we are ready. Wid your right hand you manipulate de lighter. But one momint, pleess.'

He skipped over to the bed and picked up the chopper. He came back and stood beside the table with the chopper in his hand.

'We are all ready?' he said. 'Mister referee, you must say to begin.'

The English girl was standing there in her pale-blue bathing costume right behind the boy's chair. She was just standing there, not saying anything. The boy was sitting quite still, holding the lighter in his right hand, looking at the chopper. The little man was looking at me.

'Are you ready?' I asked the boy.

'I'm ready.'

'And you?' to the little man.

'Quite ready,' he said and he lifted the chopper up in the air and held it there about two feet above the boy's finger, ready to chop. The boy watched it, but he didn't flinch and his mouth didn't move at all. He merely raised his eyebrows and frowned.

'All right,' I said. 'Go ahead.'

The boy said, 'Will you please count aloud the number of times I light it?'

'Yes,' I said. 'I'll do that.'

With his thumb he raised the top of the lighter, and again with the thumb he gave the wheel a sharp flick. The flint sparked and the wick caught fire and burned with a small yellow flame.

'One!' I called.

He didn't blow the flame out; he closed the top of the lighter on it and he waited for perhaps five seconds before opening it again.

He flicked the wheel very strongly and once more there was a small flame burning on the wick.

'Two!'

No one else said anything. The boy kept his eyes on the lighter. The little man held the chopper up in the air and he too was watching the lighter.

'Three!'

'Four!'

'Five!'

'Six!'

'Seven!' Obviously it was one of those lighters that worked. The flint gave a big spark and the wick was the right length. I watched the thumb snapping the top down on to the flame. Then a pause. Then the thumb raising the top once more. This was an all-thumb operation. The thumb did everything. I took a breath, ready to say eight. The thumb flicked the wheel. The flint sparked. The little flame appeared.

'Eight!' I said, and as I said it the door opened. We all turned and we saw a woman standing in the doorway, a small, black-haired woman, rather old, who stood there for about two seconds then rushed forward shouting, 'Carlos! Carlos!' She grabbed his wrist, took the chopper from him, threw it on the bed, took hold of the little man by the lapels of his white suit and began shaking him very vigorously, talking to him fast and loud and fiercely all the time in some Spanish-sounding language. She shook him so fast you couldn't see him any more. He became a faint, misty, quickly moving outline, like the spokes of a turning wheel.

Then she slowed down and the little man came into view again and she hauled him across the room and pushed him backwards on to one of the beds. He sat on the edge of it, blinking his eyes and testing his head to see if it would still turn on his neck.

'I am so sorry,' the woman said. 'I am so terribly sorry that this should happen.' She spoke almost perfect English.

'It is too bad,' she went on. 'I suppose it is really my fault. For ten minutes I leave him alone to go and have my hair washed and I come back and he is at it again.' She looked sorry and deeply concerned.

The boy was untying his hand from the table. The English girl and I stood there and said nothing.

'He is a menace,' the woman said. 'Down where we live at home he has taken altogether forty-seven fingers from different people, and he has lost eleven cars. In the end they threatened to have him put away somewhere. That's why I brought him up here.'

'We were only having a little bet,' mumbled the little man from the bed.

'I suppose he bet you a car,' the woman said.

'Yes,' the boy answered. 'A Cadillac.'

'He has no car. It's mine. And that makes it worse,' she said, 'that he should bet you when he has nothing to bet with. I am ashamed and very sorry about it all.' She seemed an awfully nice woman.

'Well,' I said, 'then here's the key of your car.' I put it on the table.

'We were only having a little bet,' mumbled the little man.

'He hasn't anything left to bet with,' the woman said. 'He hasn't a thing in the world. Not a thing. As a matter of fact I myself won it all from him a long while ago. It took time, a lot of time, and it was hard work, but I won it all in the end.' She looked up at the boy and she smiled, a slow sad smile, and she came over and put out a hand to take the key from the table.

I can see it now, that hand of hers; it had only one finger on it, and a thumb.

ROALD DAHL

Roald Dahl was a spy, ace fighter-pilot, chocolate historian and medical inventor. He was also the author of Charlie and the Chocolate Factory, Matilda, The BFG and many more brilliant stories. He remains the World's No.1 storyteller.

CHARMING BAKER

Born in Hampshire 1964, Charming Baker spent much of his early life travelling around the world following his father, a commando in the British Army. At the age of twelve, he and his family finally settled in Ripon, North Yorkshire. Baker left school at sixteen and worked various manual jobs. In 1985, having gone back to college, he was accepted onto a course at the prestigious Central Saint Martin's, where he later returned as a lecturer. After graduating, Baker worked for many years as a commercial artist as well as developing his personal work.

Solo exhibitions include the Truman Brewery, London, 2007, Redchurch Street Gallery, London, 2009, New York Studio Gallery, NYC, 2010, Mercer Street, London, 2011 and Milk Studios, LA, 2013. Baker has also exhibited with the Fine Art Society, collaborated with Sir Paul Smith for a sculpture entitled 'Triumph in the Face of Absurdity', which was displayed at the Victoria and Albert Museum, and continues to be committed to creating work to raise money for many charities. He has recently been commissioned to be a presenter on *The Art Show*. His work is in many international collections.

Although Baker has produced sculptural pieces in a wide and varied choice of materials, as well as many large-scale and detailed drawings, he remains primarily a painter with an interest in narrative and an understanding of the tradition of painting. Known to purposefully damage his work by drilling, cutting and even shooting it, Baker intentionally puts in to question the preciousness of art and the definition of its beauty, adding to the emotive charge of the work he produces. Indeed Edward Lucie-Smith has described Baker's paintings as having, something more, a kind of romantic melancholy that is very British. And sometimes the melancholy turns out to have sharp claws. The pictures make you sit up and examine your conscience.

Charming Baker lives and works in London.

CRUELTY
Tales of Malice and Greed

Even when we mean to be kind we can sometimes be cruel. We each have a streak of nastiness inside us. In these ten tales of cruelty Roald Dahl explores how and why it is we make others suffer.

Among others, you'll read the story of two young bullies and the boy they torment, the adulterous wife who uncovers her husband's secret, the man with a painting tattooed on his back whose value he doesn't appreciate and the butler and chef who run rings around their obnoxious employer.

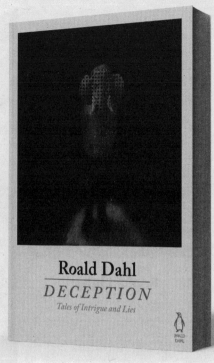

DECEPTION
Tales of Intrigue and Lies

Why do we lie? Why do we deceive those we love most? What do we fear revealing? In these ten tales of deception Roald Dahl explores our tireless efforts to hide the truth about ourselves.

Here, among many others tales you'll read about how to get away with the perfect murder, the old man whose wagers end in a most disturbing payment, how revenge is sweeter when it is carried out by someone else and the card sharp so good at cheating he does something surprising with his life.

Roald Dahl

L U S T

Tales of Craving and Desire

LUST
Tales of Craving and Desire

To what lengths would you go to achieve your heart's desire? In these ten tales of maddening lust Roald Dahl explores how our darkest impulses reveal who we really are.

Here you will read a story concerning wife swapping with a twist, hear of the aphrodisiac that drives men into a frenzy, discover the last act in a tale of jilted first love and discover the naked truth of art.

MADNESS
Tales of Fear and Unreason

Our greatest fear is of losing control – above all, of losing control of ourselves. In these ten unsettling tales of unexpected madness Roald Dahl explores what happens when we let go of our sanity.

Among other stories, you'll meet the husband with a jealous fixation on the family cat, the landlady who wants her guests to stay forever, the man whose taste for pork leads him astray and the wife with a pathological fear of being late.

THE COMPLETE ROALD DAHL SHORT STORIES VOL 1 & 2

'They are brutal, these stories, and yet you finish reading each one with a smile, or maybe even a hollow laugh, certainly a shiver of gratification, because the conclusion always seems so right'
Charlie Higson

In these two volumes chronologically collecting all Roald Dahl's 55 published adult short stories, written between 1944 and 1988, and introduced by Charlie Higson and Anthony Horowitz, we see Roald Dahl's powerful and dark imagination pen some of the most unsettling and disquieting tales ever written.

Whether you're young or old, once you've stepped into the brilliant, troubling world of Roald Dahl, you'll never be the same again.

BOY

'An autobiography is a book a person writes about his own life and it is usually full of all sorts of boring details. This is not an autobiography. I would never write a history of myself. On the other hand, throughout my young days at school and just afterwards a number of things happened to me that I have never forgotten . . .'

Boy is a funny, insightful and at times grotesque glimpse into the early life of Roald Dahl. We discover his experiences of the English public school system, the idyllic paradise of summer holidays in Norway, the pleasures (and pains) of the sweetshop, and how it is that he avoided being a Boazer.

This is the unadulterated childhood – sad and funny, macabre and delightful – which speaks of an age which vanished with the coming of the Second World War.

'A shimmering fabric of his yesterdays, the magic and the hurt' *Observer*

'As frightening and funny as his fiction' *The New York Times Book Review*

'Superbly written. A glimpse of a brilliant eccentric' *New Statesman*

GOING SOLO

'They did not think for one moment that they would find anything but a burnt-out fuselage and a charred skeleton, and they were astounded when they came upon my still-breathing body lying in the sand nearby.'

In 1938 Roald Dahl was fresh out of school and bound for his first job in Africa, hoping to find adventure far from home. However, he got far more excitement than he bargained for when the outbreak of the Second World War led him to join the RAF. His account of his experiences in Africa, crashing a plane in the Western Desert, rescue and recovery from his horrific injuries in Alexandria, flying a Hurricane as Greece fell to the Germans, and many other daring deeds, recreates a world as bizarre and unnerving as any he wrote about in his fiction.

'Very nearly as grotesque as his fiction. The same compulsive blend of wide-eyed innocence and fascination with danger and horror' *Evening Standard*

'A non-stop demonstration of expert raconteurship'
The New York Times Book Review

STORIES ARE GOOD FOR YOU.

Roald Dahl said,

*'If you have good thoughts, they will shine
out of your face like sunbeams and you
will always look lovely.'*

We believe in doing good things.
That's why ten per cent of all Roald Dahl income*
goes to our charity partners. We have supported
causes including: specialist children's nurses, grants for
families in need, and educational outreach programmes.
Thank you for helping us to sustain this vital work.

Find out more at roalddahl.com